MISTY REVENGE

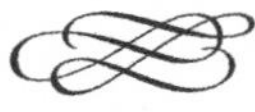

LINDA RAWLINS

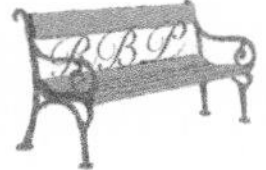

MISTY REVENGE

Misty Revenge
A Misty Point Mystery

By Linda Rawlins

E-Book: 978-0-9600549-2-3
Paperback: 978-0-9600549-3-0

Discover other titles by Linda Rawlins at
www.lindarawlins.com

ACKNOWLEDGMENTS

2020 was a sad year for humanity. Anxiety, loss, fear, grief and uncertainty from multiple sources. The world was turned upside down with many struggling to move forward. It was an exceedingly difficult year for me personally and even more so to write a book. I was absorbed by my other profession, healthcare.

When asked if I incorporated elements of the pandemic into Misty Revenge, the answer is no, for two reasons. The first is that my books are meant to be a simple place for my readers to escape. Cozy mystery is a fantastic genre for readers to disappear into a story.

The second reason is the same. Writing my books are a place for me to escape when I get caught up in the rest of my world.

For this reason, I must thank my team once again for pushing me to continue writing despite how exhausted I was physically or mentally for they know it is therapy for me as well to embrace creativity.

Thank you to my mom, Joyce, who from the beginning of my writing career, has always been there. Always encouraging, cheerleading and making sure she pushes me to continue. She also gives the first read and does a great job with suggestions for contents, edits and direction. She does have experience in this and in one way, I'm thankful she is a taskmaster.

My first readers, Sandy, Anita, Lorraine, Krista and Joe – your feedback and reviews are so important! You catch the things I've never considered.

To Dr. Joe for keeping the rest of the world spinning in the right direction.

To Aunt Helen for all the celestial work!

To a fantastic computer team with whom I was lucky enough to train this year. Vicky G, Cyndy S, Debbie Z, Joanne L, Lori T, and Lauren A. Training with this team was most certainly a highlight! Always clean your keyboard and your mouse!

To the rest of the Riverbench Publishing team including Krista, Matt and Ashley for everything else which happens from covers, blurbs, websites, social media to marketing and publicity. I can only thank you from the bottom of my heart. I know you are all responsible for the clouds!!

To my many readers, librarians, booksellers and friends, thank you for reading and sharing my stories. I love hearing from you and your encouragement inspires me daily!

Happiness is the new rich.
Inner peace is the new success.
Health is the new wealth.
Kindness is the new cool.

-Syed Balkhi

To all
Frontline Heroes
including those that help keep
the home fires burning.
Your dedication and bravery are astounding.

* * *

To Anita –

"Kindness
is the most important tool
to spread love among humanity."
RAKtivist

CHAPTER 1

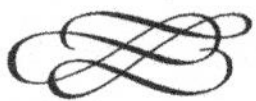

"It's beautiful."

"Isn't it? This ballroom will comfortably seat 200 guests and potential donors for your charity event." Fiona Cochran smiled at Megan Stanford as she grabbed her by the hand and guided her inside the room. Will you be having a band or a DJ? Dancing?"

Megan looked around the ballroom of the Misty Point Country Club and tried to visualize a large group of people celebrating life, laughter and hope. Pure Horizons Environmental Group was a great charity and Megan Stanford was proud to be the honorary chair. Her grandmother, Rose Stanford, had been instrumental in setting up the charity as part of her large philanthropic foundation.

When Rose passed away a year before, she left her foundation, and the responsibilities to Megan, if she chose to accept it. Megan happily made her decision and had spent the past year learning about the various Stanford Foundation Grants. She hoped to be as charitable as her grandmother was. Rose had also left her Grand Victorian Mansion, Misty Manor, to Megan as well.

"I'm not sure what entertainment we'll have," Megan said. "The committee will be meeting soon. I want to bring some preliminary information to the group. We'll make decisions after some discussion."

Fiona shook her head. "I understand. Do you know when the event will be?"

"I'm looking to book for next year. We already have our event scheduled for this year, but I'm trying to get ahead of next year. I've heard you need to book a room far in advance if you want to have an event at this country club."

Fiona nodded. "That's absolutely true. We have many weddings scheduled, especially if you aim for warmer weather." She gestured toward the floor to ceiling windows on the far side of the room. "As you can see, the view of the beach is what makes our country club one of the most striking wedding destinations in New Jersey. Many couples love having their wedding celebration on the beach. The venue is lovely ninety percent of the time, but if there is a bad weather day, we have enough beautiful rooms inside the building to accommodate the event. Most guests are surprised by the beauty of the Jersey Shore."

"I know that's true," Megan said as she nodded. "And that's also the point of our charity. We want to keep our part of the ocean beautiful. We've made strides with plastic and other forms of garbage on the beach, but we need to do more."

"I understand and applaud that," Fiona said as she used two fingers to rub her temple.

"Are you okay?" Megan asked as she looked at Fiona.

"Oh, I'm fine," she said. "I think I may have caught a bug, just vague symptoms every couple of days." Fiona leaned toward Megan and laughed. "To be honest, it's occasionally a little stressful working on weddings."

"I can only imagine."

Both women jumped when they heard loud voices in the next room.

"Where is she?" A woman screamed. "She promised me I could bring lavender vases to the wedding. Now my florist is telling me, no."

"She's with another guest at the moment," said another female voice with a hushed reply.

"I don't care. I want to talk to Fiona right now."

"Oh my," Megan said. "Someone sounds unhappy."

"That's one of our future brides," Fiona whispered. "A case in point. It's difficult to please everyone when we schedule an event. I'm not sure what the actual problem is, but if you'll excuse me, I should go address the situation before she gets worked up."

"Of course," Megan said. "Do you mind if I walk through the room for a bit before I leave?"

"Not at all," Fiona said. "We'll touch base again very soon. I'd like to answer any questions you have and get you set up for your charity event as soon as possible."

"Thank you," Megan said. "I appreciate your help."

"I'll call you as soon as I can," Fiona tossed over her shoulder as she walked toward the foyer.

CHAPTER 2

Megan walked across the ballroom and stopped at the wall of windows. She looked out toward the beach and watched the waves rolling toward the shore. Beautiful curls of foam fell to the sand, disappeared and came back again. The water looked noticeably clear with the sun pouring through the waves. The sand was clean and had obviously been raked that morning. Extra efforts made by the country club ensured the sand and facilities near the ocean were as clean and accommodating to guests as possible.

Pure Horizons started their environmental campaign a couple of years prior and the public beaches in Misty Point were much cleaner as a result. Recently, with help from the Stanford Foundation, they were able to buy a new beach rake for the town tractor and ban plastic from the beach. Each morning, someone from the Misty Point Public Works Department spent time clearing the sand of all debris. Misty Point had received an accommodation from the county for their effort and drawn more tourism as well.

Moving forward, there were plans to keep their beach and the rest of their town as clean as possible. If successful, Pure Horizons could expand to other parts of the State and Coast of New Jersey.

"You promised me," a female voice yelled from the next room. "You promised me."

"Please, calm down," Fiona said from the hall. "I have no control over what your florist is capable of. As a matter of fact, I did not recommend her to you. She's not one of our usual vendors."

"I don't care," the voice yelled. "I want lavender vases."

"Perhaps you could use another florist?"

"Hardly, I've already had to pay this one a lot of money and I want what I want."

Megan heard Fiona sigh.

"Why don't we go to my office and discuss this?"

"No, I want to discuss this right now, right here. Let everyone hear us so they'll have an idea of how much this place stinks."

"That's hardly a fair thing to say," Fiona countered. "We didn't choose the florist, Miss Goren. Why don't we call her together and see if we can work this out?"

"Fine, you'd better work it out or else." Megan cringed as she listened to their steps fade down the hall.

"Well, she's a piece of work, isn't she?"

Megan jumped when she heard the voice by her side. Her cheeks flamed as she didn't want anyone to think she was eavesdropping, although it was obvious everyone had heard the conversation.

"Sorry, I didn't mean to scare you."

Megan looked at the woman standing next to her. She was in her twenties with brown lanky hair. "I'm sorry, I was so distracted by that woman threatening Fiona, I didn't hear you come up beside me. Did you hear her?"

"Who could hear anything with Bridezilla screaming like that?"

Megan smiled despite herself. "She was loud and threatening."

The girl smiled back and stuck out her hand. "Hi, my name is Julie. Julie Bratton."

"Hi, how are you, Julie? Do you think Fiona's okay in there? Should we check on her?"

"I'm sure she's fine. That bride is in here at least once a week screaming about something." Julie smiled and shrugged to ease the situation. "I'm Fiona's assistant," Julie said as she grabbed Megan's hand and shook it.

"Very nice to meet you," Megan replied.

"Can I answer any questions for you? Were you and Fiona able to finish the tour?"

Megan paused for a moment. "No, we were just starting with the ballroom when the bride started calling for her."

"Debbie."

"Excuse me?" Megan asked.

"Bridezilla's real name is Debbie Goren."

"Oh, I understand now," Megan said with a smile.

"Anyway, I can tour you around the country club and answer any questions you have," Julie offered again.

"If you have time and don't mind, that would be great," Megan said.

"Great, let's go." Julie grabbed Megan's arm and pulled her across the ballroom. "We could go outside and look at the beach venue and then I want to show you the reception area, the private meeting rooms and the refreshment lounges."

Megan smiled as she looked at her watch. "I'm game if you are. I've got another forty-five minutes."

"Fantastic, let's go," Julie said as she led Megan out of the room.

Thirty minutes later the two women walked back into the ballroom. "Thank you, Julie. This venue is as gorgeous as everyone has said it is."

"Have you picked a date yet?"

"I have a date in mind, although I haven't run it by the board, so it's not a solid date. I also must discuss the budget for the event. I'm hoping we can get a small discount as it's a non-profit event."

Julie smiled excitedly as she listened to Megan. "Let's go look at the schedule and pencil something in. Once you meet with the committee we can always adjust if we need to, but it's better to be penciled in then not in the books at all."

Megan thought for a moment. "Okay, that sounds fine as long as I don't have to leave a deposit. I've got to have a consensus from the board."

"No problem," Julie said. "On the way to the office, I want to tell you about our upcoming food tasting. I want you to be happy about your choice to book here, so why don't you bring a few of the board members, or all of them for that matter. I think once you've sampled a few of our chef's specialties, you'll be incredibly happy that you've booked with us."

"That sounds like a great idea, Julie."

"Let's admit it, the happier you are, the more you'll recommend us to your friends, so it only makes good business sense."

Megan smiled and nodded. "I see your point."

The pair continued to discuss the food tasting as they walked toward the beautifully appointed office to schedule a date.

CHAPTER 3

"So how was it?" Amber asked as she placed a large box of envelopes on the cherrywood desk in the library of Misty Manor.

"The ballroom was beautiful especially with the view of the ocean. I didn't get much time to speak to Fiona about the event, but I got a nice tour from one of her assistants. I'd love to schedule next year's charity gala there, but it will depend on the rate we get."

Megan reached down to scratch the top of Dudley's head. Megan had adopted the Boxer after a recent emergency at the Hand in Paws Animal Clinic. She agreed to shelter the dog and a cat for several weeks but when the problem was solved, Megan didn't have the heart to send them back to the shelter.

"We can certainly look at different times and days for better rates," Amber suggested. "My company does that a lot. We'll change an event from one weekend to the next if we get a better rate."

"I think we have a good amount of flexibility with the date," Megan said as she unpacked the envelopes. "I'll see what Fiona can do for us. In the meantime, we need to concentrate on this year's event."

"We're getting there, boss." Amber smiled as she walked across the room to grab another box of envelopes.

"Are you ready to present at the meeting tonight?"

"I think so," Amber said as she stood up straight. "About this year's event, Tommy and the Tunes are set to provide the entertainment. Doogie has a presentation about potential ocean waste and the environmental impact if we don't stop polluting the coast. Georgie will help out wherever she's needed."

"That is so nice to hear and I know their contributions will be great, but we'll have to see what else the committee suggests at tonight's meeting and then decide on what makes the most sense. We'll figure it out. At least we have the date and the venue for this year and I'm sure everyone will have a great time and all for a good cause," Megan said with a smile.

"I want to know whose idea it was to make up 1000 envelopes with information about the coast." Amber scowled as she picked up a box of educational sheets.

Megan laughed. "These are the fun jobs that no one shows up for." Dudley nudged her leg with his head. She put her right hand out and stroked his head.

"That's okay, you can tell me more about the country club while we put everything together. I was invited to a wedding there. It was for one of my work colleagues, but I was out of town and missed it. I haven't been invited to anything there since, but I've heard it's a fantastic venue. The view and the food are supposed to be the best in the state."

"You're in luck. I've been invited to a food tasting and I'm asking you to join me," Megan said as she began to fold a bunch of flyers.

"What do you mean?"

"Julie, the assistant who showed me around, invited me to come to the food tasting. She said I can bring as many friends or committee members as I'd like."

"That sounds great," Amber said. "I'd love to go."

"Go where?"

Megan and Amber looked up to see Georgie walk into the library. Georgie and Amber had been lifelong friends with Megan. They went to school together and had been near inseparable since Megan returned to Misty Point.

"Georgie, where have you been?"

"It's the end of beach season. There's a lot to accomplish to get the lifeguard schedule organized, with all the kids going back to college."

"Kids?" Megan laughed at she questioned Georgie. "It wasn't too long ago when we were in college."

"I know, it's been seven years, but quite frankly, college kids are looking younger and younger to me each year."

Megan nodded. "I'm beginning to agree with you there."

"So, what are we doing today?" Georgie asked.

"We're stuffing 1000 envelopes for the Pure Horizons Environmental meeting tonight. We want the committee members to share information about Pure Horizons to year-round residents of Misty Point," Amber said.

"We need as much support as we can get for the fund-raiser as well as the programs we're suggesting to protect the environment."

"That sounds great," Georgie said. "I'm on board with all your ideas and you'll have my complete support at the committee meeting."

"I'm happy to hear that," Megan said. "Amber says she's ready with her comments."

"True that," Amber laughed. "I had some of my corporate peers review it for an independent opinion."

"And?"

"They liked it but admitted there will be an uphill battle especially if there's any money to be made."

"That's for sure," Megan said. "One of the biggest projects I'd like to gather more support for is the expansion of the bird sanctuary near the marsh."

"What's holding you back?" Georgie asked.

"The financial group who wants to bring in fill and build commercial buildings there. Not only will it ruin the natural environment, but it's also not safe for residents especially if we face another big storm like Sandy. There are a lot of issues, but I'll let Amber discuss it at the meeting. Eventually, we'll have to face off with the planning board in town."

Georgie nodded as she pulled out a chair at the large cherrywood table in the library. Amber tossed her some papers. "Here, take some of the envelopes and flyers and start stuffing."

"Will do," Georgie said as she looked around. "The Misty Manor library is so beautiful, I'm willing to spend any time in here."

Megan smiled as she looked around the beautiful library lined with cherrywood bookcases in her family's Grand Victorian home. Misty Manor was originally built by her great-grandparents in the early 1900's. Megan's great-grandfather, John Stanford was a sea captain, who had been given a very large parcel of land on the Jersey Shore as a gift for completing an important transatlantic voyage for a rich Philadelphia man in the late 1800's. John named the area Misty Point and over the last hundred years the town had grown and thrived. Portions of the town were sold to accommodate year-round residents as well as the boardwalk and public areas, but the majority of town property continued to be owned by the Stanford family, which was inherited by Megan when her grandmother, Rose, recently died.

The Grand Victorian, Misty Manor, and a beautiful lighthouse were built on a small hill by John Stanford as a wedding present for his wife, Mary. Mary was Megan's great-grandmother. It was the hill that saved Misty Manor, one hundred years later, when Hurricane Sandy hit the coast of NJ.

"Yes, it's truly one of the most gorgeous rooms in Misty Manor if not all of Misty Point."

"Did you ever dream that you'd grow up and inherit Misty Manor as well as most of the town?" Georgie asked as she leaned over and grabbed another pile of empty envelopes.

"Are you kidding me?" Megan asked as she organized her pile. "It's still feels like a dream. I remember what the coast looked like when I was growing up. I love how the town has matured and the residents are great, but part of me wants to preserve some of the original beauty and nature of the Point. We can't let them build near the marsh."

"I take it you don't own that land?" Georgie asked.

"No, but I'm pretty sure it's in an environmentally protected area," Megan said. "Sadly, builders will continue to challenge the area unless we make sure it stays protected. I have to say, I don't trust our wonderful mayor to keep the land the way it should be."

"Trust him?" Amber laughed as she screwed up her face. "I'm pretty sure he's part of the finance group trying to buy it."

"That's the reason we're having the Pure Horizons meeting tonight and keeping the fundraiser in town," Megan said.

"I don't know," Georgie teased as she tossed her head. "We had a lovely offer to use a very large and expensive yacht."

Megan chuckled. "Yes, but the yacht is fifty miles away. If we're fighting for the environment in Misty Point, what better place to have the event but in Misty Point?"

"Logically, that makes sense, but it was a really large yacht." Georgie offered a slight frown with her pleading.

"I'd rather the owner offer a nice donation to the cause," Megan said. "I guess Amber and I know where to take you for your next birthday."

"Yes, we'll gather all the guys and find the perfect yacht to have dinner," Amber agreed.

Georgie shook her head and laughed. "Sure, we all know the boat is most likely going to be the size of a dinghy and the cuisine will be fast food or pizza anyway."

"I promise I'll arrange a small tour on someone's yacht to thank you both for taking the time to volunteer and help out with Pure Horizons. Now, let's get to work."

CHAPTER 4

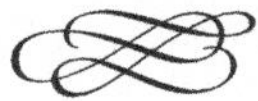

Two hours later, Megan filled a glass with ice and poured a generous amount of iced tea. They had worked steadily to stuff the 1000 envelopes and ready them for the meeting that night. Amber and Georgie had left to shower and dress for the meeting. Amber worked in corporate and would never consider giving a presentation to a group of people without wearing a power outfit. On the other hand, as the lead lifeguard on the beach, Georgie was more comfortable in swim or active wear.

Megan turned when she heard the phone ring. Walking into the foyer, she put her glass down and picked up the phone.

"Hello?"

"Miss Stanford?"

"Yes, can I help you?"

"It's Fiona, from the Misty Point Country Club. I wanted to reach out and apologize for being interrupted earlier today."

"Oh, no problem, Fiona. Thanks for calling. How's your headache?"

"She left several hours ago," Fiona said with a laugh. When Megan didn't respond she hurriedly went on, "I'm sorry. The headache in my temple feels better."

"I'm glad to hear that," Megan said. "The bride did sound aggravated."

"She tends to blow off and then calms down afterward. As a matter of fact, she came back and gave me a box of chocolates to ask for forgiveness."

"That's nice. Did you arrange the lavender vases?"

"Yes, we did. Thankfully, I was able to locate a supplier who will drop them off at her florist. Problem solved."

"That's very sweet of you," Megan said. "I've heard planning a wedding is quite stressful."

"That's an understatement," Fiona said. "Anyway, I feel bad we didn't get to finish the tour."

"That's okay, Julie came in when you left and took me around."

"Julie?" Fiona sounded surprised.

"Yes, she said she was your assistant."

Megan noted a pause before Fiona answered. "Yes, you could say that. She didn't mention to me that she toured you through the building."

"Oh, well not only that, but she invited me and any number of guests to the food tasting next week. We even choose a tentative date for our event, but I told her I have to bring the information to the committee. That's why I didn't leave a deposit. I still need rates and more information."

"I understand completely," Fiona said, her voice subdued. "I'm sorry she didn't think to mention it to me."

"Will you be at the food tasting next week?"

"Yes, I'll definitely be there," Fiona said enthusiastically.

"Great, Julie said I can bring some of the committee members. I hope that offer still stands. Perhaps you can give us a tour so we can see the ballroom in action."

"That sounds like a perfect plan," Fiona said. "If you have any questions before then please call me directly. It's easier when you use one planner. We all have a different perspective and it's better to keep everything streamlined."

"I will," Megan said. "You were the person I was referred to, so I'll make sure I speak with you directly."

"I appreciate that," Fiona said, sounding mollified.

"We have a committee meeting tonight," Megan said. "I'll let them know of our initial discussion and then I'll call back if there's a question that can't wait. Otherwise, please plan for five people to come to the food tasting. I'm not sure who'll be with me, but I'll keep it to five people."

"That's wonderful, but if you need an extra guest, feel free to bring them along. Thank you, Ms. Stanford. I'm looking forward to seeing you next week."

"You're very welcome, Fiona. I'll see you then."

Megan hung up the phone just as the doorbell rang.

CHAPTER 5

Megan opened the door and was excited to see Officer Nick Taylor standing at the door. In his arms, was a beautiful Golden retriever puppy. Dudley ran to Megan's side and starting dancing at the sight of the puppy. "Oh Nick, how adorable." Nick Taylor was a handsome officer whom she happened to be dating.

"Isn't she beautiful?" Nick asked as he scratched her neck.

"Whose puppy is that?"

"I have a friend who's trying to convince me to keep her." Nick looked down at Dudley. "What do you think? Should I keep her?" Dudley started to whine as he crouched on his rear legs.

Megan opened the door wider and stepped back. "Don't just stand there. Come in."

Nick crossed the threshold. The Golden retriever started wiggling in his arms, so he gently leaned forward and let Dudley smell her. After a minute, he put the puppy on the ground and Dudley continued to nuzzle the dog. Nick stood up and looked at Megan. "I think they'll be fine."

"I don't understand. I thought you said having a dog was a problem since you're at the police station more than home."

"That's the interesting part. I was speaking to someone about what the police department would need to start a K9 unit. I'd have to present the information to the Chief and town council since it would involve funds for training, insurance, and shelter."

"That's not a problem. I'm sure the Stanford Foundation would offer a grant for the project if they don't approve it for the town."

"We have a way to go before we get to the town presentation. I just went to get some initial information. The most common breeds used for a K9 unit are German Shepherds, Retrievers, Belgian Malinois and Bloodhounds. While I was there, the guy handed me a Golden retriever that had just been dropped off. The dog has no home, so he wants me to adopt the dog or drop her off at the Hand in Paws Animal Clinic in our town."

"Oh Nick, the shelter is almost full again. I don't know if they could take her."

"Then you're going to have another guest in Misty Manor tonight, that is, as long as you don't mind."

Megan started to pet the Golden. "She's beautiful. Does she have a name?"

"Not that I'm aware of. She was dropped off with a bow around her neck but nothing else."

"You'll have to name her, then."

"If you have room for her to stay tonight, I'll think it over. If she goes to the clinic, I'll let her adoptive family name her."

Megan laughed as she gestured at the foyer of the grand mansion. "Well, it's not like we're crowded. We have plenty of room, but we have to go to the Pure Horizons committee meeting tonight. I don't know if you want to leave her alone with Dudley and Smokey.

"If worse comes to worse, I'll be happy to stay here and watch the dogs," Nick said with a shrug.

"That's okay, you can both go. We'll be fine."

Megan and Nick turned when they heard Marie's voice call down the hall.

"Oh, thank you so much," Megan said as she walked over and hugged her friend and housekeeper. Marie had been a friend of her parents since they were young and offered to help Megan care for her dying grandmother when Megan returned to Misty Manor. Once Rose was gone, Megan asked her to stay on, more as a friend, than a housekeeper. Marie agreed but earned her keep by cleaning the rooms in Misty Manor and cooking some amazing meals.

"It's been getting too quiet here with just the few of us," Marie said. "We've got a ton of rooms in this house and only a couple are being used. I'd like a little lively company from the dogs."

"Marie, I've been asking you to sell your house and move here permanently, but you keep refusing," Megan said.

"Well, I'm not ready to part with my childhood home, yet," Marie said before she slyly looked at Nick. "Besides, I'm thinking, one day, I'm just going to be in the way."

Megan reddened and placed her hand on Marie's arm. "You'll always be welcomed here."

Nick laughed as he said, "If we ever ask you to go out for milk, you'll know what we mean." He gave her a wink that made both Marie and Megan blush. Megan grabbed him by the arm. "It's a good thing you're so handsome or I'd boot you right now but keep the dog."

"I have no doubt of that," Nick said with a laugh.

Marie shook her head at the pair. "What about dinner tonight? Are they feeding you at the meeting?"

"I think we're having snacks, but if we can get out of here on time, we're going to stop and pick up a sandwich. That will give us a chance to talk before the meeting."

"Okay, I'll just whip something up for the animals then."

"Don't forget Smokey. That cat will haunt you if you forget him."

"There's not a chance in hell that Smokey would let me forget him," Marie said. "I'm just his servant, as you well know."

Megan and Nick smiled as they watched the two dogs nuzzling in the foyer. Their smile turned to laughter as they noticed the cat on the other side of the foyer arching his back.

"There she is now," Megan said as she cooed to the cat. "It's okay Smokey, it's just a little puppy." The cat looked up at Megan, doubt in his beautiful green eyes.

"Nick, I'm going to run upstairs and change. I'll be back down in a minute and then we can get going."

"Fine, I'll wait here and play with the dogs until you come back."

Megan gave him a peck on the cheek. Nick watched as Megan ran up the beautiful grand staircase to the third landing and race off to the side to find her room. Nick was honestly awed every time he took in Misty Manor. The Grand Victorian was one-hundred years old and a beauty of a home. A grand staircase, made of cherrywood, set off the foyer decorated with marble and granite. The house had four floors and the attic led out to the roof which held a widow's walk with gorgeous views of the ocean. The fourth floor also had a full glass turret from which Megan could relax, read and watch the water when the weather was bad. Beyond the glass room, the entire floor served as a full, large attic, filled with treasures and secrets they hadn't begun to explore yet.

The first two floors of Misty Manor were simply amazing and served as a quasi-hotel in the early nineteen-hundreds when Megan's wealthy sea-captain great grandfather and his lovely bride, Mary, hosted wonderful parties for very influential friends. Their son, George, married and brought his wife, Rose, into Misty Manor. Sadly, George met a tragic end and died before his parents, so the house was left to Rose when they died. Megan's father was only a small child at the time. Megan's great-grandparents, John and Mary, trusted Rose wouldn't sell the home and move. Rose honored them by keeping the home in the family, but years later, due to some family issues, Rose had bypassed her son in her will and left Misty Manor to her granddaughter, Megan, when she died.

Nick continued to absentmindedly pet the dogs and looked up when he heard Megan descend the stairs. She had changed into a lovely dark blue dress and looked regal which only made sense as she served as the chairperson of the Pure Horizons charity. Megan had agreed to take on the role as chairperson for all her grandmother's charities which were set up and supported by the Stanford Foundation.

"Okay, I'm ready," Megan said as she stopped in the foyer and gathered her purse. "I'm nervous about this meeting. Everyone has been so emotional about preserving the marsh as a permanent bird sanctuary."

"Where there's money, there's grief. The people from the financial group figure the birds will find a new home."

"Oh, Nick, there's so much more to it than that. Amber is prepared to speak to the fact that commercial building in the marsh will ruin the ecosystem. The bird sanctuary will only be a small part of how the community will be harmed. Plus, from what I've read, it's not safe to build there, even with fill."

Nick shook his head. "I can't believe that group has actually proposed to fill in the marsh, especially with what we went through with Hurricane Sandy. The next big storm will knock it all down."

"There are people who still haven't made it back to their homes," Megan said as she frowned. "We can't set ourselves up for that ever again."

Nick opened the front door. "We'd better be going. You don't want to be late."

Megan turned toward the kitchen and yelled out. "We're leaving Marie, thanks for watching the dogs and I appreciate all you do."

Marie popped her head out of the kitchen to say goodbye. Three animals were close behind her and carefully watching the piece of ham in her hand. She waved at Megan and Nick and shooed them toward the front door. "You go, have a great time. We'll be fine."

Laughing, the pair left the manor.

CHAPTER 6

"Are you sure we have time?"

Nick shot Megan a glance. "We'll make time. You must eat. Who knows how long this meeting will last? I don't want you getting dizzy during all the yelling."

Megan's eyes widened. "That's so true, it's not even funny."

Nick chuckled and pulled his Camaro over to the curb. He jumped out of the car and helped Megan out of her seat. Pulling her close, Nick kept his arm around her waist on the way into the Deli. "When was the last time you had a sub from Shore Subs?"

"It's been awhile," Megan said with a smile. "I didn't realize they were still in business. Are they just as good as they were?"

"Even better. You order what you want, and they can load it with whatever seasonings you like." Nick kissed three fingers and gestured toward the Deli.

Megan was still laughing as they went inside. They pulled up to the counter and waited for the tanned college student to take their order.

"Can I help you?"

"I'll have the number seven," Megan said after scrutinizing the menu board. "Just a half sandwich, please."

"Toppings?" The bored counter clerk stared as he waited for an answer.

Megan thought one moment. "Lettuce, tomato, onions, and oil and vinegar. Oh, and don't forget the oregano."

"You got it," he said as he looked over at Nick.

"I'll take a number twelve."

"Loaded Cheesesteak," the student said as he nodded. "Good choice."

Nick paid the bill while Megan collected napkins and drinks and choose a table in the corner. A few minutes later, Nick arrived with sandwiches in hand.

"Oh Nick, I told him only half."

"This is half," he replied as he put the plates on the table.

Megan shook her head and took a bite of her sub. "This sub is huge. I'll eat some and wrap it for later unless you want it?" She held it out to him.

Nick shook his head. "I've got my own, thanks."

After several mouthfuls, Megan nodded as she looked at her food. "You were right, Nick. This sandwich is even better than before."

Nick chuckled as he continued to eat his meal. "So, tell me again. What's going on in this meeting tonight?"

Megan chewed as she planned her explanation. She put her sandwich down and took a moment to sip her soda.

"The issue is this. We've got to preserve the shoreline. You grew up here, so you know the bird sanctuary as much as any of us. Hell, we hiked there as kids. Over the years, the area has changed just like the coastline near the beach. Hurricane Sandy certainly didn't help. It's been several years now and the wildlife at the marsh is just returning to normal."

"That sounds logical," Nick said as he popped the last bit of sub in his mouth and then wiped his hands on a napkin.

"Yes, except there's a private financial group that is trying to change the zoning laws in town so they can purchase a good portion of the marsh and build. They're using lower taxes as an argument to convince town people."

"That's not good," Nick said.

"Tell me about it, plus they're trying to influence the planning board with a few gifts and dinners."

"Really, not good."

"So, since the town is not championing a defense of the bird sanctuary, the Pure Horizons Environmental Group has decided to step in and fight them. We can lobby just as hard at the county and state level."

"Oh boy, another disagreement in town." Nick shook his head.

"You can bet on that, but one utterly worth fighting. Those of us that love the Jersey Shore will do whatever we can to preserve it. This group wants to make a fast buck by constructing a sub-quality building in an area that may be problematic long term. I'm not sure they can build a stable foundation without bringing in fill and totally changing the landscape. They make their money and get out. We'd have to clean up the mess with a lot of taxpayer dollars when the next big storm comes along."

"That's a problem," Nick said as he shook his head. "Do you know anyone in the private financial group?"

"No, but I'm trying to find out. Teddy is coming to the meeting tonight. I'm hoping he can find some information. He won't present anything at the meeting, but it would let us examine some motives."

Megan wrapped her sandwich and placed it back in the bag. "I'm too aggravated now to finish eating."

Nick sighed as he watched her push the bag aside. "Who'll be there tonight?"

"Amber is making a presentation about land value and ecosystems. Doogie will be talking a bit about the ocean, beach and the bird sanctuary. Then we'll have an open discussion which is why I'm happy you'll be there. Some unofficial police presence will hopefully discourage protestors."

Nick smiled as they stood. "I doubt there will be any problems, but I'll do what I have to do to keep everyone calm."

He snaked his arm around Megan's waist as they walked to the car.

For a moment, she let her head rest against his hard chest and felt secure.

CHAPTER 7

As Nick drove toward the Misty Point library, Megan silently reviewed the agenda and who would be present in the conference room. The committee was growing and now full of inspired residents' intent on keeping the shore a beautiful place, but there were always those members who were not entirely open to change or new innovative ideas. All appointees were of a volunteer nature and generally the group collaborated well, but things got heated at times as everyone had different ideas of proposed goals and methods.

Georgie and Amber, her two friends from high school, were the first to join when Megan was installed as chairperson. Some older committee members had retired when Rose died, and others were thrilled the committee continued to grow.

Megan was grateful for her two friends and that they had chosen to stay in their hometown. Georgie had spent more time on the beach than at home during high school and never left after graduation. She was now the highest-ranking lifeguard in Misty Point, NJ and spent her time on education, schedules, and beach safety. She trained the new lifeguards and made sure they were competent to guard precious lives. She was perfect for Pure Horizons.

Amber had been the Prom Queen and always one of the most fashionable students. Her makeup was always beautiful. Just enough to look gorgeous but not too heavy or overdone. It was no surprise she did well at career day, looking the consummate professional and easily impressing corporate recruiters which led her to a career in administration. Recently, she started dating Tommy McDonough who worked various jobs around town to stay afloat, but his recent claim to fame was his music group, Tommy and the Tunes. They were becoming more famous than ever and able to book larger venues each season.

Both friends were speaking at the meeting tonight. Georgie was giving a real time report of the conditions at the beach and marsh. Amber was ready to speak about those ecosystems in more detail. Georgie had recently started dating Doogie Portman, a famous surfer who established his reputation in Misty Point. Since then, he had traveled to many coasts and won prestigious awards for surfing but then settled back to Misty Point as his career began to slow down. Doogie also happened to be an expert at sunken treasure ships, ocean life and many other things related to oceanography. Doogie would say a few words about the cleanliness of the ocean but have a more detailed talk at the big charity event.

Another person at the meeting would be the Misty Point Mayor, Andrew Davenport. A long-time thorn in Megan's side, she wished he hadn't felt the need to join Pure Horizons and she had a hard time believing his concern had anything to do with the town or the coast. His family had been involved in her grandfather's death and Megan was happy his jerk of a son was still in jail for accosting and threatening her life as well.

On the other hand, Megan was happy that Theodore Harrison Carter, the attorney who had represented her grandmother's estate for years and championed her trusts and foundation, would be there to represent the organization against any crazy ideas. When Rose died, he agreed to continue to serve with hope that his son could eventually take over for him as legal representation for the foundation and estate of Misty Manor.

Pure Horizons had grown, and opinions had become much more diverse. She tried to meet and introduce herself to each new member but there was never enough time to get to know everyone as well as Megan would have liked. Serving as the chairwoman, Megan knew the group needed to feel united over the ultimate decisions that were made.

Thankfully, Nick was there to watch the crowd. There were definite advantages to having a police presence at public meetings.

"Penny for your thoughts?"

Megan turned toward Nick and blinked, realizing she had not heard anything he said in the last ten minutes. "I'm sorry, what did you say?"

"I asked what's on your mind. You're noticeably quiet tonight."

Megan offered a quirky smile. "I'm just thinking about the meeting. I hope we don't have anyone looking for a fight. If our members don't agree, how can we come together on a unified front to fight the private equity group trying to get rid of the marsh?"

Nick reached over and grabbed her hand. "It will be fine. Let's see what happens and then we'll deal with it."

"I hope so, Nick. I really hope so."

CHAPTER 8

They reached the library and Nick parked the car. "Wow, the parking lot looks pretty crowded."

Megan frowned as she looked around. "There's way too many people getting involved in this."

"Things will be fine. Let's go in and get this party started."

They locked the car and walked into the library. The community room was in the back of the library and Megan walked in to see Amber and Georgie already greeting other members. There was a table covered with a beautiful sea blue and green tablecloth. Platters of cookies, brownies, cheese and crackers were on the table and looked delicious, but it was the smell of the freshly made coffee that always drew Megan in. She normally didn't drink a lot of coffee at night, but the Pure Horizons meetings were an exception.

She placed her things at a seat in the center of a table in the front of the room. The board sat in the front of the room while the members sat in fabric chairs facing them. Megan then walked over to the coffee pot and poured a cup of coffee. She added vanilla flavored cream and sipped. Within seconds she was joined by Amber and Georgie.

"We're glad you made it," Amber said. "Everyone is excited about this project."

Georgie popped a brownie bite in her mouth and nodded toward the mayor. "I don't think the esteemed Andrew Davenport looks so happy."

Megan slowly turned around to act casual. She spied the mayor speaking to another man across the room and using his head to nod in her direction. Megan didn't recognize the other gentleman from town, but Misty Point had grown. There were plenty of people Megan didn't know.

"I sneaked up behind him a little while ago," Georgie continued. "I don't know who he's talking to, but I don't think he's happy that so many residents have already gotten behind this meeting."

"That's too bad, if it's true, because he's likely to see many of us at the planning board meeting when it comes up." Megan threw her stirrer in the garbage and turned back to the table. "We're just going to talk about our town and what can happen when you upset the balance of mother nature. The residents can offer their opinion, so we'll see if we're united. Whether there are ten members of Pure Horizons or one hundred, we'll still question whether it's safe to change the zoning laws near the marsh to allow more construction." She looked at her watch and nodded to Nick who was at the other side of the table grabbing a couple of chocolate chip cookies. "Okay, let's do this."

Megan walked to the front table and sat down with other members of the board. Amber and Georgie sat in the first row and looked around the room to watch if others were getting the hint. Nick popped the last cookie in his mouth and then leaned against the wall with his arms folded across his chest.

Megan looked up and down the table and when the entire board was seated, she reached down and rang a small bell she brought to meetings with her. Hearing the sound, the few guests who were still lingering by the food scurried to a seat and fell silent.

"Good evening," Megan said as she looked around. "My name is Megan Stanford and I'd like to welcome you to the monthly meeting of Pure Horizons. I see a lot of new faces in the crowd. For our first-time visitors, Pure Horizons is a non-profit committee dedicated to keeping the ocean, the beaches and environment of Misty Point and other parts of the state clean and renewable. This committee was started by my grandmother, Rose Stanford, as part of the Stanford Foundation. The foundation continues to support the committee along with other activities run by Pure Horizons."

A woman shot her hand up in the air.

"Yes? Do you have a question?" Megan asked the woman politely.

"I'd like to know what kind of things Pure Horizons does?"

Megan paused for a second and nodded. "Okay, this isn't normally the open part of the meeting, but to answer your question Pure Horizons sponsors education about the shore, as well as sponsors environmental walks, beach cleanup and decreased ocean pollution. We also donate when new flora needs to be planted to protect the shore. For instance, there was a lot of indigenous planting that needed to be done after Hurricane Sandy."

"Fine, that's wonderful," the lady said and crossed her arms.

Megan looked to her right and saw Teddy furrow his brow. She was familiar with that look and knew it usually indicated he was concerned about possible trouble brewing at the meeting. Thankfully, they had him on their team acting as legal expert.

"To continue, can I have a motion to open the meeting?"

They received a motion which was seconded, and Megan looked at Betty to see if she had been able to record the names and the time before she continued. Betty had retired from town hall a couple of years ago and was a cracker jack at meetings. When Betty nodded, Megan continued to explain the agenda. The committee worked through their reports and Megan announced both Amber and Doogie when it was time for their presentation.

The audience listened to everything they said and there was a robust Q & A after their talks. Once they were done, the committee discussed goals and next projects including the marsh and proposed change of the zoning laws. The gentleman who was with the mayor raised his hand and when he was recognized said, "I'm just wondering, Ms. Stanford. What's the benefit to you if this change does or doesn't go through?"

"I'm sorry?" Megan said as she shook her head. "I don't understand the question."

"Well, I'm sure you wouldn't be this passionate unless there was something in it for you in the long run."

Megan was taken aback as her cheeks flamed. "There is no gain for me either way. I simply want to see the town protected and kept clean."

"Sure, the town you happen to own most of." A few gasps were heard in the crowd as heads turned to identify who would say such things at a private committee meeting.

Teddy raised a hand toward Megan, indicating he would handle the remainder of the conversation.

"Excuse me, sir. Can you state your name and address for the record?"

The man did not speak but glared at Teddy instead.

Teddy tried again. "Would you mind giving us your name and address for the record? Are you a resident of Misty Point or perhaps the press?"

The man, who remained agitated said, "I'm trying to establish who will gain or lose if this plan goes through or not." Megan glanced at Nick who stood up straight and walked closer to where the man was sitting as Teddy continued to speak.

"Miss Stanford does not own the property that is in question. It's owned by the town as part of preserved land. The town has the burden of proof of need to open such property to private use. Keeping land in its natural state is vital for water quality, wildlife, flood control, clean air and tourism which is a big part of a shore town's economy. Those are the issues at stake here, not Miss Stanford. If you have any further questions, please see me privately after the meeting."

The man turned absolutely red. "I'll get my answers where and when I'm good and ready to get them and not from some empty suit who'll just try to dance around me with legal crap." Pushing the empty chair in front of him, he stood up and strode out of the meeting.

Teddy glanced at Nick who followed behind to make sure he left the library property.

Embarrassed and with warm cheeks, Megan reviewed the Pure Horizons main event for the summer, inviting everyone to attend and help support their mission. The meeting was then officially closed, and everyone dispersed to chat or grab more snacks from the table. Megan stayed in her seat, waiting for Nick to return.

CHAPTER 9

"Don't worry about that idiot." Megan looked up to see Teddy by her side.

"He was so rude," Megan said, her hands trembling slightly.

"I don't know if he's just another person who believes everything is a conspiracy or if he was put up to this foolishness by the mayor. They were deep in conversation before the meeting started."

"Yes, I did see that as well."

"Megan, don't pay him any attention. Let's continue on our path and honor the goals and ideas started by your grandmother. I'm sure she is very proud of you at this moment for protecting the town and continuing to support her favorite charities. There are many people in town who rely on these grants and donations. Half of them don't even realize where they're coming from. What's important is we continue to help the community even if everyone doesn't see it that way."

"You're right, Teddy," Megan said as she gave the elderly gentleman a big hug. When she released him, Nick was on his way over. Amber, Georgie, and Doogie were waiting by the side.

"Is everyone okay?" Nick asked as he snaked his arm around Megan's shoulders and gave a squeeze.

"Yes, we're all fine," Megan said as she smiled at Nick. "I know you can't be here in your official duty, but did he cause any trouble or just leave?"

"I watched him pull out of the parking lot," Nick said as he smiled. "I was able to get his plate, so I'll look into that in the morning."

"Don't do anything that will get you in trouble. He can have his nasty opinion. I just want to make sure he's not a threat to anyone."

Nick cocked his head to the side without saying anything, but Megan watched the meaningful look between Nick and Teddy. She realized they were considering him more of a threat than they wanted to admit. Megan made a mental note to follow up with Nick after work tomorrow and see what he was able to find out.

Megan turned to Teddy. "How do you think the meeting went over?"

"I think it went well. The talks were highly informative and the literature for the attendees, as well as the community at large, was an excellent idea, especially giving them independent websites to obtain more information." Megan smiled at the attorney. He was still a dapper gentleman, with proper suit and silk tie in place, even for an evening meeting. His son, Jonathan Brandon Carter, although extremely handsome, would dress more casually at these types of meetings.

"Thank you, Teddy. I'm sure we'll get some feedback." As their conversation ended, Megan could see the room had cleared, and she looked up to see her friends waving at her and pointing to their watch. It was time to go. Megan turned back to Teddy. "We're going to get a bite to eat and discuss the meeting. You're welcome to join us unless you're meeting Jonathan?"

Teddy laughed. "That would be difficult. He's back in London, my dear. I appreciate the invitation but believe me you don't want these old bones holding you and your friends back. Go eat and enjoy your dinner." Teddy leaned down and gave Megan a peck on the top of the head, the same way he'd been doing since she was a little girl. "I'll be calling you soon so we can continue to plan. I meant what I said. I know, deep in my heart, that Rose is smiling in heaven as well as shedding a tear or two with pride. Keep doing what you know is right and you'll be fine."

Megan was surprised when she felt a lump form in her throat. She missed her grandmother and would give anything to have her at her side this very moment. "Thank you, Teddy. Be safe and I'll talk to you soon."

Teddy turned and shook Nick's hand which Nick appreciated very much. He was aware that Teddy had been hoping there would be a relationship between Megan and Jonathan, but Nick would have been very intent on not losing Megan again. She had refused to go to Prom with him years ago and instead went with Mayor Davenport's son. Nick felt so defeated that she had chosen a weasel over him, he didn't ask her out again until she returned from Detroit to take care of Rose. Thank goodness he was around to protect her when the Mayor's son tried to kill her. He was not going to let her go easily.

When Teddy walked away, Megan grabbed his hand and walked over to her friends. "You guys still up for pizza?"

Georgie started laughing. "Is that a real question?"

Megan rolled her eyes. "Someday, we'll grow up. Let's go to Antonio's."

The group drifted out to the parking lot and everyone jumped into their cars. It was only a couple of blocks to Antonio's and it would have been simple to walk there, but it was always walking back that could be a problem depending on the time. It would be a different story, if it were a warm, beautiful night, highlighted by a full moon, and a gentle wind. Both would allow a vision of the ocean, combined with the smell of the brine and the sound of the ocean waves breaking on shore.

"What are you thinking about?" Nick asked as he laughed.

Megan shook her head. "Oh nothing, my mind is drifting through a lot of things tonight."

"Well, try to relax and enjoy yourself." Nick pulled into a parking space and turned off the car. After securing the brake, the two got out and met their friends in front of the pizzeria. Doogie had his arm around Georgie. Amber purposely stood off to the side, not to cramp their style. Tommy wasn't able to come to tonight's meeting as he had a gig near Seaside, but he'd planned to call as soon as he was free.

"Hey, my favorite group," Mary, their favorite waitress, said as they walked inside. "Where do you want to sit?"

"How about our usual booth in the back?" Megan leaned toward Mary. "We have some talking to do."

Mary smiled as she grabbed menus from a pile on the stand near the door. "You got it." The group followed her as she led them to the isolated table. Although it was sparkling clean, she pulled out a rag and wiped it down again. When the gang was seated, she pulled out her pad and pen. "Do you know what you want?"

"A pitcher of Diet Coke to start," Amber said. "I'll take a small salad with red wine vinegar and just a drop of oil."

Georgie rolled her eyes at Megan. When Mary looked up at the rest of the group, they didn't hesitate to order several delicious pizzas, meatballs and wings. Within a flash, Mary was back with red plastic cups filled with ice and several pitchers of diet soda with lemon. She brought two pitchers of cold water with lemon as well.

Once everyone had a drink, Megan asked the same question. "Well, how do you think the meeting went?"

"I think it went very well," Georgie said, "except for the jerk." She turned to Amber and Doogie. "Both of you gave great talks. I'll admit I was a little nervous it would be boring, but it was very interesting and informative. I think every guest there tonight was ready to sign up and give us support."

"Thank you," Amber said as she preened. "I'm so glad the library had the ability to show the presentation on the screen. That made things so much easier."

"I'll agree with that," Doogie said. "I'd like to use that room to teach the local kids more about oceanography. I think there's a decent group that would be interested."

"That sounds like a great idea," Megan said. "Anything to bring the community back into the library. Let's talk to Lindsey. I'm sure she and the rest of the librarians would be on board to have a great educational program." Megan thought for a minute and smiled. "Hey, let's record your lectures and then you can start a video channel on social media. You can invite your followers to follow environmental suggestions as well."

The rest of the group nodded and suggested they start a video channel about the town in general. They could post videos about the lighthouse, town history, boardwalk and a few promos for tourism and Pure Horizons. "Let me talk to Teddy about that," Megan said with a laugh. "Although I might do better talking to some of those young lifeguards for tips." The group talked about the meeting for a few more minutes but stopped when their food arrived. The pizza disappeared quickly as they laughed and enjoyed their time together.

"Speaking of eating, I wanted to invite you all to join me for dinner next week," Megan said as she gathered their attention. "Amber, make sure you bring Tommy as well."

"At Misty Manor?" Georgie asked.

Megan shook her head.

"What's this all about?" Georgie asked, eyebrows raised.

"You heard me talk about the Misty Point Country Club tonight. I tentatively booked next year's event there, but we still must vote on the date and price. In the meantime, the manager, Fiona, invited me and several board members to their food tasting. I wanted to invite the group to go and see what you thought of the place."

Amber smiled as she said, "I've heard the weddings are beautiful so I'd love to go but shouldn't you be taking the board members?"

"I did ask a few of them at the meeting," Megan said as she picked up her glass of water. "One or two said yes and Teddy said he would love to come. The others either had plans or didn't want to go. They said I could bring unlimited guests and I'm sure Fiona wouldn't mind a few others. Of course, I'll call her to make sure."

"It sounds great," Amber said as she sat up straight. "I wonder what one wears to a food tasting. Did she give you any hints about proper attire?"

Megan turned to her. "I never even thought about asking that question, but I'll ask when I confirm." She turned to Nick. "Do you think you'll be able to come?"

He shrugged. "I have to check my schedule. I'll do that at the station tomorrow. Hopefully, I'm not scheduled to patrol the boardwalk that night."

"I hope you're free," Megan said as she turned to the group. "I hope you're all free. It may be fun, and I think it would be good for Tommy and the Tunes to meet Fiona. I'm sure she can recommend the band if Tommy wants to play there."

Amber thought for a moment. "I'll be sure to ask him. I'm sure the exposure couldn't hurt but they're really not a wedding band."

"Well, just talk to Fiona and see what she says. I'm sure they have other events there all the time. Anyway, I think it could be fun."

"Sure, I'm in," Georgie said as she poured herself some diet soda.

"Me, too," Doogie said as he popped the last piece of his pizza in his mouth.

"And you couldn't keep me away," Amber agreed. "I'll talk to Tommy tonight."

Megan turned to Nick. "I'll check my schedule and let you know tomorrow."

"Great, then maybe we can go to the boardwalk afterwards."

Mary started clearing the table and dropped the bill. Once they settled, they walked to their cars.

Nick opened the door of his Camaro and helped hand Megan inside. She put her belt on while he circled the car and jumped into the driver's seat. Megan slid her window down and put her face toward the surf. "It's such a beautiful night. It's a shame we couldn't have spent the night near the beach enjoying the sound and smell of the surf."

"There's no reason we can't go now," Nick said as he raised his eyebrows.

Megan thought for a moment before Nick nudged her. "C'mon, you live near the ocean, but you rarely enjoy it. Let's go for a walk."

He drove toward Misty Manor and parked near the end of the boardwalk. Hand in hand, they walked in silence toward the water. As they walked, they pointed at the lighthouse. The light flashed in the lantern room and looked bright as ever despite being 100 years old.

"Uncle Billy's keeping the lighthouse in order," Megan said as she smiled. Uncle Billy was a good friend of the Stanford family and looked out for Rose for years once George disappeared. He was welcome to live in the lighthouse as long as he wanted.

Megan stopped near the surf, took her shoes off and stood with her feet in the water. She faced the horizon and watched the moon reflecting on the water. Nick gently stood behind her and wrapped his arms around her waist. Megan leaned her head back against his strong shoulder as they watched a few boats in the far distance. "It's so beautiful and relaxing at this time of night."

"Couldn't agree more," Nick said as he whispered in her ear. The wind blew wisps of her hair around them. He began to nibble Megan's earlobe and trailed kisses down her neck. Megan giggled until Nick turned her to face him. Their lips met with a passion as the surf crashed around them and splashed at their feet. Nick kissed the hollow of her neck as she held him tightly. His hand slid to her low back as their senses blended with the sand and the reflection of the moon off the sea.

CHAPTER 10

"You look gorgeous," Megan said as Amber twirled.

"Thank you," Amber preened. "It took me a while to figure out what to wear."

Megan smiled as she looked down at her own outfit. She wore a nice dress, but nothing fancy.

"Amber, I love that color on you and your outfit will blend in beautifully with the ballroom. Everything there has been done in shades of blue and seafoam."

"I can't wait. I'm so excited."

Megan turned when she heard the doorbell ring. Through the windowpane to the side of the door, she spied Georgie and Doogie on the porch. "You guys look great," Megan said as she pulled the door open.

"Thank you very much." Georgie and Doogie stepped into the foyer. They were also in casual dress. "Amber, you look fantastic, as usual."

"I haven't dressed up in a long time. It feels nice to fuss on occasion," Amber said as she smiled.

Georgie turned to Megan. "Is Nick coming?"

"Yes, thankfully he was able to adjust his schedule and should be here any minute. Why don't we wait on the porch? It's a beautiful night."

"Sounds great," Amber said. "Tommy should be here soon."

Megan turned and shouted to Marie that they would be on the porch. Marie stepped out of the kitchen and waved. Her full apron was tied over her clothing as she concentrated on cooking a delicious meal for later in the week. "Okay, I'll be there in a moment, but everything is set up and waiting."

The group landed on the porch and watched the ocean for a few minutes. The wind was mild, but strong enough to carry the scent of brine and suntan lotion to the house. They watched the waves and foam roll to shore until Megan caught sight of Nick's car pulling in the driveway. After parking, Nick and Tommy both jumped out and joined the group on the porch.

Nick pulled Megan into a tight hug and kissed her on top of her head.

Tommy ran over to Amber and pulled her close. "You are a sight to behold." Amber blushed as they hugged.

Megan held Nick's hand as she called the group to walk to the end of the porch. Marie had set up a table with plates of cheese and crackers. A bar was tucked under an eave, stocked with ice and glasses.

The group sauntered over, and Nick slipped behind the bar. He spent a few minutes opening cold beer for the guys and pouring glasses of wine for the ladies. They nibbled on a few crackers while they sipped their drinks.

"So, how does this food tasting work?" Tommy asked as he pulled on his beer.

"I'm not sure, but I believe they invite guests as if they are having a wedding. They want the guests to have a general sampling of hors d' oeuvres, entrees, salads and desserts. Their goal is to entice you to schedule your event there and prove that it will be worth it."

"I've heard the food is excellent," Amber said. "They put on an elegant, classy event. That's why I've been dying to go."

"I'll introduce everyone to Fiona. She's the manager of the country club," Megan said as she sipped her wine. "Tommy, you may want to ask her about putting you on the recommendation list for events. I know your band is booked for some larger gigs, but it may not hurt to get some recommendations until you're fully booked. I think most of the guests who attend gatherings there are fairly influential."

"I agree completely," Tommy said as he nodded. "I brought along some cards, just in case."

Nick looked at his watch and corked the wine just as they finished their drinks. "Our ride should be here soon. I just got a text. We don't want to be late to the party."

"Yes, because I have no idea if they serve at a specific time or if it's a timeless buffet," Megan said with a shrug.

They placed their glasses and bottles on the bar. Marie had already come to the deck and collected their dishes as they walked down the steps toward the driveway.

After a few minutes, a black SUV pulled up and a driver stepped out. The man was big and powerfully built. He was dressed in black cargo pants and a tight T-shirt. "Hey, Nick," the man said as he approached and shook his hand.

"Luther, great to see you," Nick said as he stepped forward and slapped his shoulder. "Thanks so much for doing this."

"Hey, anytime. I owe you this and more," Luther said as he gathered the group toward the car and opened the back door. Nick made introductions all around. Finally, he turned and said, "This is Megan Stanford."

"Happy to meet you," Luther said. "Nick has told me a lot about you."

"Oh, he has, has he?" Megan said as she turned to Nick.

Nick shrugged. "Guilty."

"To be honest, everyone is asking him about you. We were worried when Rose died. Didn't know what would happen to Misty Manor and the town. Nick says it's all going to be fine so we should stop worrying."

Luther helped to hand the women inside the SUV and the men followed. Nick sat in the front seat with Luther.

"Where are we heading?" Luther asked as he started the ignition.

"The Misty Point Country Club," Nick said. "They're having an event this evening. I couldn't fit everyone in the Camaro."

"No problem, this way you can enjoy yourself as well. It's only a couple miles away from my house, so just give me ten minutes or so notice when you're ready to return to Misty Manor."

"Thank you, Luther," Megan said. "I appreciate this."

"Anytime, Megan. As a matter of fact, anytime you need a driver or a bodyguard for that matter, give me a call. Nick is a great guy and I'll do anything for him."

"Thanks, Luther. I'll keep that in mind." Megan smiled.

Luther started the car, slipped on a dark pair of shades, and began the drive.

Within ten minutes, they arrived at the Misty Point County Club. A young valet approached the driver's door. Luther shook his head wordlessly and the valet backed off. Luther got out of the car and opened the driver's back door at the same time Nick got out and opened the back-passenger door. The group climbed out of the car and gathered under the portico roof in front of the luxurious entrance.

Luther slapped Nick on the side of his arm. "Text me when you're ready. Make sure you give me at least ten minutes."

"Will do, thanks," Nick said as he watched Luther get into the SUV and drive away. Joining his friends, Nick held out his arms and started to direct them inside the gorgeous facility and toward a very strange evening.

CHAPTER 11

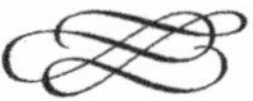

The multi-story lobby was impressive as the group walked inside. They were greeted by a maître d who directed them toward a table which held many seashells. Each shell had a name written on it. When they located the shell with their name, they picked it up. Inside the shell was a number which indicated what table they were seated at, as well as a small baggie which contained sand and a fragrant pink candle.

"What a great idea," Amber said. "Are we all at the same table?"

"I think we're all at Table Four," Megan said as she peeked at everyone's shell. "How lovely."

As the group moved forward, they were met by a waitress holding a tray of glasses filled with strawberries and champagne. She handed each person a glass to enjoy while they made their way to their table.

"This is delicious," Georgie said. "Next time we sit on the porch at Misty Manor, let's have a tray of these babies."

Megan laughed at Georgie's enthusiasm. "You got it. I'll make sure I tell Marie about it as soon as we go home."

The group reached their table and arranged their seats. Laughter filled the room. There was a tinkling of glasses and bits of happy conversation flowed through the air. Their table had a gorgeous sea foam linen tablecloth with a blue silk topper. The centerpiece was a clear glass vase filled with a combination of white roses and ferns. Positioned around the floral arrangement were several clear glass holders with lit candles inside. The candlelight was thrown around the room by the reflection of the crystal chandelier overhead. "This place is beautiful," Amber said as she looked around. "If this is what they do for a food tasting, I can only imagine what a fancy wedding looks like. The place even smells good."

Megan laughed as she looked at her friend. "I agree with you completely. I admire your analysis for consideration but why don't you just relax and enjoy the evening."

Amber sighed, "Okay, but the analysis is all part of my work."

Megan squeezed her arm. "I know, I know. So then, let's continue."

The table was set with delicate china decorated with a small pattern of seashells. Across the plate, was a formal menu listing the multiple courses of tonight's dinner, including several choices for the entrée.

"Wow, this meal sounds delicious," Tommy said. "The band is usually watching everyone else eat while we play. I'm going to enjoy this tonight." He elbowed Amber and said, "You think I could have all of these entrees tonight?"

"No, not without being obvious. Let's order something different for me and I'll give you my food, too."

He smiled and she realized he was teasing her.

"What looks good to everyone?" Megan asked as they continued to preview the menu. "The appetizers look phenomenal. I'll be full by the end of the first course."

Georgie looked up. "That's why we brought the men."

"True, that's very true," Amber laughed.

"Hello, my name is Skylar. Welcome to the Misty Point Country Club. Can I get anyone a drink?" The group looked up and saw a lovely young waitress standing between Georgie and Doogie. She was dressed in black pants with a fancy silk peacock blue top and stood poised to take their order.

"I'll take another glass of champagne and strawberries," Georgie said as she drained the first glass and put it on the table.

"Of course," the waitress said. "If you're interested, I can bring a pitcher of Bay Breezes to the table. Very refreshing."

"That sounds, great," Amber said as she looked at the waitress.

The waitress looked at each member of the table, to confirm they all agreed. When she looked at Nick, he said, "I'll take bourbon, neat."

"Of course," she said. He was rewarded with a warm smile from Skylar before she left to fill their order.

"The room's filling up," Nick said as he continued to observe the guests.

"I'm surprised you noticed," Megan said with a smirk. She nodded her head to the side. "Don't look now, but Mayor Davenport just walked in with a bunch of his cronies," Megan whispered. "Thankfully, they're seated on the other side of the room."

"I wonder why they're here," Nick said as Skylar was back placing their drink glasses in front of them as well as the pitcher of Bay Breezes.

"Maybe, as dignitaries, they get invited to every food tasting to keep connected with the community." Megan took a sip of her drink and placed her glass back on the table.

"There you are." Megan turned when she heard a voice.

"Teddy, how are you? I'm so glad you were able to come. Are you sitting at our table?"

Teddy looked down at his shell. "It says Table Four, so I guess I'm the guest that will complete your seating." Teddy looked to see the empty seat located across the table.

Doogie jumped up and pulled his chair back. "Here, why don't you take my seat? That way, you'll be next to Megan and I'll sit on the other side of Georgie."

"Are you sure?" Teddy asked. "I don't want to displace you."

"No, not at all," Doogie said. "This makes more sense since you two can talk about whether the country club will meet the needs of Pure Horizons as well as a host of other things you must need to discuss."

"Thanks so much," Megan said as she squeezed his arm. "I appreciate this."

"My pleasure," Doogie said. "I'm thankful you invited me tonight as your guest." They spaced the chairs to allow plenty of room at the table and Doogie settled himself in the chair on the other side of Georgie.

Teddy made himself comfortable in his chair next to Megan while the rest of the group continued to enjoy their drinks and exchange pleasantries.

Minutes later, Megan tapped Nick and Teddy on the arms and pointed at Fiona Cochran. "There's the manager. The woman in the green dress. She'll be over at some point during the evening and probably offer to give us a tour of the club." The three watched as others entered the room and circled near her. Megan recognized Julie Bratton, her college aged assistant. She was dressed up compared to when Megan saw her last, but still looked frumpy compared to Fiona. Her hair was in a messy bun. She didn't wear makeup except for a small amount of lipstick. Megan continued to watch as the crowd filtered in and sat at their assigned tables.

"What do you think so far?" Georgie asked as she continued to sip her strawberry champagne.

"I can understand why it's so hard to book here. It's just as lovely as everyone says and we haven't tasted the food yet. I'm sure the service is top notch as well."

"We'll have to learn more about the cover band," Amber said as she pointedly looked at the trio in the corner. "I have to admit that group plays great jazz."

A shrill laugh caused them to look up. "What was that?" Tommy said as they looked across the room.

"Oh, that's Debby Goren," Megan said. "She's the bride who was complaining the day I originally came here to tour. It's looks like she's here with her mom."

Nick shook his head. "I don't think she's complaining now. Perhaps, that's her normal tone. I feel bad for the groom."

Megan elbowed her date. "Nick, be nice."

"I am. I'm showing compassion for the guy."

"Fiona told me that Debbie came back with a big box of chocolates to apologize for the day she yelled at Fiona."

"That was civil of her. I don't know why people think it's okay to be rude and obnoxious. Sometimes a big box of chocolates isn't enough to make it right."

Megan nodded while looking at Nick. "Interesting. I'll keep that in mind, Nick."

Nick picked up his glass and sipped his bourbon.

The group continued to watch the room as it filled with guests. "I can't imagine all these people are looking for a venue or have an event," Teddy said with a frown.

"I'll ask Fiona about it when we have some alone time," Megan said as she reached out and grabbed Teddy's arm. "Look over there. Isn't that man the jerk from the meeting last week? You remember? He was rude and refused to give us his name."

Teddy took a few moments as he watched the man. He slowly nodded. "Yes, I believe that is him."

"I'd love to know what event he's here to plan," Megan said. "And look, there he is laughing with the mayor."

Teddy's nod was so slight, Megan wasn't sure if she saw it or not, but Teddy looked as if he was taking notes. They watched the pair walk over to the bar and request a drink. The bartender placed two napkins on the bar and then a glass on each napkin. He poured a drink in each glass and finished by placing a small piece of lime on top. The three men then engaged in conversation for ten minutes or so. Laughing, the bartender poured another drink as soon as their glasses were empty.

"It looks like they know each other," Teddy said as he watched the group.

"It sure does," Megan said as she lifted her Bay Breeze for a sip. Her attention was brought back to the group when Amber grabbed her wrist.

"Hey, do you have to go to the ladies' room?" Amber opened her eyes wide and winked at Megan. "You have to go to the bathroom, don't you?"

"Ah, sure, yes, I think I need to go," Megan said as she put her drink down and leaned to her side to pick up her purse. Amber, Georgie and Megan all got up together and headed toward the side door. When they passed into the hall, Megan turned to Amber and said, "What's up?"

"I wanted to look around while everyone is distracted. I want to see more than this room. You took a tour. Show us where everything is."

"What? I can't take you into other rooms. What if they're locked or worse yet, being used for an affair?"

"Since when do you get nervous?" Amber asked.

"I don't know. I guess because I've already had a tour and I don't want to get caught. Fiona was very willing to tour us around and if she's busy, I know her assistant, Julie, will take us. I promise I'll get you a tour."

Disappointment crossed Amber's face.

"Since we're up, let's go to the bathroom. You're going to be amazed at how beautiful it is. The whole bottom floor of the country club is a place to relax. There's a fireplace down there with big armchairs. A nice place to escape from an event or make a phone call. We'll start there," Megan promised.

The trio walked down two flights of stairs covered with deep carpet. There was an option of an elevator for guests who were disabled. The lobby on the lower floor was also covered by the ornamental rug. Amber saw the armchairs near a fireplace which would be lovely in the cold months.

A door in the back corner led to a game room for young children and teens. An unobtrusive place to unwind and play some ping pong. There were plenty of chairs and tables for games of the digital type and one old-fashioned pin ball machine.

In the middle of the lobby were the doors leading into the restrooms. Each restroom had multiple private lavatories with doors covered with wooden slats and beach decorations. There were counters along the wall, behind blue-green glass sinks, which held tissues, lotion, and various other sundries.

As the girls were washing up, Fiona burst through the door. A look of exasperation crossed her face. "I've got to hide for a moment. If anyone asks, you didn't see me come in here." She then ran to a corner privy and locked the door.

Within seconds, the entrance door opened, and Debby Goren came barreling through. She noticed Megan and her friends and pulled up short. "Oh, I'm sorry. I was looking for someone. Did anyone notice a woman come in here? A blond with thin hair? Now that I think about it, I think she has some bald spots."

Megan recognized the woman's voice and shook her head side to side. "No, I'm sorry. I didn't see anyone who looked like that."

"Are you sure? She's the manager of this dump. She was in the ballroom and I think she took off when I went over to talk to her about my wedding." Debbie looked at Georgie and Amber who also shook their heads to indicate they hadn't seen her.

"I could have sworn I saw her run in here, but I was at the top of the stairs," Debbie mused to herself. "Maybe I should look under the stall doors."

"I think you're going to have trouble with that," Megan said as she threw her deluxe hand towel in a bin. "The wooden lattice goes to the floor."

Debbie looked at one of the doors. "Damn, you're right."

"You know, we were just looking at the game room. There were some kids in there," Georgie said with a shrug. "Maybe she's over there."

Debbie snapped her fingers. "Good idea. Believe me, I'll find her and when I do, I'll have some choice words for her."

"Great," Megan said with a lopsided frown.

"Good luck," Amber called as they watched her bang out of the door.

Megan sauntered over to the closed door that Fiona had hidden in. After a minute, she spoke to the door. "Fiona, she left the bathroom, but she may be across the lobby."

They heard a faint voice. "Thank you so much. That woman is so obnoxious. I don't have time for her complaints today."

Georgie was at the main door. She opened it an inch, wide enough to peek out. She held her hand out towards Megan and Amber as she kept watch.

"Fiona don't come out yet. We're watching her in the lobby."

After another minute, Georgie started to beckon everyone with her hand. "The coast is clear, she just went upstairs."

Fiona gingerly opened the door and stepped out.

"Are you alright?" Megan asked as she watched her.

Fiona straightened her dress and grabbed a cloth to wipe her face of perspiration. She washed her hands and turned.

"Yes, thank you. And thank you so much for covering for me. It's been a long day, I'm exhausted, and we have to start the program. If she had caught me, everyone would have heard her yelling like you did the last time you were here. That's the last thing I need tonight." Fiona leaned against the granite counter for a second.

"Do you want us to escort you back to the ballroom, so you'll have cover?" Georgie asked with a smile.

The girls laughed.

"I'd love that, but I have to make a phone call. I'll hop into the private office across the hall, and then slip into the ballroom through a private door. You can all go back up. Thank you for the offer. I appreciate the protection."

"Okay, if you're sure?" Megan looked one last time at Fiona's face for assurance.

"Yes, I am. I'm sorry she's ruined every visit you've had here. When the tasting is in full swing, I'll bring you and your friends for a long private tour."

"Yay," Amber cheered as she lifted on her toes and quietly clapped her hands together.

"Normally, I can handle most pushy women," Fiona said with a frown. "But I swear that woman will be the death of me."

CHAPTER 12

Megan and her friends returned to the ballroom and took their seats.

"Hey, we were just going to send a search party," Nick laughed as Megan settled in.

"Did you get the tour you wanted?" Teddy asked as he turned to Amber.

"Not yet, but Fiona ran into the bathroom because Debbie Goren was chasing her, so we helped her hide," Amber said as she picked up her drink and took a sip.

"What?" Nick turned to Megan.

"Oh, forget about it for now," Megan said as she waved him off. "I'll spell it out when we can talk more freely."

The party relaxed and within ten minutes Fiona returned to the room. She walked to the area where the band was playing and was handed a microphone.

She introduced herself and spent some time talking about the history of the country club and Misty Point concentrating on Megan's great grandparents and Grandma Rose. She elaborated on the honored events they had held and the celebrities that passed through over the years. She then asked her staff to join her and they lined up near the band. She took the time to introduce each staff member.

Megan made it a point to memorize the bartenders name, Lionel White. Nick would be upset but she'd see if she could dig up some information on him. Maybe she could politely ask Fiona when they went for their tour. Fiona might know the name of the obnoxious man who huddled with them as well. Megan tried not to get her hopes up and turned her attention back to the presentation.

"We'd like to take this opportunity to thank you for spending time with us at the Misty Point Country Club. We'll be offering many selections so try to sample each and every one, so you'll know how exquisite the food is. We'll all be available for questions and small tours. It would be our honor to host your event and I believe you will be incredibly happy with the outcome. Thank you very much for being our honored guests this evening."

Debbie Goren started to rise from her seat and held her arm up to ask a question. Fiona quickly turned to the band and gestured for them to start playing music. She then walked over to Debbie, took her elbow and guided her out the main door of the ballroom toward her office.

Megan jumped when Skylar appeared at her side. She held a large tray with platters of hors d'oeuvres to be served to each table. When everyone had made their choice, Skylar confirmed their choice entrée. They were offered a taste of each selection or could choose a specific dinner.

The group enjoyed the next several hours as they tasted samples of appetizers, salads, and multiple drinks with champagne. The band played soft jazz in the beginning and would switch to dance music while waiting for the next course to arrive. The couples headed out to the dance floor to work off the food.

"Where did you learn to dance?" Megan asked Nick as he led her to the music.

"Various place," Nick answered with a smile. "You think I didn't know how to dance?"

Megan shrugged. "I don't know. We've never been in that type of situation before."

Nick laughed. "We would have been if you went to the Prom with me."

Megan gave him a mock frown. "Don't spoil the evening, Nick Taylor." They continued dancing for a few more minutes before Megan said, "There doesn't seem to be as many opportunities for couples to dance as there was when I was a kid."

"The world moves on," Nick said as they adjusted to the next song. Doogie and Georgie went back to the table. Amber and Tommy stayed on the dance floor. The next song was a ballad and as they neared the table, Teddy stood and asked her for the honor of a dance.

Megan shyly agreed as Teddy took her hand. "I used to dance with your grandmother," Teddy said as he enjoyed memories of Rose. "She was a beautiful dancer. You know, you look a lot like her when she was young. Teddy pulled back and looked at Megan. She loved you so much."

Megan was temporarily speechless and felt a lump in her throat. Although she had come a long way, she still felt guilty she hadn't come home right after college to take care of her, but Rose would have been the first one to throw her out of Misty Manor and tell her to go live her life.

"Thank you, Teddy, and thank you for taking such good care of her over the years. Especially, while I was gone."

"It was my honor and pleasure," Teddy said with a smile. They stopped dancing when the music paused. Teddy gave her a slight bow to thank her. "I'm afraid I have to leave. It was a nice evening and I have no doubt having next year's event at the country club will be nothing short of a very classy affair. Thank you for extending one of the invitations to me."

"Thank you for coming for dinner, Teddy. I value your opinion."

Teddy gave her a quick kiss on top of her head. "Good night, my dear."

Megan watched him leave and made her way back to the table.

"He is just too cute," Georgie said. "He adores you."

Megan laughed. "He loved my grandmother and to be honest, he was the grandfather I never had. Hell, he was more of a father to me than my father ever was."

"It's time for your next entrée," a voice said over a microphone. "Please find your way back to your seat and enjoy."

CHAPTER 13

The group sat at the table and pulled their chairs close. Skylar, along with another server, arrived at the table with platters of food. They each had a plate with a generous piece of beef, fish and chicken. A little more than enough for them to taste the savory selections and enjoy their meal.

As the table was cleared, waitstaff rolled trolleys of dessert into the room. Skylar reappeared at their side with silver pots of coffee and tea as well as cream and sugar. Another waitress arrived at the table and was serving the group their dessert requests.

Megan stood when Fiona neared the table to greet them.

"Well, what do you think?" Fiona asked as she turned to Megan and the group.

"It's all wonderful," Megan said. "My friends would still like a tour, but between you and me, I can't wait to hold next year's Pure Horizons event at the country club."

Before Fiona could respond, Skylar appeared between them with a small silver tray. "Sorry to bother you, but the pastry chef demanded I bring this tray to the both of you."

"What's that?" Fiona asked as she looked at the tray.

"This is a brand-new dessert which the chef hasn't made for the

Club yet. He wanted the two of you to have the honor of the first taste. It's a new Chocolate Truffle creation. He said there is a secret ingredient that makes it irresistible."

"It certainly looks delicious," Megan said as she looked at the tray.

Skylar placed the tray on the table and with a napkin, handed a truffle to each of them. Fiona took a bite and gave a small appreciative moan as she looked at Megan. She then turned to Skylar and said, "You tell the chef this truffle is one of the most delicious desserts I've ever tasted."

"Hey, are you two going to share or eat them all by yourself?" Tommy called out.

Megan turned to look at him. "There's plenty on the platter. You'll get yours in a second or two." Megan turned back to Fiona. "I swear, you'd think these men are never fed."

Fiona offered a broad smile, however it didn't reach her eyes. Instead, her face showed faint dark circles that her make-up was no longer capable of covering.

"How did things go with Debbie?" Megan asked tactfully as she placed her truffle on the table. "I hope it all worked out."

"Yes, we resolved today's crisis," Fiona grinned. "To be honest, I sat and ate the chocolates she gave me as she voiced her very strong opinion as to how I should be doing my job."

Megan chuckled. "You must meet some interesting characters."

"You can say that again," Fiona said as she suddenly grimaced and leaned forward.

"Are you okay?" Megan asked, concerned she was in pain.

Fiona held a hand to her lower chest and stomach for a second. "Yes, I'm sorry. Must be too much chocolate. I'll be okay in a minute. I just haven't been feeling that well, lately."

"Have you seen your doctor?"

"No, I keep promising myself to make an appointment, but you know how that goes. The next day comes and you feel better, so you move on with the other 1000 things you have to do."

"Yes, I know what you mean, but maybe this time you should pick up the phone and make that appointment."

Fiona smiled at Megan. “I will. You’re very kind to worry about me. Now let’s do something for you and your friends.”

“Great,” Megan said as she waved the rest of her friends over. When she turned back, Fiona was very pale and had perspiration lining her forehead. “Fiona? Are you okay? Maybe we should schedule the tour for another day. You really don’t look well.”

Fiona didn’t answer and stared straight though Megan. She was clearly not focused. Megan turned to Nick. “I don’t know, but I don’t think she’s doing too well.”

Nick took a step closer to the manager. “Are you having chest pain?”

Fiona placed her hand to her chest, looked down as if she were going to vomit and then crumpled forward onto the floor.

“Oh, no,” Megan cried and knelt on the floor with Nick at her side. They called her name, but she didn’t answer them. Nick tried to feel her pulse but when he found her wrist, she pulled it back. At least they thought she did until they noticed her body was fully writhing in front of them.

“Is she having a seizure?” Georgie asked from behind them.

“Call 911,” a voice yelled out from the group.

“Let’s give her some space,” Nick said as he tried to wave back the crowd that was forming around them.

Within a few minutes the seizure stopped, and Nick rolled Fiona onto her side. He began to feel for her pulse again but could not find one. He rolled her onto her back and assessed her again. An EMT in the crowd ran over and helped him administer CPR but Fiona continue to lie on the rug, her skin bearing a pale gray pallor. She didn’t move and when the men paused for a second her head rolled to the side. Megan would never forget the sightless eyes staring in her direction. What looked like foam or spittle formed at Fiona’s mouth.

“Nothing,” the EMT said as he checked for a pulse. “Let’s try again.” Together they continued to perform CPR until the police arrived followed by EMT’s.

Megan and her friends backed up behind the table and watched in horror as the team continued to work to save Fiona’s life. Everyone saw a member of the ambulance squad look at the other and shake his head. The group watched in horror as the EMT's pulled up her chin, inserted a metal blade in her mouth and stuck a plastic tube into her throat. They pulled a metal wire back out and attached a bag which someone started squeezing as another paramedic listened to her lungs with a stethoscope. The tube was taped in place and within seconds the team lifted her on a gurney and rushed her out the door.

"Oh, Lord, they've intubated her," Georgie said with a frown.

"What does that mean?" Amber asked from behind her.

"It means she's not breathing on her own," Georgie said. "I've seen it done a couple of times on the beach. Not good. Not good at all."

"I have to sit down," Megan said as she started shaking. Someone in the ballroom was making an announcement for everyone to return to their tables and collect their things which seemed appropriate as the event was nearing the end before Fiona had her spell.

Nick walked over to the group. "They're taking her to Coastal Community but honestly they don't think she's going to make it."

"If you ask me, it looked like she's already gone," Megan said, tears forming in her eyes.

Nick saw her shaking and wrapped his arms around her. "I'm sorry you had to see that. It's very disturbing when you're not used to it."

"I wouldn't want a job where I'd be doing that all the time."

"I get it," Nick said. "I really do, and I can't tell you that it gets any easier."

"Here," Amber said as she thrust a cup of tea at Megan. "Maybe this will help you focus on something else."

Megan took the cup of tea and sipped. After a few minutes she relaxed and stopped shaking.

"Better now?" Nick asked as he tipped up her chin.

Megan gave a loud sigh. "Yes, I guess so, but this night will haunt me for a while."

"I hate to have to do this, but I'd like you to try," Nick said as he grabbed his pad.

"What?"

"So I have the facts right, please tell me what you remember. I want to know everything about tonight."

"Why?" Megan asked, her face unsmiling.

"Because that's what we should do in case the doctor has a question. Sometimes, families want to know about the final moments of their loved one. So, let's write down some facts. Tell me what you remember."

CHAPTER 14

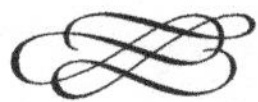

"You were there, Nick."

"I wasn't paying attention to Fiona until you called me, so tell me what you know."

"Okay." Megan paused to gather her thoughts. "Fiona walked over to the table. She had promised us a tour. Amber was dying to see the whole place. Oh, that was a bad choice of words."

"Go on," Nick said as he continued to write.

"She was at the table and wanted to know what we thought of the country club. I told her we still wanted a tour, but we were impressed and would be thrilled to hold our next event here."

"Then what?"

"Let me think a minute."

"We were just getting our desserts off the trolley cart," Georgie piped in. "The rest of us were chatting about what to taste and that the guys wanted four different things. Then Skylar brought a special tray to you and Fiona from the chef, remember?"

"That's right," Megan said. "Skylar interrupted us and said the pastry chef had sent out a special tray of a brand-new chocolate truffle dessert. Skylar said there was a special ingredient and he wanted Fiona and I to be the first ones to try it."

"Did you eat one?" Nick asked.

"Come to think about it, I took one, but I didn't get the chance to bite into it. Fiona ate hers right away so she could give feedback to Skylar for the chef." Megan quickly glanced around the table before pointing." There it is. That's the truffle I choose."

Waitstaff were buzzing around the room picking up dishes. Nick jumped up and grabbed the small plate with the truffle as well as the half-eaten one that was bitten into by Fiona. He grabbed a plastic bag for leftovers and put the plate inside.

"Did you two eat anything else in common?"

Megan shook her head. "No, I never got to eat that. I have no idea if she ate anything else during the night, but I doubt it. She didn't look like she felt well. Isn't that right?"

Georgie and Amber nodded. "How could she eat after that rude lady threatened her in the bathroom?"

"What was that all about?" Nick asked.

"Oh, it was that bride," Megan answered. "The woman who was loud. I'm pretty sure her name is Debbie Goren. She was here screaming at Fiona the first day I came to look at the place and then she was looking for Fiona tonight. She said she was going to give her some choice words when she saw her. Anyway, Fiona ran into the bathroom and we helped her hide. Fiona did say the woman would be the death of her, but she was just saying that because she was too tired to handle her attitude tonight."

Megan sat up straight. "Wow, I forgot."

"What?" Nick asked as he stared at her, waiting for her to continue.

"Well, like I said, Debbie Goren was here screaming at Fiona about lavender vases the first time I was here. I wound up leaving while she was engaged but she called me later. I asked her how it turned out and she told me that Debbie had given her a large box of chocolates to apologize. And then tonight, Fiona told me that while Debbie was yelling at her in the office, she ate several of the chocolates to distract herself. Do you think that's significant?"

"I have no idea," Nick said. "We could go into her office and check for the box. Maybe she was allergic to something in all this chocolate. We could bring it to the hospital."

"I guess so, but honestly I don't think Fiona was healthy."

"Remember that Debbie said she had bald spots when she talked to us in the bathroom," Amber said over Megan's shoulder.

"That's right," Georgie nodded. "She did comment on her hair. Can you believe it?"

"Fiona had some dark circles around her eyes, and she did tell me she'd been having some stomach trouble," Megan added. "As a matter of fact, when she first came to the table, we were talking about how she needed to make an appointment with her doctor as she hadn't been feeling well for a while."

"Maybe she has thyroid disease," Amber said. "One of my coworkers had that and her hair was a problem."

Nick nodded. "That information should help the doctor. Maybe they'll find something in her tests."

"I certainly hope so," Megan said. "When will we know anything?"

"Technically, we wouldn't officially be told anything because that information is protected. Maybe I can call and get an update later."

"Would you do that?" Megan asked. "I feel so bad for that woman."

"I'll try," Nick said as he put his pad and pen away. He gathered the truffles and then looked up. "Are we ready to go?"

"I sure am," Megan said as she put her teacup down and grabbed her purse.

"Please wait a minute," Amber said. "Tommy is over there talking to someone in the jazz band."

"That's fine," Nick said. "It will give me a few minutes to find the chef and ask what the special ingredient was."

Megan looked across the room and saw Tommy with the jazz band. Behind him, Julie was collecting papers from the front of the room. Megan made a note to give Julie a call in a day or two. Something was odd about this situation and Megan was trained as an investigative reporter. Maybe it was time to turn back to her skills and dig for a little information.

CHAPTER 15

A few minutes later, the group gathered and went out to the parking lot and stood in front of the entrance until Luther pulled up in the black SUV.

"What the hell is going on here?"

Nick turned to Luther. "The manager appeared to have an event and started to seize or have a heart attack in the ballroom."

"Oh, snap," Luther said.

"They took her to Coastal Community."

"Hope she's okay," Luther said as he helped everyone into the SUV and slid into the driver's seat. Looking over toward Nick, he asked, "Where we headed?"

"I think we need to get back to Misty Manor. Let everyone get settled. I need to go to the hospital and drop something off. If they want to go to the boardwalk, they can walk from the house."

Luther threw the car in gear. "You got it."

The group was quiet as they drove toward the house. No one had the desire to walk the boards after what had happened at the club. They quickly reached their destination and climbed out of the SUV. After hugs and kisses all around, everyone promised to call if they heard anything about what had happened and left.

Nick and Megan walked up to the porch. He placed his hands on her hips and leaned in for a kiss followed by a great bear hug.

Megan pulled back after some time. "So, what's on your mind, Nick Taylor? I can smell your thoughts burning and it's clear you don't plan on coming inside."

Nick shrugged. "I thought I'd follow up with the squad and see if there's any new information."

Megan watched his face closely. "You're going to the hospital, aren't you?"

When Nick didn't immediately respond, she said, "Of course you are. You're going to drop off the truffle and talk to the guys."

"Busted, but I want to find out if there was anything else to follow up on."

"Okay, let's go."

"What?" Nick's face held a bemused look.

"I said, let's go. There is no way you're going to the hospital without me. I may be able to get more information than you anyway depending on the people there."

"Excuse me?"

"I was an investigative reporter. Do you have any idea how much information you can collect in a hairdresser's shop or a waiting room for that matter?"

Nick shook his head. "Remind me to never turn my back on you or try something sneaky."

"You'd better believe it," Megan said. "Marie's watching the pets." She grabbed Nick's hand and pulled him toward the stairs. "C'mon, let's go."

They jumped into the Camaro and Nick drove to the hospital. Although it was late at night, there were many cars in the parking lot near the Emergency Room. They found a space and went inside. When a security guard stopped them, Nick flashed his badge and said he had information for the doctor. After receiving directions, they walked toward the doctor's lounge in the middle of the Emergency Room.

When they arrived, the room was empty. "I've always wondered what was in the lounge," Megan said. As they gazed around the room, they noticed bulletin boards with schedules, a small refrigerator, various wrapped snacks on a side table as well as a large coffee machine offering choices of automated coffee, cappuccino, expresso or hot water. The table and the chairs were standard plastic, suitable for residents to work on their documentation. A couch sat in the corner, for an emergency nap when necessary. "Not very luxurious."

"Please, sit down," Dr. Curtis Jeffries said in his low mellow voice as he entered the room and waved toward the plastic chairs. "Would you like some coffee?"

"No, thank you," Megan said while shaking her head.

"I assure you, it's not bad. They make a fresh batch for the night shift. The snacks are stale." After filling his cup, Dr. Jeffries sat at the table. His dreadlocks were pulled back from his forehead with a headband and he had a green surgical hairnet over his entire head. He sipped his coffee and then looked at Megan. "It's nice to see you on this side of the ER." He grinned when Megan blushed.

"I'm happy to be in the lounge, rather than one of the cubicles," Megan said with a lopsided smile. This place is scary to me."

"I understand," Dr. Jeffries said with a nod.

"We asked to see Fiona Cochran, but they told us to wait here instead. The receptionist said you were still working with her."

"We appreciate you bringing us into the lounge instead of the waiting room," Nick said. "We can see you're busy tonight."

Dr. Jeffries took another gulp of his coffee and shook his head. "I'm glad you're here. I had some questions and was wondering if you could give me a little more information about what happened tonight."

Nick looked at Megan and then nodded to indicate she should take the lead. Speaking slowly, she led him through the events of the night including Fiona's nausea and apparent seizure. She described everything they did up until the time the Emergency medical team arrived.

"This happened after she ate her dessert?"

"Yes, it was a new chocolate truffle by the chef," Nick said with a nod.

"Did anyone else have the truffle?" The doctor asked.

Megan shook her head. "No, it was offered to me, but I didn't get a chance to try it before everything started happening." Megan looked at Nick with a raised eyebrow. "That's funny you ask. The chef said there was a special ingredient, but we couldn't find him in the aftermath, and we weren't sure if it could be related so we took the truffle and came here to give you a sample. We thought you could test it in case Fiona is allergic to one of the ingredients. Why are you asking?"

Nick pulled the baggie with the truffle out of his pocket and placed it on the table.

Curtis shrugged his shoulders. "No specific reason, but something seems off. I was wondering if she has any chronic illness or other disease. Eating the truffle doesn't seem to explain it all."

"I've only met her a couple of times, but it does seem she wasn't feeling well over the last couple of weeks. As a matter of fact, she mentioned she was thinking of calling her doctor for an appointment so something must be wrong. Maybe you can do some tests while she's in the hospital." Megan watched Curtis as he sipped his coffee again. "How is she doing?"

Curtis put his coffee on the table and looked up at Megan and Nick. He reached his large brown hand over to Megan and covered her forearm. His voice was warm and soft. "I'm sorry to say this, but she didn't make it."

Megan shook her head as she tried to take in the news. "What?"

"We worked on her for a long time and you saw they worked on her in the field. We pronounced her about 25 minutes ago. We have not been able to locate any family or next of kin and I wanted to get more information on her and what happened tonight."

Megan took a couple of deep breaths and Nick slipped his arm around her to bolster her up. "Are you okay? Do you need some water?"

She shook her head side to side and took a deep breath. "I'm okay. I feel bad for Fiona. Where is she now?"

"The medical examiner just picked her up," Curtis said. "I'm sure they'll have some questions as well once they do the post." Looking toward Nick, he picked up the baggie with the truffle. "I'll make sure the coroner gets these truffles."

Megan looked at Nick. "You know, we never did get the box of chocolates from Fiona's office. Should we go get them?"

"What's that all about?" Curtis asked.

"Fiona was eating from a box of chocolates that was given to her from an angry client. They had words in her office and Fiona said the only way to tolerate listening to her was by eating the chocolates as the lady was yelling."

"Was she drinking?"

"No, I don't think so. Technically she was working the crowd to encourage everyone to book their event there."

"How many chocolates did she eat?"

Megan shrugged her shoulders. "I have no idea, but she did say she was eating those chocolates, then she had the truffle. She hadn't been feeling well for a couple of weeks before that. What does that all mean?"

Curtis smiled at Megan. "I have no idea. She could have had a heart attack. Maybe she had other problems, but I don't think one night of rich chocolates could kill anyone unless they were laced with something."

Megan looked at Nick. "We have to get those chocolates."

"We can't just walk in and pick them up. We have to get a warrant unless someone willingly hands them over, but it's 11:00 p.m. at night and I doubt anyone is there."

"Let's ride by and see. Maybe someone is working late after an event like that. Maybe they're still cleaning the place up or getting ready for another event for tomorrow."

Nick shrugged. "I guess it couldn't hurt. Let's go."

Curtis emptied his coffee cup as they all stood up. "Thank you for coming in. If you do meet anyone in there, please ask if she has any next of kin or an emergency contact in her employee record. We need to find someone to notify or the medical examiner will do it officially."

"What should we do with the chocolates?"

Curtis spread his arms. "I'm sorry about your friend, but everything is now in the hands of the medical examiner so anything or any information you find should now go directly to them. I know Nick is aware of how to get it there. I'll make sure the truffles get there, because they're coming back to the hospital for another patient, but from this point on, you can work directly with them."

Nick stuck his arm out and shook hands with Curtis. "Thanks so much. I appreciate your help."

"I'm sorry, my friends. I hope everything works out."

Nick put his arm around Megan's waist and guided her out to the parking lot.

"What was that all about?" Megan asked as she turned toward him.

"What?"

"That look Dr. Jeffries gave you when he shook your hand just now."

Nick shook his head. "I don't know what you're talking about."

"Hmm, I wonder. You better not be holding out on me, Nick Taylor." Nick unlocked the car doors and guided Megan into the passenger seat. He waited until she put on her seat belt and then closed the door. Moving around the vehicle, he jumped into the driver's seat and did the same. Within minutes, they were off toward the Misty Point Country Club.

CHAPTER 16

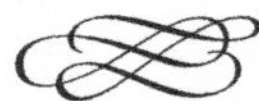

Pulling into the parking lot, they spied a box truck near the building as well as two cars in the parking lot.

"Maybe someone is still here," Nick said as he parked the car. The two jumped out of the car and went to the front door. Nick pulled the door to find it was locked. "I didn't think the front door would be open, but it was worth a try."

"Let's go around the side," Megan said. "We'll use the delivery entrance. Maybe they're still cleaning up."

Rounding the corner of the building, they passed in front of the box truck and noticed a side door was open with light pouring through the frame.

"Nick, it's open. Let's get in there."

Nick crossed in front of Megan and passed through the doorway. There were several people working in the kitchen, stacking dishes and sweeping the floor. Through a window in another door, Megan could see someone in the ballroom changing tablecloths and arranging the chairs around the tables.

Sensing a presence, the two people in the kitchen stopped what they were doing and stared at them. Megan could sense their anxiety.

"Hi, sorry to interrupt but we were at the event earlier tonight and we forgot something. We were wondering if we could pick it up?"

The workers looked at each other and one said, "Please stay right there while I get Mr. Darcey." She turned and ran out of the kitchen.

The other worker continued to stare.

"Just curious. Who is Mr. Darcey?" Megan asked with a shrug.

The girl was uncomfortable, but she answered. "He's the director of the country club. He stays here until we're done cleaning at night."

Within a minute, the other worker returned with a nice-looking middle-aged man save for the dark circles under his eyes. He walked right up to them. His expression was guarded. "Sorry, we're closed."

Nick extended his arm. "Hi, my name is Officer Nick Taylor. I'm with the Misty Point Police Department."

The man relaxed and shook Nick's hand. "Mark Darcey, I'm the Director here."

"I'm sorry about the late hour," Nick said. "Is there somewhere we can talk?"

Mark hesitated for a minute then waved them forward. "Yeah, let's go to my office." He led them through the ballroom, down a hall and into a small office. He gestured to a pair of comfy chairs and he sat down behind the desk and absently rubbed his face. He pushed a few things around to straighten his desk and then looked up. "I assume this has to do with what happened tonight. How is she?"

Nick nodded. "Yes, we're here about Fiona. Are you close to her?"

Mark paused for a second to consider the question. "She's the best manager I've ever hired. I guess we're friends, but I don't see her outside of work too often."

"I see, Mark. Can I call you Mark?"

The man shrugged. "Sure."

"Is Fiona married or does she have family? The hospital wanted to call someone, but we didn't have any information for them. They asked us to check for a relative or family."

Mark shook his head. "I've never heard about any family. I haven't seen her with a boyfriend, and I know she doesn't wear a wedding ring."

"Could you check her employment chart? See if she listed an emergency contact?"

Mark paused for a moment. "Ah, sure, of course. Before I continue, could you show me some ID? You can never be too sure these days."

Nick pulled out his wallet and produced his police identification and his badge.

Mark seemed satisfied. "Thanks, I appreciate it." He retrieved a set of keys from a desk drawer and then shrugged. "The HR person usually handles these files, so you'll have to give me a few moments."

"Take all the time you need," Nick said, throwing a hand up for emphasis. "I'm very appreciative that we were able to speak with you at this time of night. I wouldn't push, but it's important."

Megan didn't want to interrupt as she knew Mark was responding to the fact that Nick was a cop. Technically, the ER physician had enlisted the police department's help in the matter. Nick didn't look official as he never changed from the clothing he wore to the dinner.

Mark got up and opened a file cabinet. He pulled out the drawer and started to sort through files. He looked genuinely concerned for a moment and then smiled with relief. "Here, I found it." He pulled the manilla file folder and turned around to offer it to Nick.

Opening the folder, Nick pulled out the usual forms with demographics. He quickly copied Fiona's address, telephone number and an emergency contact. He also spotted a copy of her driver's license and copied her number. Rifling through the file, he didn't find anything else that would be significant at the moment.

"Thank you for this information," Nick said. "This is a big help and the only information we have so far."

"My pleasure," Mark said. "I hope she pulls through okay. Did they figure out what happened yet?"

Nick was thoughtful a moment. "No, they're still looking into things which is why they asked if we could get some information for them." He turned and scrunched his eyebrows at Megan. She widened her eyes in response.

"Well, if there's anything else I can do, please let me know," Mark said as they all stood.

"There is one more thing," Megan said as she smiled at Mark.

"Yes?"

"Fiona mentioned she had been eating some chocolates tonight while she spoke with someone in her office. The ER physician was wondering if that could have been a problem and asked if we could bring them to the hospital. The other thing is she obviously wasn't able to bring her purse to the hospital and they need her insurance information. Do you think you could let us into her office so we can check?"

Obviously uncomfortable, Mark wasn't sure what he should do. "I'm a little uncomfortable letting you take her purse. No offense, I believe you're with the police, but this is a little odd with the hour and all."

Nick nodded, "I understand. I can come back tomorrow in uniform. Let me know what time is best for you. Just please keep her office locked up until I come back."

Mark looked at his watch, clearly conflicted about what he should do. "Okay, how about this? I'll let you in to her office to see if we can find the insurance card, but I'll keep the purse here until she calls me for it."

"Can we take the chocolates?" Megan asked.

"Uh, sure, you can have them if they're there," Mark said as he looked at Nick. "Do we have to do anything official or is it okay to just take them?"

"I'll file some paperwork," Nick said. "Not to worry."

Together, they walked to Fiona's office. Mark used his keys to open the door and turn on the lights. A gold box of chocolate was sitting on her desk with the lid askew. Nick walked over and used a pencil to fully open the lid. There were originally 15 chocolate candies in the box but only four remained.

"Is everything okay?" Mark asked with eyebrows raised.

"Yes," Nick smiled. "Just being cautious."

"Okay, if you say so," Mark said as he watched them. "What about the insurance card?"

Nick nodded and used his pencil to open the bottom drawer of her desk. Snuggled inside was her purse. He opened the bag and found her wallet. Using a tissue, Nick pulled it out and opened it. He found her license and insurance cards. "Do you mind if we take a copy of these? Then we'll leave everything here as long as you keep the office locked."

"Sure," Mark said as he took the cards and the license and made copies. While he was engaged, Nick looked through her credit cards and cash which looked untouched. There didn't seem to be any special cards or notes shoved into her wallet. There were no medical appointment cards. Taking a quick peek, he didn't notice anything amiss in her purse. He pulled out his phone and took some photos of the purse, the chocolates, the desk and the room.

Mark returned and handed them the photocopies. They returned everything as they had found it and put the purse back into the desk. Nick picked up the chocolates and together they left the room. Mark made sure the door was locked and promised it would remain untouched until Fiona called, or an official request came in from the police department.

They walked through the ballroom and to the kitchen. The tables had all been covered with lilac tablecloths and a beautiful china laid out. The kitchen was cleaned, and the workers were waiting to be excused. Mark nodded and hurried the girls out the door. He then turned to Megan and Nick to help usher them out as well.

"Thanks once again for helping us out," Nick said. "We appreciate it and we'll be in touch."

"You're welcome. I hope she feels better soon and tell her we're all praying for her."

"Will do," Nick said as he guided Megan through the doorway and waved goodbye.

"What was that?" Megan asked when they were out of earshot. "Why didn't you tell him she was dead?"

"Because I don't have the authority to do that," Nick said. "We don't give out information until we've notified the next of kin or arrived on an official police visit. We're pushing the envelope as it is. We got the chocolates and I'll bring them to the Medical Examiner's

Office tomorrow. I got a look in her purse, but to be honest, I'm not overly worried about the hospital's ability to bill her insurance right now."

Megan frowned. "Okay, fine."

"Don't tell anyone she's dead until we know what we're dealing with."

"What do you mean?"

"We still don't know if she had a heart attack or an allergic reaction."

"Okay, I hear you. I won't say anything to anyone until you tell me it's okay."

"That would be refreshing," Nick chuckled. "Is there any chance you'd listen if I asked you not to get involved?"

"According to you, there's nothing to get involved with yet," Megan mocked.

"I'm serious. Leave anything that needs to be done to my department. I'll let you know when we have information."

When she didn't answer, Nick persisted. "Megan?"

"Oh, okay, but you better promise to let me know what's going on."

Hands up, Nick said, "I promise, okay?"

He helped her get into the car and then strapped himself in. Starting the car, he turned to her and asked, "Feel like taking a little walk to calm down?"

Megan was so upset she wanted to run home, but when she turned to him and saw his expression, she changed her mind. She checked her watch. "Sure, let's go for a walk on the boardwalk. Everything is closing down so it should be quiet."

CHAPTER 17

The next morning, Megan rolled over in bed and was met with a big wet tongue licking the side of her face. She put her hand up. "Dudley, stop it." Excited to hear her voice, Dudley edged closer and landed a large paw over her side. He then began to lick her ear. She tried to hide under the covers, but the dog kept pawing the blankets until she couldn't escape.

To make matters worse, Smokey jumped on the bed as well. The cat silently crept up to the pillow on top of her head and eventually stretched out.

"Well, I guess it's time to get up then," Megan said as she rolled out of bed. Dudley watched, ready to spring off the bed the minute Megan gave a signal that she was ready to go downstairs.

She picked up her robe and took a hot shower. When she was done, she wrapped her wet hair in a towel and threw on a pair of jeans with a T-shirt. The pets followed her downstairs to the front door. Throwing open the door, she stepped onto the porch as Dudley ran down the porch steps to relieve himself in the buffer of grass before he hit the beach to chase a few seagulls.

Megan leaned on the front porch post and breathed in the smell of the brine. She enjoyed the breeze against her face as she watched the waves race to shore. Each time they broke, she watched the water splash and land on the wet sand. The white noise of the surf combined with the refreshing wind made her want to recline on the porch and go back to sleep but she knew her friends would be over soon.

As she stood there, she felt Smokey making figure eights around her ankles and lower legs. She continued to stare out and reflect on the day before. The whole situation with Fiona felt surreal, yet the knot in her gut told her Fiona was dead. She had clung to Nick when they returned home, needing that tight embrace to remind her that she was still fully alive, but very tired.

When Dudley finished playing, he returned to the porch and they all went inside toward the kitchen.

Marie was either sleeping or hadn't arrived yet. She may have been at the market. Megan told her she had an open offer to stay at Misty Manor. She understood that Marie didn't want to sell her childhood home in Misty Point. Marie was a great help watching the animals and pampering Megan whenever she got the chance. She helped her keep the rooms clean and prepared scrumptious meals, but Marie had a life as well. Megan wanted it understood that her offer to Marie was not for personal reasons but to let her know how thankful she was to her for taking care of Rose. She had been a great help to Rose in her final months helping to make sure she was comfortable. Marie had been a friend of her parents as well, although that situation was still sordid. Maybe one day the truth would come out.

Megan fed the pets and then put up a pot of strong, rich coffee. She ground her own beans and enjoyed the aroma as she placed the grounds into the coffee maker. Adding the proper amount of water, she waited for the pot to brew.

A small time later, she poured a fresh cup, added a small amount of cream and sugar and enjoyed her first sip. As she walked toward the library, she heard voices on the front porch. Looking through the window, she saw Georgie and Amber walking up the stairs toward the front door. Megan flung the door open to greet her friends.

"Good morning, ladies."

"Good morning," Georgie said. "You're looking rather tired today."

"I'll echo that," Amber observed. "Although I can understand it after that wild night."

"You're telling me," Megan said. "I don't ever want to go through that again."

"So where did you and Nick go last night?" Georgie asked. "You weren't here because I called, and Marie said you never came into the house."

"No, we didn't come in. We went to the hospital. Nick wanted to drop off the truffle Fiona had eaten. While we were there, we met with the emergency room physician, Dr. Curtis Jeffries." Clearing her throat, Megan ushered them into the solarium. "Have a seat. Do you want coffee?"

The girls both asked for a cup, so Megan ran into the kitchen and retrieved mugs with coffee and brought them into the solarium on a tray which also held a small pitcher of cream and sugar. After she served the coffee, she sat at the table with them.

"You avoided it long enough," Georgie said as she sipped from her mug. "Did she make it?"

Megan looked down at the table and shook her head. "No, she didn't. By the time we got to the emergency room, she had already passed. They tried but they couldn't save her."

"That's so sad," Amber said. "What happens now?"

"Dr. Jeffries asked Nick if the police could help them find a next of kin so that's what Nick is working on today."

The women finished their coffee and placed their mugs on the table. "What are we doing today?" Georgie asked. "What's the plan?"

Megan gathered up the mugs and loaded them on the tray. "Well, I want to get some information about the marsh to bring to the next meeting. I thought we could go there and take some photos today. That would make a presentation easier to understand. What do you think?"

"I think it's a great idea," Georgie said.

"Before we go, tell me more about the marsh," Amber said. "I want to be informed in case anyone asks me a question."

"Okay, the area we're talking about is a salt marsh. It's an area of coastal wetlands that are flooded and drained daily with salt water brought in by the tide. The salt marshes are very important because they protect the coast from flooding and erosion. The salt marsh is an important habitat for fish and other natural resources."

"I do know that it smells like rotten eggs," Georgie laughed. "Especially when it's low tide."

"That's because the bottom is made up of decomposing plant material. The oxygen level is extremely low and that's why it smells when there's a low tide."

"Doogie told me that we would have had more damage from Hurricane Sandy if we didn't have the salt marshes and tidal creeks," Georgie said as she nodded her head.

"From what I've read, that's very true and that's why we have to fight to keep it the way it is," Megan said. "We can't let them change the zoning laws and we can't let them fill it in."

"Doogie said the same thing. Building there would be a quick, get-rich scheme for a financial group that leaves after the damage is done while the homes sink into the land and the coast is ruined in many different ways. We need to protect the natural environment."

"Well, then let's get out there, take some photos and hopefully come up with a strategy. Maybe we can call a conservation or preservation group," Amber said. "I can get behind that."

Megan laughed as she lifted the tray and carried it into the kitchen. "Let me take care of the animals and we'll be on our way."

CHAPTER 18

Nick pulled the glass door open and walked into the station. Wearing his uniform, he looked very official as he steered toward the Captain's office.

"About time you got here," Davis said as Nick walked in.

"I come bearing gifts," Nick said as he placed a box of donuts on the desk as well as two large paper cups full of coffee.

"And my favorite donuts from what I can see," Davis said. "I appreciate it, Nick. The swill around here is disgusting."

Nick laughed as he pulled his coffee from the holder. "Don't you make anything at home before you leave?"

"Nah, too much of a pain in the ass. The missus used to make coffee every morning but now that I'm alone, I don't bother."

"Don't be a sourpuss," Nick said with a smile

"Hmmm," Davis said as he picked up the coffee and enjoyed the flavor. Nick watched as he leaned back in his creaky, old, wooden chair.

"Is your back hurting you again?" Nick asked with concern. "You seem more uncomfortable lately."

"Something's acting up. I'm gonna have to go see the doctor again.

Maybe, I'll go for the X-rays this time. Anyway, enough about that. Now that you're here, tell me what the hell's going on."

"You heard about the County Club?"

"How could I not? Everyone's talking about it. I heard you went back there last night after hours. Not too happy about that. And there she is right back in the middle of things again," Davis said, referring to Megan Stanford. "I know she's your girlfriend, but this has to stop."

"It wasn't like that. As a matter of fact, she was barely involved."

"I doubt that," Davis said shaking his head. "So, what the hell happened?"

Nick took a bite of a Boston crème donut and washed it down with a gulp of coffee. "Well, we were all at the Misty Point County Club last night. The Stanford Foundation supports the Pure Horizons Environmental Group, and they were scouting a place for next year's fundraising event. The manager, Fiona Cochran, invited everyone to a food tasting. There were a lot of people there checking it out for weddings and what not." Nick took another bite and spoke with his mouth full while gesturing with the donut. "Anyway, toward the end, Fiona bites into a special chocolate truffle, then gets nauseous and passes out. We call 911, then she starts seizing. The medics came and worked on her, but they couldn't save her."

"So, it sounds like a medical problem. What's all the hullabaloo about?"

"Earlier in the evening, a bridezilla was acting out and there was some unrest. We were wondering if she had a heart attack from the stress, but then someone suggested it was an allergic reaction. Anyway, I grabbed the truffle to bring to the ER in case it was of help, but she was gone by the time we got there. Dr. Jeffries had unofficially asked if we knew of a next of kin or had any other info. Since the staff was still cleaning up, we stopped in and spoke with the Director, a Mark Darcey.

"I know, he called me," Davis said with a pointed look.

Nick nodded. "I figured he would. He gave us some information and let us take the box of chocolates she was eating. I was going to see

Chen and drop it off, if that's okay with you. I want to give him the info we got last night. He's got to call someone for notification."

Captain Davis shook his head. "That medical examiner creeps me out."

Nick dusted the crumbs off his hands. "I know what you mean, but Chen is a good guy."

"So, this is still a medical incident."

Nick nodded as he finished his coffee. "So it seems, but it was upsetting to the guests because it was a dramatic situation which happened in front of 150 people or so last night. And let it be known, Megan was no more than an invited guest who happened to be there."

Captain Davis grumbled. "Hmmm, I wonder." Davis grimaced as he sat forward and stood.

"Maybe you should call that doctor now," Nick suggested. "Can't do anything about you being a curmudgeon, but maybe he can make you more comfortable."

Davis turned to Nick. "What about the mayor? I heard he was there."

Nick paused before he answered. "Yes, the mayor and a few of his friends were at the event. We're quite sure he's behind this new petition to change the zoning laws so they can fill in the salt marsh."

"Any confrontations there?"

"No," Nick sighed. "The only thing that was odd was the pastry chef sent out a special dessert for Fiona Cochran and Megan. Fiona collapsed right after eating that dessert. I couldn't find the pastry chef afterwards, but it appears that he's part of the mayor's group."

"As I said, she's right back in the thick of things," Davis frowned.

"We don't know that," Nick protested.

Davis returned to his seat. "Let me know if Chen has anything important to say. Now, get out."

"Thanks, Boss." Nick left the office and headed toward the parking lot. Hopping into his cruiser, he drove toward the Medical Examiner's Office.

He found a space in the empty parking lot and turned to gather the chocolates. The building was a one story, gray structure. No windows, no markings. Nick felt it was creepy just parking there. He got out and went inside the building. Surprisingly, the inside was very modern. He had to sign in and was led to a hallway which housed two locker rooms and several autopsy suites. When he caught sight of Chen washing his hands in a large silver sink, Nick walked over to greet him. Chen, dressed in scrubs and still wearing a paper cap over his hair, looked up and nodded.

"You brought me candy? It's not my birthday and I am spoken for."

Nick started laughing as he held the gold candy box. "Sorry to hear that. Actually, I'm here to drop off the box of candy that Fiona Cochran was eating chocolate from last night."

"And I hear you're responsible for sending the truffle as well?"

"Yes, that was me," Nick said.

"I've heard too much dessert would kill you, but I don't think anyone meant it in the immediate sense of the word." Chen shook out his hands and then took his time drying them on a clean towel. He made sure every finger, crevice and nail were clean and dry.

"We just wanted to make sure she didn't have an allergic reaction or something."

"Why is this case bothering you?" Chen asked.

"What do you mean?"

"You seem unsettled about this lady. We have plenty of patients with heart attacks, especially when they're running a 5K or drinking on a hot beach, but you're never this tenacious about it."

Nick shrugged. "I don't know, something feels off. I don't think she's got much medical history, but she went from being okay to dead. Although, she admitted to Megan that she hadn't been feeling well for a while."

"Ah, Megan Stanford," Chen said with a smile.

"Don't start," Nick said with a frown.

Chen put his hands up in mock defense. "Not me, I'm just saying it's a good thing she's got a cop for a boyfriend. She keeps busy. Actually, she keeps me busy."

Nick turned to the side and tossed the gold candy box on the counter. He turned to find Chen grinning.

"Is there anything else you can tell me about last night? Did you or Megan notice anything specific or out of place?"

Nick shook his head. "The whole night was off. We were there for a food tasting. They hold it twice a year for couples planning a wedding or guests planning an event. It should have been a nice time, but it wasn't. Fiona was working, trying to impress everyone. She was being stalked by a bridezilla. Also, there was some political nonsense going on. The band and the food were good. Fiona spoke a bit and then they served dessert. Fiona and Megan were speaking when a waiter brought them a special tray which the chef said had a special ingredient. Fiona ate the whole truffle, then started having stomach pains and keeled over."

"Did Megan have a truffle?"

"Thankfully, no. She was about to when she was sidetracked by something. They were still on the table, so I grabbed them just in case. From what Megan said, Fiona choose the truffle she ate so there was nothing specific about the truffle itself unless she had a reaction."

"Well, I can have all this stuff tested. You would be amazed at what we find. Sometimes certain foods are covered with bacteria or have other things added to them." Chen shrugged. "Or they can be fine except for an ingredient someone has an allergy to."

"Are you finished with the post?"

Nodding, Chen said, "Yes, I finished this morning."

"What do you think? Did you find anything suspicious?"

Chen paused for a moment. "I'm not sure what you mean suspicious. It's not like she had a knife hanging out of her back. I did note one physical finding but I'm not sure it had anything to do with her death."

"Does it confirm anything?"

"Not necessarily," Chen said. "Do you know if this woman had any history of kidney disease?"

Nick shook his head. "No, that's the point. We don't know much about her."

"Did you find a next of kin?"

"Haven't spoken with anyone yet. There was an emergency contact listed in her work chart, but we haven't gotten hold of anyone yet."

"I haven't done a notification because I have no names, no background," Chen said with a frown. "And no one has called looking for her, either."

"The emergency address is in another city, so we called and asked them to send a squad car. They haven't gotten back to us, yet." Nick said.

"If you do hear from anyone, ask if she had kidney disease," Chen said again. "Some of the findings, the hair loss, bruising and fingernail changes can be from kidney disease."

"Can it be anything else?"

"It could be a lot of things. Anything from chemo to certain diseases to potential poison," Chen said. "I didn't see anything on the body that would define it either way. We ran toxicology and sent specimens but it's going to take time to get the results. I can tell you it wasn't an allergic reaction. Her airway wasn't swollen and there's no evidence of hives."

"Could someone have poisoned the truffle?"

"Could be anything," Chen said. "Not to cause trouble, but if that were the case, do we know for sure that Fiona was the intended target? Maybe she just had the bad luck of eating first."

Nick paused for a moment, reality hitting him in the head as he thought the scenario through.

Chen saw his expression and lightly tapped his arm. "Listen man, I can see the wheels moving in your head. Let's not get ahead of ourselves. We don't know that it's poison. We don't know anything yet. Let's wait for the tests. We need tox screens on the lady, the chocolates and I need to find some medical history. I have a call in for Curtis Jeffries. I want to see if they ever found any medical history in the computer. If people live in an area long enough, they have tests or go to the doctor's office at some point."

"I'm not following you," Nick said looking confused.

"Most of the hospitals and doctors' offices are from the same network. That's one important concept about digital medical records, they never go away. In the network, all the records are connected so if she has been in the hospital or a physician's office, it's likely the records would be linked unless she made specific arrangements for a visit not to be visible. She must have had a physical or something in the area. I'm not sure that the ER clerk had time to search before the poor lady died. I want to make sure we check everything we can."

"I see."

"In the meantime, you need to find the next of kin. See if there's any history of anything. Cancer, chemo, kidney disease, anything." Chen paused for a second. "You're the police. Can't you run her driver's license and social security or something?"

"Yeah, we can do a lot of things. I'll talk to Davis. It seems we need to make this an official investigation to get closure."

"Sounds like a great idea to me," Chen said. "I've got your number and you've got mine. If anyone finds anything, we'll talk. In the meantime, I've got another, ah, client to attend to." Chen started to chuckle and walked toward the locker room.

"He's one creepy dude," Nick muttered to himself as he made his way out of the building.

CHAPTER 19

Megan drove along the bay and pulled off the road into a small dirt lane that led into the marsh. They found a small, expanded parking area and the three women got out of the car. Megan had her phone ready to take photos and perhaps some measurements. They walked to the center of the parking area and turned to examine the wetlands.

"I can see why they would want to build here," Amber said. "There's a beautiful view of both the ocean and the bay if you're facing the right direction."

"Yes, I see your point, but I'm looking at the water and thinking of all the fish and wildlife that live here."

Georgie swiped at an insect buzzing her face. "Yes, it's wonderful except for the bugs and smell of rotten eggs."

Megan started laughing. "You have no idea how many different things are happening simultaneously to create this ecosystem."

"Go ahead, professor," Georgie said as she continued swiping at insects.

"Well, first there are estuaries, the place where freshwater meets the ocean. We have quite a few in New Jersey, near the Hudson, Hackensack, Passaic, Shrewsbury, Navesink and Raritan Rivers. Every day, the tide brings salt water into the area and fresh water comes from the rivers. They mix all the time. You'll see different fish and birds in those areas. There are creatures who live in the mud and their presence attracts bigger animals, who come to the water line to fetch a little snack."

As they walked, Megan stopped to take a few photos of the water, grasses and scenery. She turned to Amber. "I have a good job for you, if you're willing."

"Sure, how can I help?"

"You'd be great at checking with the Environmental Protection Agency and maybe something like Fish and Wildlife Service. I know they're always concerned about the swamp lilies and I'm sure some endangered plant or wildlife has to be registered in this area. Maybe that's what we can use to stop the town from rezoning and letting them build here."

"That's exactly the thing I'm good at," Amber said. "I'm on it."

"I'm quite sure Doogie can give you some insight or some numbers to call. Hell, he probably knows an environmental lawyer, but I imagine Teddy can get some good referrals as well," Georgie said.

"Teddy is all over this," Megan said. "He's very keen about keeping the shoreline as natural as possible. Teddy is the one who taught me about the different marsh levels."

"What do you mean?" Amber asked, trying not to step in an area consisting of mud.

"Well, the low marsh is completely underwater almost all the time and usually hosts a lot of grasses and weed. The middle marsh is submerged part of the day depending on the tide and the rivers. The high marsh is only covered with water when the heavy rains or floods comes in."

"Are there snakes?" Georgie asked looking down at her feet.

Megan thought for a moment. "Amber, can you look into that when you do your research? I thought I had heard that snakes are an endangered species in New Jersey. There are other states who have a lot more snakes when it comes to marsh or watery areas, but you never know."

A variety of birds flew overhead sounding bird calls as they looked for food. "It is very pretty in a certain way," Amber said. "Although I wouldn't be walking through here on a daily basis, I'd hate to see it disappear or become polluted.

"And that's what was happening fifty years ago," Megan said. "The New Jersey water was getting so dirty, consumers had to be careful about what they ate. After a few laws were passed, the waters improved. Conditions are better now. It's very hard to regain what was lost back then but at least it's not disappearing like it was. Even more reason for us to prevent commercial building." Megan took a deep breath. "I'm glad we came out here. We have some photos and an action plan."

"I'll ask Doogie for his thoughts as soon as we get back," Georgie said as they walked toward the car.

"I'll contact those agencies and get more information," Amber said as she opened the door.

"And I'll contact town hall and see when the next zoning board meeting is coming up," Megan said. "I'm sure the Mayor will be happy to hear we all plan to attend."

Megan started the car, carefully turned around on the dirt parking area so her tire wouldn't get stuck in the muck and headed back to the road along the bay.

CHAPTER 20

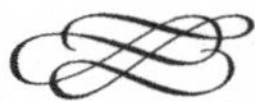

Nick walked back into the police station to see Davis. He looked through his door window and was waved inside. He was carrying a bag with sandwiches.

"You must want something big to bring breakfast and lunch the same day," Davis said as he eyed the bag Nick was holding. Although it showed no markings, he thought he could smell cooked onions and spices.

"Well, I wanted to bring you up to speed on the case," Nick said as he opened the bag.

"What case?"

"Fiona Cochran," Nick said as he extracted the food.

"Chili dogs? They smell great," Davis said.

Nick handed two over. "Chili, mustard, sauerkraut and the best beef hotdogs in the area."

Davis spread a napkin and pushed papers away from his blotter. "Okay, now what do you want?"

Nick took a bite and wiped his hands. "I went to see Chen. He's asking for help. He finished the post but he's holding the death certificate until he gets more information."

"What's he looking for?"

"He said he found a few odd things so he's looking for either medical history or a next of kin or someone who could help him with some information. Do you know if they found anyone at the address we have on file?"

"Haven't heard a damn thing," Davis said. "We asked the locals to do the notification, but I haven't heard back from anyone."

"Do you have the name of the detective it was assigned to?" Nick asked as he chewed. "I'd like to call and see if they were successful. Maybe I can get a name and contact them myself to get some info for Chen."

"Is that what you're looking for, my blessing?"

"Guess so. I know there wasn't any criminality to this death, especially since it was witnessed by a hundred people or so, but it needs some work. We need to know who the hell Fiona Cochran was."

"You're going to have to start the old-fashioned way," Davis said. "Run her name. See if she has a record, a rap sheet or whatever. Maybe she ran away from an abusive husband. Knowing Chen, I'm sure he took her fingerprints. Run them too."

Nick nodded as he finished his chili dog. "That's the answer I was hoping you'd give me. Something sounds off so I just want to do some basic digging. Chen's going to need the information to properly sign off on the death certificate anyway."

"You've got my blessing, so go. By the way, my favorite donut is chocolate frosted."

"Gotcha," Nick said as he smiled and walked out the door.

CHAPTER 21

Megan finished her shower, wrapped herself in a towel and opened the bathroom door to go to her room. Dudley and Smokey were waiting outside, eager to be by her side. "I'm sure the two of you could smell the marsh the minute I got into the house." She dressed in shorts and her favorite T-shirt and put her wet hair up in a pony.

When she turned around, she spied two dogs and the cat. "Wait a minute. When did Nick's dog get here?"

The dogs answered by running around her legs as she walked down the hall. Smokey followed behind as the group descended the staircase together. Megan walked toward the kitchen and found Nick eating a sandwich at the dining room table.

He looked up and shrugged. "Marie said I looked hungry and made me a sandwich."

"If I didn't know Marie, I'd say that was one of the weakest excuses I'd ever heard."

Nick shrugged and whispered, "I already had two hot dogs, but I didn't want to hurt her feelings."

As Megan shook her head, Marie walked into the dining room. "Megan, would you like something to eat, perhaps a sandwich? I know it's near dinner and you were busy today or do you two have more formal plans for tonight?"

"Not a single thing planned," Megan said. "I'd love to have a sandwich."

"Great, you sit right there. I made a nice pot roast today. I'll bring you a platter, meat, veggies and some fresh bread. You can cut the carbs if you want or have it on a sandwich. I'll bring some extra for Nick."

"Sounds great, Marie. Thank you very much. It sounds delicious," Megan said with a smile.

"You are most welcome, Megan. In the meantime, you three come with me and I'll have your dinners ready as well." Marie left the dining room, and all three animals ran after her anticipating savory treats for tonight.

Megan turned in time to see Nick pop the rest of his sandwich in his mouth. Megan was surprised he didn't eat more on a daily basis, but he was meticulous about his diet and exercise. He ran daily, worked out several times a week and filled out his uniform in ways that occasionally sent her heart singing.

"Don't get me wrong, I'm very happy to see you but what brings you here tonight?"

He dusted the crumbs off his hands into a napkin. "First, I wanted to see you."

"Good answer," Megan replied with a smile.

"I didn't have time to shop and was hoping Marie would feed me."

Megan frowned as she squinted at him.

He started to laugh. "It's true, I didn't shop but I wanted to let you know that I went to see Chen today. He isn't signing Fiona's death certificate yet. He wants the police to look for more information."

"Why? The death wasn't an obvious heart attack or allergic reaction to something?"

Nick shook his head. "He said there were a few things on her post that could be related to chemo or kidney disease. But the same things could be related to poisons or pesticides as well. He wanted to see if we had any news on the notification yet."

"Well, that's disturbing," Megan confided.

"I talked to Davis. He's going to let me start a basic investigation."

"What does that mean?"

"I'm going to New Paltz, NY. That's where Fiona listed the emergency contact address. I want to see if there's anyone we can talk to. Someone must know if she had medical issues."

"Great, when do we leave? I'll ask Marie to watch all the animals."

"We? What do you mean we?"

"New York is a 120-minute drive and I've heard New Paltz is a beautiful area. You could use some company. Maybe we could stop in to Mohonk while we're there."

"Did you miss the point that this would be an official police investigation?"

"Oh please. It's not like someone came down from New York and killed her. You're looking for medical history, not a killer. Let me come with you."

Nick was thoughtful for a moment. Davis wanted his inquiry to be casual. "I'm not taking an official cruiser. I'll let you drive with me, but if there's any issue, you're sitting at the police station while I check out the house."

"Are you nuts?" Megan asked.

"Me? You've been back to Misty Point for a couple of years and have gotten into more trouble than I care to count. You've already been the victim of several murder attempts and quite frankly, your position and your money make you more of a target every day. Those are my terms. Take it or leave it."

Megan was fuming, her face flamed red. "Fine, I'll take it, but I'm going to want a drive by of the house at least. I want to see what it looks like."

"We'll make a pass before I drop you off," Nick said. "But we don't know who lives there, or what their relationship to Fiona was."

"Maybe you should call and see what the status of that notification is," Megan said.

"It's late now and I won't get the right info. It doesn't matter, I want to go up there. Are you free tomorrow?"

"Yes, I can be," Megan said. "What time are we leaving?"

"I'll be here to pick you up in the morning. I can try to call them while we're on our way up."

"You got it. I'll be ready," Megan said with a firm look.

"Here you go," Marie said as she walked into the dining room with a couple of platters in hand. "Fresh pot roast with carrots, mashed potatoes with gravy and some corn bread on the side."

"Marie, you didn't have to go through all this trouble for me" Megan said as she jumped up to help Marie with the platters.

"Nonsense, you need a healthy meal and I'm sure Nick will be able to fit in another small plate."

Megan helped to place plates, utensils and napkins on the table. Dudley and Nick's dog watched from the doorway. Marie placed a large serving fork on each platter and left the dining room with both dogs in tow.

"Wow, that looks great," Nick said. "She's killing my diet but at least it's healthy food."

"Better than pizza," Megan agreed as she plated food for the two of them. "Nick, do you think there could have been any poison in the food at the country club?"

Nick shrugged. "I wouldn't think so unless someone was randomly hoping to pick someone off. It's too unpredictable to assume someone would eat a particular dish. Allergies are a different issue though. Although Chen was certain she didn't have an allergic reaction. He said he didn't notice the normal signs of one on the post."

Megan was thoughtful as she ate. "I'd hate to think we're doing all this just to find she did have a heart attack. She looked pretty healthy but who knows, right?"

"You do have a way of attracting killers into your universe," Nick said dryly.

He chuckled when Megan frowned.

Placing their utensils on their plate, they pushed back from the table. "I hate to eat and run but honestly, I've got to go."

"Do you?" Megan asked looking up at Nick.

"Yeah, I've got to go to the station and get some paperwork done.

Davis will let me go tomorrow as long as I don't let other things fall behind."

Megan tried not to show her disappointment. "Why don't you leave your dog here?"

"Bella," Nick said with a smile.

Megan laughed. "Thanks, I'll walk you out."

"That's the dog's name. Bella for beautiful."

"Oh, I get it now," Megan said as she nodded.

Together they walked to the front porch and stopped near the steps while they looked out at the ocean. The day had been beautiful. There was a warm breeze, and the ocean sent large waves crashing to the sand. The water lunged forward and then was pulled back. Seagulls circled above crying out. It would have been a perfect time to take a long walk along the water's edge with the dogs, but it wasn't meant to be.

Nick seemed to feel it too as he reached around Megan's waist and pulled her close. After a minute or two, he turned to face her. Megan's heart did a flip when she saw his handsome tanned face looking down at her.

"You know we haven't had much time to ourselves lately," Nick said as he placed his forehead against hers.

"I know," Megan said. "There's already too much committee work and drama going on around town."

"Maybe we can have a nice time tomorrow. We'll stop for lunch and make a day of it. You're right, this is mostly information gathering, not a pursuit."

"I'd like that, Nick."

"When this is all over, let's spend some alone time working on us." Nick lowered his lips to hers as he held her in a tight bear hug. He kissed her gently at first then his lips demanded more. With a moan, he pulled back and held her to his chest.

Megan wished time could stop at that very moment. She was glad he couldn't feel her heart beating.

With a heavy sigh, Nick ran his fingers through her hair and smiled. He kissed her quickly on the lips. His voice was rough when he said, “I’ve got to go. I’ll be back to pick you up in the morning.” He ran down the steps of Misty Manor but turned back to wave as he reached the bottom.

At that moment, Megan’s breath caught short as she looked at him. She realized she was falling in love with him. She would be crushed if he decided to stop seeing her. She turned back to Misty Manor, went inside and closed the door.

CHAPTER 22

Morning dawned bright the next day and Megan was ready when Nick pulled up in the Camaro.

"Hey, good morning," Megan said as she hopped into the car.

"Good Morning to you," Nick said as he looked over and smiled at her. She fastened her seat belt and Nick pulled out of the driveway. "Hey, I want to thank you for taking care of my dog last night. I wound up staying late at the station."

"Oh please, Marie had the time of her life with those animals last night. She's thrilled to have the company this morning as well. I can't see Bella being all alone in your house when she can be playing with Dudley and Smokey. Plus, I'm happy to see you gave her a name. What a sweetie."

"Believe me, Bella and I really appreciate it," Nick said. He pulled onto the New Jersey Parkway and headed North toward New York State. "You know this is a two-hour trip?"

"I know," Megan said with a smile. "It's not the trip, it's the company. What difference would it make if we were hanging out at the beach or driving. Besides, I think it's nice to take a little trip out of town."

"That's fine because we have to go all the way up the Parkway and then the NY Thruway."

"A lovely ride, though," Megan countered. "I've always wanted to see Mohonk Mountain House. I heard it's a beautiful place to relax. I've heard there's a beautiful view of NY State from the top of the mountain. They have some walking paths and a great restaurant, but it's fancy."

"I didn't bring my fancy clothes today but, maybe, one day, we can make a longer trip," Nick said with a smile.

"That would be fun. Did you know the movie for Stephen King's, *The Shining,* was filmed in New Paltz, NY? In the book, the story takes place in Colorado, but the film featured Mohonk."

"Really?" Nick laughed at Megan's enthusiasm. "Tell me more."

"Okay, I will. Another show, *Upload,* an Amazon Prime series features the exterior of Mohonk Mountain House."

"Well, aren't you just full of information?" Nick laughed as they traveled up the highway.

Megan watched the scenery fly by. She enjoyed the heady feeling of wind blowing through her hair as the car sped along the road. Their time was relaxed as they chatted about various things. Megan watched Nick at the wheel. His strong arms seemed to be an extension of the car. The machine and driver working as one. It was also the first time they had left Misty Point for a private trip together. She turned to watch the scenery while enjoying every minute of it.

Two hours later, they rolled into the town of New Paltz, NY. Nick turned into the police parking lot, parked the car and turned to Megan. "Please stay in the car for a few minutes. I want to go inside the station and see if they were able to make the notification. I'm telling them it's official business so I can't have you with me."

"Okay," Megan said as she looked at him.

"Okay? That's it? No fight, no argument?"

"Nope, I told you I would respect what you're doing here so I'll wait right here. There's some beautiful scenery. I'll just relax."

Nick shook his head in disbelief as he quickly jumped out of the car. He didn't want to take the chance Megan would change her mind. Walking into the station, he caught the attention of the desk officer.

"Can I help you?"

"Hopefully," Nick said as he flashed his badge. "Name is Nick Taylor. I'm with the Misty Point Police Department in New Jersey. We called to see if you would assist us with a notification of a deceased person. I happened to be in the area today and was wondering if you had any luck."

The other office remained silent until Nick had finished. "Name again?"

"Mine or the deceased?" Nick asked.

"Let's start with yours."

"Officer Nick Taylor, Misty Point Police Department, NJ."

The officer picked up the phone and called someone in a back room. He spoke into the phone in hushed tones and hung up. "Someone will be out in a moment to speak with you."

Nick nodded. "Thanks, I appreciate it."

Moments later, a door opened, and a middle-aged officer looked out at Nick. He introduced himself and invited Nick to his office. Once he had settled at his desk, he asked, "How can I help you?"

Nick explained the situation and asked about the notification. He didn't miss the strange look that fleeted across the face of the officer.

"Who did you say died?"

"A woman by the name of Fiona Cochran. She was the manager of the Misty Point Country Club," Nick explained. "She collapsed during an event at the facility and was sent to the local hospital but didn't make it. The medical examiner asked for some help making a notification and wanted us to get some medical history. He hasn't signed the death certificate yet."

The officer nodded. "That name isn't familiar to me and I've been here a lot of years."

Nick pulled out his phone and gave the officer the address Fiona had listed for an emergency contact. "That went with a last name of Hawk."

"Now that name I've heard of."

"Do you know if anyone was able to speak to them?"

The officer shook his head. "I'm not sure, but there's no them. Only one living in the Hawk house is an 80-year-old lady. She had a son, named Ozzie. He's no longer with us."

"As in he moved?"

"No, he died," the officer said. "Can't say much except he was an unsavory fellow."

"Would you know how this Fiona was connected to the family?"

"Honestly, I've no clue."

"Did anyone contact Mrs. Hawk?"

The officer tapped into his computer. "I'd have to check to see who took this call. I'm not sure if they were able to connect or not. Mrs. Hawk is not exactly a social creature plus she's getting up there in years. There's a good chance, it hasn't happened, yet."

Nick paused, feeling a strange vibe from the conversation. "Is she dangerous?"

"Not as far as I know, she's just not easy to pin down."

Nick scratched the back of his neck. "Well, then while I'm here, maybe I'll take a swing by the place. It would be helpful if I could find any medical information for the coroner. It might be a bust, but it's worth a try."

The officer nodded. "Sure, do me a favor and let me know if you connect. I'd like to know what's going on."

Nick nodded as he stood and extended his hand. "I'll be sure to do that. Thank you for your time, Officer …?

"Maywood and you're welcome. Let me walk you to the door."

CHAPTER 23

Nick walked through the parking lot and slid into the Camaro.

"Well, how did that go?"

"I'm not sure," Nick said as he started the car. "There was a strange vibe coming off the officer I spoke to."

"Were they able to make the notification?"

"Apparently not. He said the only person living at the address we gave him is an eccentric woman in her 80's. She had a son named Ozzie Hawk who died, but he didn't say how. He also said she's not easy to track down and suggested she wasn't inclined to entertain visitors."

"And Fiona?"

"He didn't recognize the name and has no idea what their relationship was."

Nick turned out of the parking lot. "I'm going to drive by, and we'll look at the property. This whole case gets stranger by the minute."

"Okay."

"Remember, if I stop, you're to stay in the car," Nick said as he turned to Megan. "Otherwise, I'll come right back here and drop you off."

Megan rolled her eyes and turned to look out of the passenger side window. She watched the countryside, green fields, trees, and apple orchards roll by as Nick continued through winding roads.

He slowed as they neared the address announced to them by the GPS. There was a house set back quite a way from the road. A lone battered mailbox sat crookedly on a broken post at the edge of the dirt drive. To the side and behind the house was a pond. Nick turned into the long dirt drive and slowly crossed over various ruts and bumps as he made his way up the drive.

"I get what he was saying when he talked about the property," Nick said as he checked out the place.

"I'm not getting warm and fuzzy either. It certainly doesn't present the most welcoming front," Megan added.

Nick slowed as he approached the end of the drive. He put the car in park, turned off the engine and sat for a few minutes, watching the area.

"Seriously, I want you to stay in the car. For some reason, the place gives me the creeps. If something happens, you need to drive out of here and get help immediately."

"Nick, maybe we're overreacting," Megan said.

"You promised you'd stay in the car if I didn't drop you off at the station. I'm holding you to it or I'll never talk to you about an investigation again. Agreed?"

Megan was silent for a moment before she threw her hands up. "Okay, agreed."

"Here, I want you to have the number of the police station. Put this into your phone." Megan rolled her eyes again, but she tapped the number into her contacts as he rattled it off.

"Hey, many times you don't need to do anything but it's when you're unprepared that you die. If you're going to be with an officer the rest of your life, you're going to have to get used to that."

"Oh?" Megan raised her eyebrows in question.

Nick leaned over and gave her a quick kiss on the cheek and hopped out of the car. He walked toward the front of the house and looked for a doorbell. Not finding any, he began to knock on the front door. He waited several minutes and tried again.

Megan watched as he stepped back to look at the windows. Movement from the side of the house caught her eye as a woman peered around the frame. She was only a few feet from the car and held a metal rake in her hands in a defensive position.

"Whatever you're selling, I'm not buying," she yelled. "You'd better get off my property now if you know what's good for you."

Nick turned toward the voice and held his hands up. "Mrs. Hawk? Are you Mrs. Hawk?"

"Who's asking?" Her whole body tensed, her mouth a firm line.

Nick slowly walked toward the woman. "My name is Nick Taylor. I'm an officer with the Misty Point Police Department."

"Stay right there," she yelled as she pointed the rake in his direction. "That's close enough."

Nick stopped moving as he continued to watch the woman. "I'd just like to ask you some questions."

"Never heard of Misty Point and I ain't talking to nobody. Now get off my property."

Megan couldn't help herself and opened the car door. She slowly stepped out. "Mrs. Hawk? We just want to talk about Fiona."

Surprised, the woman quickly turned to face Megan. She was now holding the rake forward and looked back and forth between Nick and Megan.

"I don't know any Fiona. Least ways, not anymore."

Trying to calm the woman, Nick began to walk toward the car. He stood next to Megan near the door of the car.

Megan whispered. "She's tough but she's frightened."

Nick's jaw tightened. "We'll talk about this later."

"Mrs. Hawk, Fiona was sick. We need to talk to you about her."

"The Fiona I knew went away a long time ago and if you ask me, it was good riddance. Now get off my property. I got nothing to tell you people."

Megan tried once more. "Mrs. Hawk, did the Fiona you know have any medical problems?"

"I don't know and if she didn't, I'd be glad to give her a few. If you're associated with Fiona, you're the last people I want to talk with."

Mrs. Hawk started backing up and disappeared behind the back of the house.

"Should we follow her?" Megan asked.

Nick shook his head. "And do what? The woman clearly doesn't want to talk to us. Even if we calmed her down, she probably wouldn't remember anything. Hell, we don't even know if we're talking about the same Fiona. Something doesn't add up. Let's go."

Nick and Megan got back into the Camaro. Nick started the car and backed up until he came to a wide enough part of the drive to turn around. He pulled out of the lane and onto the main road. His fingers gripped the wheel, his body tense and he was silent.

"What?" Megan asked as she watched him.

He continued to set his jaw and grip the wheel with one arm. After a few moments of dead silence, he quietly said, "I told you to stay in the car. As a matter of fact, I didn't even want to bring you to the house."

"She was just a scared, little old lady, Nick."

"Do you know how many little old ladies carry guns? If she were packing and she looked just mean enough, you could be dead. You have to stop doing this, Megan."

"Nick, I'm not doing anything except trying to help settle this mystery with Fiona. I didn't go out and look for this. She died at my feet."

"I get that, but you need to start trusting professionals to do their job. As much as you have some intuition, you are not trained. You could get yourself killed or others." Nick looked over at Megan pouting in the passenger seat. She looked out the window as the scenery flew by, tears running down her cheeks.

"I was trying to help."

Nick kept driving. After a few minutes, he reached over and grabbed her hand. She continued to look out the window. "I can't do this with you if there's a chance you could get hurt. I've been in the hospital with you several times already. I couldn't go through losing you."

Megan was silent as she listened to Nick. She squeezed his hand.

"Hey, I'm starving," Nick said. "How about we grab some lunch? C'mon, what do you say? You must be hungry too."

Megan slowly nodded. "I'm not sure I could eat anything right now, but I guess I could have a cup of coffee."

"That's my girl," Nick said. He continued to drive through the winding roads until they came upon a small luncheonette by the side of the road. There was a stand with baskets of apples, pears, peaches and apricots. Picnic tables were scattered under a series of trees standing guard around the building. Nick pulled into the dusty parking area and turned off the car. "Let's get something to eat. We'll both feel better."

They got out of the car and walked to the front door. The screen door opened into a small space filled with a counter, a refrigerator filled with drinks and one table on the side.

"Hello, welcome," a woman said as she pulled up to the counter. "What can I get you? Everything's homemade."

Megan and Nick searched for a menu board. "I'm sorry, what would you suggest?"

"The chicken salad is nice and fresh today. I've got some homemade vegetable soup, too. The bread is fresh from the local bakery this morning."

"Sounds good to me," Nick said as he smiled at the woman. He turned toward Megan. "What about you?"

Megan nodded. "Sure, it sounds great." They completed their order. Nick paid for lunch and offered a nice tip.

"Thank you very much. Why don't you grab a spot outside and I'll bring your lunch out to you?"

"Sounds great, thanks," Nick said as he held the door for Megan. The pair ambled over to a shady picnic table under a nearby tree.

"She was a lovely lady," Megan said as she sat down on the bench. "This place is very quaint."

"It's nice," Nick said as he sat next to her. He put his arm around her shoulders and pulled her close. "Megan, you understand what I'm trying to tell you, right? I get that you're trying to help someone, but you have to be careful. You put yourself in danger all the time and I don't want to lose you, especially after I found you again after all these years."

Megan turned to Nick and his lips found hers.

"Here you go." The woman placed two trays down on the table. "I threw in a couple slices of apple pie. Homemade this morning."

"Thank you so much. This looks delicious," Megan said as she surveyed the tray.

"You're very welcome. When you're done, I'd appreciate it if you could bring the trays up to the fruit stand."

"Will do," Nick said as he turned around to face the picnic table.

"Enjoy."

They spent several minutes eating. "This is pretty good," Megan said. "Thanks for suggesting we stop and eat. I feel better now."

"I'm more intrigued than ever," Nick said. "I don't know what the hell happened back there, but I'm going to keep looking for information."

"What else can you do?"

"I'm calling Officer Maywood and let him know what happened. Then, I'm calling Chen," he said. "As soon as I finish lunch."

CHAPTER 24

Nick and Megan returned the trays to the stand, purchased a bag full of fruit and drove the next hour in silence. The meal had been a perfect peace offering and helped calm emotions. As he drove, Nick pushed the call button on his Bluetooth and gave Chen's number. After several rings, the call was answered.

"Victor Chen, Medical Examiner. How can I help you?"

"Chen, it's Nick Taylor."

"Hey Nick, what's happening? Have you found any info for me yet?"

"No. I'm just returning from New Paltz, NY. The emergency contact Fiona listed with the director of the country club was there, but it was a bust. There was an elderly woman living at the house who said she knew a Fiona many years ago but didn't know anyone now. She wasn't cooperative so no information beyond that. We didn't get a chance to tell her Fiona died. How 'bout you? Anything at the hospitals or in the local database?"

"Nada," Chen answered. "I went into the electronic records for the local hospitals as well as the doctors' database. Found nothing which is telling. Even if the woman was on chemo but going to a specialized hospital, there's usually something in the local records. A blood test, x-rays, but there was nothing. So, what's left? I haven't signed the death certificate yet. No cause of death and I'm not sure of the manner then either."

Nick was thoughtful for a moment. "Chen, you got fingerprints, right?"

"Sure did. That's one of the first things we do."

"Well then send them over to the station. I'm going to run an official trace on her. I got a weird vibe when I spoke to the New Paltz Police. I can't connect Fiona with the woman in the house, but the officer mentioned there was a man living there who has died. Let's see if anything jumps out."

"You got it. I'll send over the scan now."

"Great, I'll get one of the guys to start running them immediately."

Nick disconnected the call and then called the station. He spoke to the duty officer, told him to look for the prints and start loading them in the database. When he was done, he hung up the phone and looked at Megan.

"Hopefully, that will get us some information. It's as if this woman never existed which is impossible. I'm glad Davis let me make this an official investigation."

"I don't even want to know, Nick," Megan said as she shook her head and looked out the passenger window. "I'm not going to ask you to share what you find."

"You promise to stay hands off?"

"I promised. It's in your hands now. I have enough to do with the Pure Horizons project."

"Okay, I'm taking you at your word," Nick said with a smile. The pair enjoyed the remainder of their ride home making small talk and enjoying each other's company.

Nick pulled into the driveway of Misty Manor and parked. Megan got out of the car. "I'll walk myself into the house. I know you want to get over to the police station so why don't you go? We can keep Bella here with us. She's probably had a great day with Dudley and Marie."

"Are you sure?"

"Absolutely, it's been a long day. Thanks for taking me along and for lunch."

Nick popped out of the driver's seat long enough to give Megan a strong hug and a kiss goodbye. "I'll call you later to make sure you're okay."

"Fair enough," Megan said as she turned and made her way inside the house.

CHAPTER 25

Dudley and Bella raced to the door when they heard Megan enter the foyer. She threw her purse on the side table and knelt to hug the dogs. Smokey sauntered out of the kitchen to observe what was happening.

"How are you? Did you have fun today?"

"Fun? They ate like they haven't been fed in weeks and then took a long nap in the sunroom. These pets are as spoiled as they come," Marie said as she approached the door.

"Hmm, I think you have something to do with that," Megan said with a smile.

"They haven't been out in a while if you want to get some air," Marie said.

"Sure, I'll take them out. Anything else happen while I was gone?"

"Yes, you got a call from the country club. Let me see." Marie fumbled in her apron and put on a pair of glasses. She pulled a note from her pocket. "Someone by the name of Julie Bratton called from the club. Said she wanted to touch base about your event."

"Oh, I haven't thought about it since Fiona died, but I guess from the club's perspective, business has to go on. Alright, I'll take the dogs outside and give her a call."

Marie handed Megan the note with the phone number as Megan opened the door and whisked the dogs toward the beach. They flew down the front steps and into the weeds near the buffer. When they were done, they trotted on the sand toward the water's edge. Megan followed behind and watched them play with the waves. She shook out her hair and enjoyed the sea breeze as it flew across her face. Seagulls flew overhead, squawking and in search of a snack.

Walking the shoreline, Megan admitted the country was beautiful and serene, but she could never imagine leaving the ocean behind. The saltwater was part of her blood. Sadness engulfed her as she fully understood why Grandma Rose had refused to leave Misty Manor during Hurricane Sandy and rushed right back when she could. She also understood why Grandma Rose refused to leave before her death. When you lived near the ocean, you became one with the water, the breeze, the rhythmic timing of the waves and the tides.

Megan reached the gazebo and sat down facing the water. Pulling out the piece of paper Marie had given her, she dialed the number.

"Hello?" The voice sounded sleepy.

"Hi, I was looking for Julie Bratton."

"This is she. Who's calling?"

"It's Megan Stanford. I'm returning your call. I'm sorry, perhaps I should have waited until tomorrow morning."

"No, no, it's fine. I ran home before dinner, so I wasn't expecting your call. Oh, don't mind me. Anyway, how are you?"

"I'm fine, Julie. How are you?"

"Good, I'm good. Um, I wanted to reach out to see what you wanted to do about your event. I mean, with what happened to Fiona, you know, we weren't sure."

"Yes, that's so sad about her collapsing," Megan said softly.

"Yeah, my boss told me she died. The medical examiner called here asking questions," Julie said quietly. "That was a surprise."

"I'm sure it was and very unpleasant at that."

"Yeah, anyway the director asked me to reach out and see if you had any thoughts about your event. It's still on the calendar and all."

"Yes, I understand," Megan said. "Tell you what, I'll talk to the other members of the Pure Horizons committee and then come by the country club so we can discuss details. How does that sound?"

"Oh, good. Real good. I'll tell him tomorrow when I go back to work."

"Great. I'll see you both soon. Get some rest, Julie."

"I will. Thanks, Ms. Stanford."

Megan didn't get a chance to respond before Julie clicked off the phone. She realized Julie was college age but didn't know if she was going to school. Megan wondered if Julie had ever experienced the death of someone close to her. Megan would be sure to speak gently to her when she went to the club.

Megan watched the dogs ran up to the gazebo and drop on the floor. They sat there panting, tongues lolling but looking happy. "Well, aren't we having a fine day? It appears you've been having fun all day. It's time we get back to Marie."

She walked along the water's edge toward Misty Manor when her cell phone rang. She answered immediately, hoping it was Nick.

"Hey."

"Hi, yourself. How did things go today?" Georgie asked.

"Oh, hi Georgie. I'm sorry I didn't check the number. I thought it was Nick."

"Sorry to disappoint you."

Megan laughed into the phone. "No, it's not that at all. Nick was following up on a few things so I thought he might call me."

"I see. Well, how did it go today? Did you find anything?"

"No, not really. Nick got mad at me for jumping in, so I promised him I'd behave from now on."

"Yeah, like that's gonna happen."

"He was upset. I'm not going to do any investigating on my own. I promised."

"We'll see. You didn't find anything? No one was at the address?"

"No, just an elderly woman who yelled at us to get off her property."

Georgie laughed. "I wish I was a fly on the wall for that one."

"No, I don't think so," Megan said. "By the way, I just got a call from someone at the country club. They wanted to touch base and see if we were still interested in having our event there next year. I told them I wanted to speak to the other members of the committee before I made any final arrangements. Are you and Amber free sometime soon?"

"I'm going to be on the beach tomorrow."

"Where else would you be?"

"I'm not officially working but we have a couple of new lifeguards so I told them I would hang out in the area. I think maybe you and Amber could use a beach day. Come down and hang with me. We can go over everything."

"That sounds good to me," Megan said. "I'd like to hear what we've come up with so far."

"Good. I'll call Amber. Let's meet around 11:00 a.m. tomorrow. We can have Antonio's deliver a pizza and salads for lunch if you want."

Megan laughed. "You'd better ask Amber first. If she doesn't have a new bikini to show off, she may run out and buy one in the morning."

Georgie chuckled. "That's true. Okay, I'll call her. I'll be at Twentieth Street tomorrow. If I don't call you back, we're on. Sound good?"

"You got it. I'll see you in the morning."

CHAPTER 26

The sun rose bright and strong the next morning. Megan enjoyed her coffee in the library while she attended to some paperwork and bills that waited for her on the desk. Grandma Rose had used a small office off the hall as her work area, leaving the library virtually untouched, but Megan felt she could use the library desk and still show the respect the library deserved. She kept the desk and surrounding area pristine and free of clutter.

The ring from her cell phone took her away from her bills. She recognized the number and answered it immediately.

"Teddy? How are you?"

"Fine, my dear. How are you?"

"Doing well. I'm trying to catch up on bills and such."

"Why don't you let me take care of that? I always handled it for your grandmother. You have tons of money. You shouldn't have to worry about those things."

"Aw, Teddy, thank you. I know it sounds silly but being aware of what it takes to run the estate and Misty Manor keeps me grounded. No one in town has any clue how much I'm worth and I want it to stay that way. That's why it's good for me to know what's going on."

"Whatever you want, but I can easily have someone in my office dispatch bills when you're ready to give that up. When you realize you're currently worth a quarter billion dollars, you won't have to sweat the mundane."

Megan laughed. "Thank you, Teddy."

"Your quite welcome, my dear. Have you heard anything more about that poor woman at the country club?"

"Oh, I didn't tell you, but she passed away in the emergency room. They worked on her for a while, but she didn't respond."

"That's a shame. She seemed like a nice woman."

"Yes, she was."

"Did they find out what happened to her?"

"No, the medical examiner is trying to find more information to help him reach a conclusion. There are no hospital records, and they can't find family so Nick is opening an investigation. Same as if she was an unidentified person."

"Hopefully, that will bring things to a close."

"Yes, we'll see."

"At any rate, the reason I called you is to let you know I did a little research on that financial group that's trying to get the zoning laws changed so they'd be able to build in the marsh."

"Good, did you find anything interesting?" Megan asked, her interest now piqued.

"Through an unnamed source who spoke with a friend of a friend, I was able to identify some members of the financial group."

"Anyone I know?" Megan asked, wondering how long Teddy would keep her in suspense.

"I believe so, remotely at any event. I was given a list of names which didn't mean much to me, so I researched a bit more. Turns out, the bartender and the chef from the country club are both principal members."

"Really?"

"So is the obnoxious man from the Pure Horizons meeting."

"How do you know that?"

"If you remember, Nick got his license plate when he followed him out that night. He ran the plate the next day. I asked him to send me his name. When I got this list, I cross-referenced his name and there he was."

"That man has a lot of nerve," Megan said, her anger rising. "And he stood at that meeting and accused me of fighting this proposal for personal gain? Look at him."

"He was egged on, of course, to specifically cast aspersions on you. And it gets worse," Teddy warned.

"Worse? How can it get worse?"

"Apparently, our esteemed Mayor is part of the group as well."

"Andrew Davenport? Are you kidding me?"

"Well, we can't say we're surprised. He's one step removed as his interest was presented through a representative, but he would reap the profits if the laws were changed and the building went through."

"Isn't that a major conflict of interest?" Megan sputtered.

"Only if someone found out," Teddy said with a chuckle.

"There has to be something we can do."

"Well, if the information is accurate and he is part of the financial group, he'd have to recuse himself from any proceedings. If not, the first thing that would happen is he would be referred to the local ethics committee. If they find he was involved to change the zoning laws to reap a profit, we'd open a criminal investigation. I'll continue to work on things from my end to see if there's something we can pursue as a conflict of interest."

"Okay, thanks, Teddy. I'm meeting with Georgie and Amber today to discuss what they found out about the Environmental Protection Agency and such."

"That sounds perfect. We'll talk again and compare notes before the next zoning board meeting."

CHAPTER 27

Megan stepped from the boardwalk stairs onto the sand at Twentieth Street. She adjusted her large hat but still couldn't find Georgie although she knew the approximate area her friend favorited at the beach. She moved through the sand and enjoyed the cool feeling as it slipped through her toes. The smell of the ocean combined with suntan lotion was familiar and pleasant. Megan felt herself relax and chided herself for living on a beach and not enjoying the benefits more often.

Looking up, she saw Georgie sitting in her favorite beach chair, facing the ocean and the lifeguards at the same time. She was there for support and advice although she didn't have to be. The ocean and beach were a permanent part of the saltwater flowing through her veins.

Megan reached Georgie and gave her friend a hug. "This was a great idea."

"I know," Georgie said with a smile as she looked up and adjusted her sunglasses. "I thought I'd have to drag you down here kicking and screaming."

"Not necessary, thank you very much." Megan pulled her big towel out of her beach bag and spread it out on the sand. Rummaging through her bag, she next pulled out sunscreen, sat on her blanket and began to apply the lotion to her skin.

"Good to see you relaxing for a change," Georgie said.

"The ocean looks great," Megan said. "So clean and refreshing. It even smells cleaner here."

"You have no idea," Georgie said as she squinted at one of the lifeguards. "Since we banned smoking and plastic, the beach has become magnificent, and we have to keep it that way."

"That's what Pure Horizons is all about," Megan said as she stretched out on her blanket. She closed her eyes and concentrated on the sound of the water flowing to and from the shore. She heard the gulls flying above and crying out for tidbits of food. The breeze felt great and she relaxed as she became one with the sand.

Georgie left to speak with one of the lifeguards and Megan enjoyed the quiet. She had just started to doze when a shadow fell over her. Shading her eyes, she looked up to see Amber had found them.

"Hey, you started without me," Amber said as she pulled a cart toward Georgie's chair.

"Moving in?" Georgie asked as she returned to her chair.

Amber made a face and shook her head. "You know I have to be careful about my skin. I need my umbrella, my glasses, my hat, my sunscreen and a special conditioner for my hair so the color doesn't turn."

Megan raised up on her elbows and watched Amber unpack. Georgie smiled as she rolled her eyes toward Megan.

"Let us know when you're settled," Georgie said.

Megan sat up. "I like your bikini. Is it new?"

Amber checked the sun to see if her towel was facing the correct direction. "This was last year's bikini, but I never got a chance to wear it to the beach. I didn't have time to buy anything new because the mall didn't open until 10 a.m. today."

"It's lovely," Megan said as she rolled over onto her stomach. "Who cares if it's last year's style? My suit is about ten years old and Georgie only wears classic lifeguard red."

"I know, it's like a second skin," Amber said.

Georgie threw some sand in Amber's direction while Megan laughed into her towel. She stretched her arms out in front of her and rested her head on them. Across the beach she heard kids laughing, people talking and a radio in the distance.

Ten minutes later, Amber had her umbrella set up and positioned with the top pointed toward the sun. Her nose was covered with a zinc oxide screen, her eyes covered by her sunglasses and her floppy beach hat firmly plastered to her head. She sat back in her low beach chair and immediately rifled through her bag to pull out a bottle of water. She turned and saw the other girls watching her. "What? I don't want to get dehydrated."

"That's very wise," Megan said as she sat up and took a deep breath. "I've forgotten how great it is to smell the ocean."

"It's very relaxing. The ocean has always had special health benefits." Georgie lifted her face toward the sun.

"Okay, so what progress have we all made since we last met?" Megan asked as she grabbed a water for herself.

Amber dug through her purse and pulled out a pad. "From what I've researched, it appears the New Jersey Department of Environmental Protection took over watch of New Jersey's wetland programs. I wrote down the Commissioner's name and number. They have a large staff so we can start making calls if we need to. We'd have to go through one of the dedicated divisions but first we would start with the town, then the county and eventually the state."

"Would they be able to build there if they get the zoning laws changed?" Megan asked.

"Not without getting the proper permits and permissions," Amber answered with a shrug. "But you know how it goes. Someone knows someone who knows someone else. It's possible a few palms get greased here and there and permits become available."

"What about Doogie?" Megan asked Georgie. "Did he have any thoughts?"

Georgie smiled. "After I was educated about the marsh and the many species of fish, birds, snakes and bugs, we talked about the implications. He said the same thing. If it's worth enough money to someone, they could make something happen if they knew the right people despite the devastation to the community in the future. By then, the investment group would have already made a profit and disappeared."

Megan took a deep breath. "Then we have to stop them now, before this gets a chance to catch on or someone bribes someone to look the other way."

"Seems that way," Georgie said with a frown.

"Teddy called this morning, and he had some interesting information about the investment group. Apparently, we know a few members."

"Who would that be?" Amber asked while adjusting her hat.

"The first one is our esteemed mayor."

"What a surprise," Georgie said sarcastically.

"Who else?" Amber looked at her with a curious stare.

"It seems the group of men we saw at the country club are all involved."

"Seriously?"

"Yes," Megan nodded. "All of them."

"Even the bartender?"

"Yes, the bartender, the chef, the mayor and that obnoxious man who was at the Pure Horizons meeting."

"Then we have our work cut out for us," Amber said. "It's time to get organized. Let's see if those flyers we sent out make a difference. We can start a petition and I can get some corporate muscle behind us."

Megan looked at her friends and smiled. "I know it's going to be work but this town and beach are certainly worth it. I appreciate your help more than you know."

"Worth every moment of it," Amber said with a nod.

Georgie looked over toward Megan. "The beach is my life as well as the community, so I would fight to stop the destruction of the natural wetlands anytime. There's a large number of people invested in protecting the beach. I'm sure they would also support the marsh. We could reach them through our email list as well as social media."

"And I know someone who would write an article for the Sunday paper about the threat to the natural wetlands," Amber said as she sat forward.

"Wow, you guys are on fire," Megan said. "I'm glad you're on our side."

Amber flipped her pad to a new page. "Okay, let's start making a list of what we need to do."

CHAPTER 28

After spending the day at the beach, Megan returned to Misty Manor and took a warm shower to wash off the sand. She felt more relaxed than she had in a long time. It was the first time she had a meeting at the beach, and she planned to do it again. She was getting dressed when she heard Marie calling to her from the hall.

"Marie? Is everything alright?" Megan asked as she dried her hair.

"It's all fine," Marie whispered. "Nick is waiting for you downstairs."

"Nick? I didn't know he was coming over."

"Looks like he's anxious to speak to you," Marie said as she took the wet towel for the wash. "I told him you'd be down shortly."

Megan gave her a strong hug. "Thanks so much. I'm lucky to have you here with me."

Marie pulled back and smiled. "I've known you since before you were born. It's my pleasure to stay here and help you. Misty Manor is a grand home and holds a lot of lovely memories for me."

Megan nodded her approval as she placed her brush on her dresser. "I'm glad you feel that way."

"Great, now get downstairs and see what that man wants."

Megan laughed as she left her room and bounced down the grand staircase into the foyer. Nick was petting Dudley and Bella at the same time. Smokey was standing near the wall, watching the pair but not getting involved.

"Hey, I didn't know you were coming over."

"Neither did I," Nick said. "I wanted to talk with you. How about we take a stroll on the beach?"

"Okay, can Dudley and Bella join us?"

"Sure can," Nick said as he opened the front door so the dogs could run out. Dudley stopped on the porch and looked back at Megan. When she shooed him on, he took off for the long grass near the beach.

Nick and Megan walked onto the porch, down the steps and toward the ocean. He grabbed her hand as they neared the shoreline.

"It's early but a beautiful evening," Nick said as he looked at her.

"Yes, it is," Megan agreed. "I was getting worried when I hadn't heard from you since we returned from New York."

"I'm sorry about that," Nick said. "I meant to call you last night but then one of the officers called out and I had to work an extra shift."

They continued to walk along the beach and watch the moon as it reflected along the water. The sound of the waves had a soothing effect and Megan felt herself yielding to the lull.

"Is everything okay?" Megan asked as she looked up at Nick.

He looked at her and nodded. "Yes, it's fine. I'm having a debate with myself. I wanted to tell you where we stand with the investigation, but I don't want you getting involved."

Megan frowned. "It's too late now. You must tell me if you found something. I clearly got your message the other day, but I think it's unfair to hide things from me. I was part of this from the beginning."

"That's true. You remember that I had Chen send me Fiona's fingerprints?"

"Of course," Megan said.

"Well, it turns out her name was Fiona Cockburn, not Fiona Cochran. In addition to that, she has a criminal record."

"What?" Megan said, the surprise evident in her voice. "For what?"

"Apparently, she was arrested for taking part in a Ponzi scheme with her so called boyfriend."

"Don't tell me, Ozzie Hawk?"

"None other," Nick said as he threw a piece of driftwood toward Dudley in the surf while Bella fought with the waves.

"What happened to him?"

"Deceased which is why his mother was so resistant to talk about Fiona. I'm sure she blames her for everything."

"How did he die?" Megan asked.

"He was murdered by one of the victims of the Ponzi scheme."

"Oh my," Megan said. "That's sounds like it was ugly."

"Yes, it does."

"Lay it out for me, Nick. Were they arrested? What happened?"

Nick looked at Megan and smiled.

"You'd better put that grin away and start talking or you're going to be in big trouble," Megan said as she punched him in the arm. Her tap didn't begin to make a dent in his tight muscle.

"And you promise to keep this quiet?"

"Yes," Megan said as she crossed her heart. "I already told you that."

Nick put his hands up for protection. "Okay, okay. It appears that Fiona worked as a sales representative in New Paltz. Making sales was her forte. Ozzie recognized that talent and invited her into whatever little game of fraud he had going on at the time. They made a lot of money but some of the investors were suspicious. There was a complaint to the police and an investigation ensued. Ozzie was caught red-handed, but Fiona's role was not as clear. They couldn't prove anything because she didn't have any evidence of receiving money. There was nothing in her bank accounts. It's possible Ozzie screwed her out of her share. We'll never know."

"Tell me more about the murder."

"The police were planning on a surprise arrest. The plan leaked from the department and one of the investors was so incensed, he decided to get revenge before Ozzie spent comfy time in jail. When the police went to arrest Ozzie, they found him murdered."

"Did they catch the person who did it?"

Nick shook his head. "No arrest was ever made but there were rumors."

"What about Fiona?"

"She was arrested and considered a suspect, but with no evidence, they had to release her. She left New York, relocated to New Jersey and remade herself by getting a job at the country club."

"How did she get a job with a criminal record?"

"I don't know. She probably had fake credentials. Jobs like that don't require fingerprints. Even if it did, her record may not have caught up with her if she was hired right away. Back then, they may never have checked the system for a record, especially if she had an alias, although they couldn't get away with that as easily now."

"That's shocking," Megan said. "No wonder his mother was so hostile. Maybe she's afraid they'll come back for her."

Nick nodded. "It's certainly possible but it doesn't appear she was involved."

"Did Chen have anything else to say?"

"No, he's still waiting for the tests and toxicology to return. Then he'll have to make a determination on the death certificate."

Megan was quiet as they walked.

"It's amazing what you don't know about someone. She seemed so nice, but I guess that's why she was so good at sales."

"That's usually the case," Nick added.

"It's interesting, because it puts a whole new slant on that scene where she ran into the bathroom and was trying to hide. We assumed it was because the bride was being a pain in the tush, but what if there was something else going on?"

"It's very possible they could have known each other or perhaps Fiona was hustling people for extra money in New Jersey." Nick looked at Megan carefully. "You're thinking way too hard right now."

"What?" Megan asked innocently.

"Don't play innocent with me, Megan Stanford. I don't want you investigating on your own, or with Georgie or Amber. The police have officially taken over this case and you don't need to be anywhere around it. Davis would have my head if you were."

"Okay, okay," Megan said. "I'm not going or calling anyone, but you can't stop me from thinking."

"I don't have much luck stopping you from anything."

They reached the steps of Misty Manor. Megan turned and looked at him from the first step. "You don't have to be insulting."

"Megan, promise me you will not act on this information. Otherwise, I will never tell you another thing. Swear to me."

"I swear I will not investigate Fiona's history. However, I do have to go to the country club to finalize the arrangements for the Pure Horizons event. The staff called me a little while ago to see if I was still interested and want me to bring a deposit." Megan realized she was stretching the truth a bit, but she did promise Julie she'd return and didn't want Nick to find out she was there from someone else.

"Then make sure someone goes with you," Nick said. "I don't think there's a threat, but I don't want you to ask questions and put yourself in danger."

"I get it, Nick," Megan said as she climbed another step before quickly turning back. "What about her apartment?"

Nick was thoughtful a moment. "What about it?"

"I just realized we never spoke of her apartment. Has anyone looked there for meds or medical records?"

"As a matter of fact, the police are combing it right now. We were able to gain access as soon as the investigation was official."

"Do you know if they found anything?"

"I haven't gotten a report yet and I'm not sure I'll share when I do." Nick reached the top step and put his hands around Megan's waist as he looked at her.

"You have to let me know if you find something medical."

"Maybe," Nick said. "I'll decide later."

"What will happen to all her things if no one claims them?"

Nick shrugged. "The team will bag what may be important and then the rest falls to the landlord. I think they may hold it for a short time and then it either goes out or maybe they donate to a charity. We only hold what we think could provide information and since we didn't witness a crime, we're not going to take much."

Nick watched Megan carefully. "I don't know what's rattling around that brain of yours, but whatever it is, forget it." He wrapped his arms around Megan's waist and pulled her tight. They embraced as the sea breeze whipped around them. The moon was bright off the water and Dudley whined as he and Bella flopped down to the porch floor. "How about we think about something else?"

Megan turned her head to the side. "I don't know, Nick. You were kind of mean tonight."

"Well then let me make up for it." He bent his head and traced his lips from her earlobe down her neck. She giggled and turned toward him. His lips found hers and all else was forgotten for the moment.

CHAPTER 29

The next morning found Megan driving toward the Misty Point Library to do research on Salt Marshes. She wanted as much information as possible to help defend the Pure Horizons stance when they went to the Zoning Board meeting. She parked and went inside and met with Lindsey, the librarian. She explained what she was looking for and Lindsey asked her to wait at one of the work-tables. Within a short time, she returned to Megan and had a variety of material relating to the salt marshes in New Jersey. To learn about protecting wetland and shallow bay habitats for water birds, the librarian asked Megan to read about the Edwin B. Forsythe National Wildlife Refuge in southern New Jersey. She also read about the New Jersey Wetland Program and the vegetation commonly associated with the Salt Marshes of southern New Jersey.

Next the librarian brought her several charts showing the Predicted Habitat Loss to Development over the next decade including the associated loss of various species and vegetation in New Jersey. Megan knew this information should be available to all before any decision was made about changing the zoning laws.

After an hour of reading, she gathered what she considered the most important data and charts and carried it up to the front desk.

Lindsey looked up at her and smiled. "Did you find what you were looking for?"

"Yes, I believe so," Megan replied. "I need to bring this information to a meeting, and I was wondering if you would be able to copy it for me."

"Of course. Do you want a digital copy or paper? Will you be projecting for the group or having an on-line meeting?"

Megan was thoughtful for a moment. "You know, I'm not sure what their requirements are. Would it be a big problem to give me a digital copy as well as paper? It's important the information is shared with those that attend and I don't want the fact that I don't have the proper display to screw things up."

"No problem," the librarian said. "Do you need it right this minute or can I have it ready for you in a day or so?"

"No, I don't need it immediately," Megan said. "You'll call me when it's ready?"

"Of course. Can you give me a minute?" Lindsey turned to check out a book for a small boy and his mom. "My, what a fun book this is."

"I love dinosaurs," the boy said as he eagerly took the book from her. "My mom says I can get a pet dinosaur if I'm good at the doctor's today."

"Oh really?" Lindsey smiled at his mother who cocked her head and shrugged.

Lindsey turned back to the boy. "Well, sometimes dinosaurs take up your whole bed and they like to sleep in the mountains."

The boy turned to his mother. "Is that true? They like mountains?"

His mother nodded at him. "Yes, I've heard that."

"We don't want him to miss his family." Sadness lined the boy's face which made Megan's heart flip.

"No, I don't think he would be happy," his mother said.

"Well, if we let him stay in the mountains, could we go visit him there?"

"Maybe, we'll certainly talk about it," his mom said as she tousled his hair.

The boy looked at the book and nodded. "Okay, it's okay if I read about him for now and one day, I'd like to go to the mountains and see if we can visit."

"That sounds like a great idea," his mom said. She turned to Lindsey and mouthed a thank you.

"You have a wonderful day and make sure you come back and choose more books to read," Lindsey said.

"We will," the boy said. "I love going to the library."

"Me too," said his mom.

The librarian handed over their books and they left the desk. She turned back to Megan and noticed she was reading a newspaper that was sitting on the circulation desk. "Oh, that lead article is about the poor woman who worked at the Misty Point Country Club. I don't think they figured out how she died yet. The paper said they're waiting for tests to return."

Megan nodded and tried not to comment. She didn't want to break Nick's confidence.

The librarian continued. "She would come in here on occasion and ask me to find books about weddings. She would always try to come up with something unique for each bride."

"She sounds like she was genuinely trying to help the brides realize their dreams," Megan said. "It's a shame."

Lindsey nodded. "Yes, as a matter of fact, I think she still has some of our books. I hope we get them back someday. I'm not sure what happened to her things."

"I met her once or twice, but she never mentioned family," Megan said coyly.

"No, I don't think she had anyone in the area." The librarian looked up from the desk. "She lived in the apartments near the beach. You know, the old apartments on the south point. Those apartments are small. I don't think they take families."

"Oh, yes I know which apartments you mean," Megan said as she filed away the information for later. "Well, I hope you're able to get your books back. If not, you can let me know and I'm sure the foundation will add extra money to the library budget this year if it's needed."

Lindsey's smile was all the reward Megan needed to know support of the library through the Stanford Foundation was appreciated.

"Thank you," Lindsey said. "I'll work on your copies as soon as possible and call you when I'm done."

"I appreciate it," Megan said warmly. Smiling, she turned and left the library.

CHAPTER 30

Megan got into her car and turned the key. The engine hesitated, but after a few prayers, she was able to get the car started. She made a mental note to bring the car to the auto dealer as soon as she could before she got stuck somewhere. She drove down Main Street and within minutes found herself traveling in the opposite direction of Misty Manor. Although she had resolved not to get involved, she told herself there was no harm driving by Fiona's apartment complex.

Megan slowed as she turned the corner. She looked for police vehicles and seeing none, continued forward. She didn't want to risk Nick or any other officer seeing her and reporting back to Nick.

She pulled into the parking lot. Getting out of the car she looked at the apartments until she saw one with a small manager sign near the entrance. Telling herself she was doing a favor for the librarian, she took a deep breath and knocked on the door. Within a minute a middle-aged man opened the door with a scowl.

"Yes?"

"Oh, hello, I'm sorry to bother you, I was looking for the apartment manager." Megan realized she was nervous.

"I'm the manager," he said. "How can I help you?"

Megan stammered as she came up with an excuse. "I was here to see Fiona Cochran. I was just at the library and she has some overdue books so I thought I would help her out and pick them up."

"Well, you're about a week too late, Lady. She's dead."

Megan stiffened at his crude announcement of Fiona's death. It was a good thing she already knew about her fate or she would have been shocked. "Oh, I'm so sorry."

"Yeah, the police just left this morning. They've been looking through all her stuff. They took a few boxes out but I don't know what they took."

Pretending not to know, Megan asked a question. "What will happen to her things now?"

The man shrugged. "I don't know. It's been a week, and so far, no one is stepping forward to claim anything."

"What happens then?"

The manager scratched his upper arm. "When someone takes off and doesn't take their stuff, I'd have to inform the police about abandoned property. If the police don't want it, we can sell it or throw it out. There's been a time or two we stored it for a month but then we usually lose money on the storage, so we don't do that anymore."

He looked up at Megan. "Hey, do you want to see her apartment? You can see if you can find the library books."

Megan didn't expect to go into Fiona's apartment but seized the opportunity. "Sure, I'd like to check if that's okay. Are you sure the police are done? I don't want any trouble."

"Yeah, they even took the yellow tape with them. They said to do whatever I want with the stuff. To be honest, I need to see if there's anything worth selling."

"Okay, sure, let's go." Megan followed as the manager led her up a flight of stairs and to a door at the end of the hall. He pulled a set of master keys from his pocket and opened the door.

Crossing over the threshold, they walked into the apartment. "Looks like a decent couch," he said with a shrug. "Maybe I can do something with that." His cell phone started ringing and he pulled it out of his pocket and looked at the display. "Excuse me a minute, I gotta take this."

"Sure, of course," Megan nodded.

As he walked out, she heard him say, "Hey, Frankie, where's my money?"

Megan turned and walked around the apartment. The living room was functional, and the furniture was good quality, but devoid of any personal items that would give a clue to family or friends. The manager was still out in the hall, so Megan went through the door into Fiona's bedroom.

The bed was made with a soft white duvet. Once again, the furniture was of good quality, but the room lacked any personal items. Megan looked over the dresser and stepped into the bathroom. A hairbrush sat on the counter with a large amount of hair in it. She opened the medicine cabinet but didn't find any medicine bottles. She chided herself knowing the police would have taken any prescriptions if there had been any.

Megan backed out of the bathroom and looked through the doorway, but the manager was still in the hall arguing with someone for his money. The next place Megan approached was Fiona's desk. She moved a newspaper and underneath it found the two library books. She picked them up. She quickly looked through the drawers but didn't find anything significant. Once again, she was sure the police would have taken any planner that listed names or addresses.

Stepping back into the living room, she stood there just as the manager returned.

"One of my tenants. The guy hasn't paid rent in three months, can you believe it?"

Megan shook her head but was without words for Frankie's trouble.

"Hey, I see you found the books. Those are the library books, right?"

Holding them out to him, she showed him the library brand on the inside cover. "Yes, they are. Do you mind if I take them back to the library?"

"No, they belong there. Just make sure they arrive there, like they're supposed to, okay?"

"Of course," Megan said.

"The rest of this crap might sell, but who's got the time to get it all lugged out? These people are all a pain in the butt. You know what I mean?"

"May I please suggest something?"

"Sure, what is it?" He stood in the living room and crossed his beefy arms over his chest.

Megan swallowed. "I work with a few charities. What if we take the whole lot off your hands? We could repurpose the furniture with families in need."

"You mean donate? I could get $500 bucks for that couch," he said pointing to the side.

"No, no, we would pay you a fee for the lot." When he didn't respond, she continued. "We'll send the movers over as well."

The manager frowned. "Why are you so interested lady? You know something I don't?"

"No, I feel bad that Fiona passed, and I do know families in need. The charity would pay you and then it would be a win for everyone."

After a moment, he nodded. "That sounds like it could work. Let me have a number and I'll call you."

Megan wasn't happy about leaving her name as he hadn't asked so far. "Can I give you the number of a man who is on the committee. Could you call him when you're ready and he'll make all the arrangements?"

"I don't care if it's Santa Claus as long as he's gonna haul all this stuff outside."

Megan took a piece of paper out of her pocket and wrote down the number of her estate lawyer, Teddy. She wrote the name of his secretary and handed him the card.

He glanced at the card and put it into his breast pocket. "Okay, I'll call you real soon. Let me confirm with the police."

Megan's stomach rolled into a knot. She didn't want Nick to find out. He would go ballistic. She had no choice but to follow him out of the apartment. They went downstairs and when they reached his apartment, she began to turn toward the parking lot.

"Thank you. I appreciate your help." She held up the books.

"You got it, Lady."

Megan got into her car and was thankful when it started without a problem. Wondering what she had just done, she put it in gear and drove away.

CHAPTER 31

Megan drove by the library on her way back to Misty Manor. She didn't want to go inside and announce where she had been, so she did the next best thing and put the books in the book drop. Lindsey didn't need to know who put them in there as long as they were returned. When she got back into the car, she had trouble starting it again. Once it turned over, she drove straight to the auto dealer to drop it off. She didn't want to be stuck somewhere she shouldn't be. Walking into the service department, she waited fifteen minutes to explain the situation and hand over her keys. Just as the service member asked if she was planning on waiting until an assessment was done, her cell phone rang. She raised her finger to the service clerk to ask him to wait a moment.

"Hello?"

"Megan, it's Nick."

"Hey, Nick. What's up?"

"Where are you?"

Megan stomach clenched. There's no way he could have heard of what she did, she hoped. "I'm at the auto dealer," Megan said. "Where are you?"

"I'm at Misty Manor. I wanted to tell you about tonight, but you aren't here."

Megan took a deep breath. "To be honest, it would be great if you could pick me up and bring me home. Are you free?"

"Sure, let me have the address. What's wrong with the car?"

"I don't know, but I went to the library to do some research on salt marshes. I had trouble starting it several times. I was afraid I'd get stranded, so I drove straight to the dealer."

"I'll be there in ten minutes," Nick said.

"Wait, what about tonight?" Megan asked.

"The gang is planning on meeting at the Clamshell so I wanted to call to see if you could go. We'll talk about it on the way home."

"Okay, see you in a few," Megan said and ended the call.

She turned back to the service clerk who was now leaning on the counter staring at her. "I'm sorry. I wasn't sure if I had a ride, but now I do so I'm not going to wait."

He nodded. "Gotcha and went back to his computer to log in her final status which immediately showed up on the digital board hanging over the counter. Megan marveled how the board always reminded her of the flight status in an airport. She went out to the front parking lot and looked for Nick's car as she waited.

She spotted the Camaro before Nick saw her and waved so he would see her. He drove up to the sidewalk and stopped a few feet away. Megan moved forward, opened the car door and popped into the passenger seat. She belted herself in as Nick took off and hit the main street.

"Thanks for picking me up. They haven't looked at the car yet, so it's possible it won't be ready for days."

"Is it the starter or battery?" Nick asked as he quickly glanced over at her.

Megan shrugged. "I have no idea. I only know that it wasn't starting well."

"Did the lights or horn work?"

"I believe so," Megan said.

"We'll have to wait until you get the phone call. If I'm with you, let me talk to them when they call."

"Okay," Megan agreed. "Where are we going?"

Nick turned toward the beach and parked in a parking lot that allowed them to see the beach. They watched the waves crash on the shore. Nick turned off the engine and turned to Megan.

"What's going on?" Megan asked as she looked at him.

"I went to Misty Manor because I needed to talk to you."

"About what?"

"A couple of things. First is that the gang wants to go to the Clamshell tonight. Tommy and the Tunes are playing a last-minute gig. Tommy reached out to me and I think Amber left you a couple of messages at the house."

"Why didn't she just text me?"

"Have you checked your phone lately?"

Megan pulled out her phone and found fourteen text messages. "Wow, I guess I didn't hear the tone."

"That's why I was worried when I didn't find you at Misty Manor."

"I get it, Nick. But I do have things to do. I'm not a fixture there." Megan immediately felt bad when she saw Nick's face especially knowing that he was concerned. "Is there something else you're not telling me?"

"Yes, and I want to tell you about it before we get together with anyone. Or before it possibly leaks out."

"You're starting to scare me," Megan said, eyes wide open.

Nick took a deep breath. "I heard back from Chen this morning."

"And?"

"He got some of the screens back and it turns out that Fiona was poisoned."

Megan didn't respond for a moment and Nick wondered if she had heard him.

"Wait, what did you say?"

"You heard me, it turns out Fiona was poisoned."

"Do you mean murdered?" Megan felt herself getting agitated. "How? Where? With what?"

"We don't know if she was murdered. It could have been accidental poisoning. But that's the point. It could have been murder. If it was, it's possible that Fiona wasn't the target."

Megan blinked. "What are you saying?"

"If you remember, the last thing Fiona ate was that special chocolate dessert the chef made. The same chef who is part of the finance group trying to build real estate in the marsh."

Megan frowned. "Do you think they would try to kill me just for fighting their plans?"

"We're talking a potential loss of millions of dollars for them. I've investigated people who were killed for a hell of a lot less than that," Nick said as he watched her.

Megan was quiet for a minute. "Did Chen have anything else to say?"

Nick scratched the back of his neck and opened the windows to allow cool air to flow through the car. "Yes, he's waiting for the rest of the toxicology screens to return."

"What's not in yet?" Megan asked, trying to understand.

"For one thing, he didn't get the results of the chocolate dessert or the box of chocolates given to Fiona from Bridezilla."

"Did he say what the poison was?"

"Sort of, but it's a bit complicated. He said he'll explain it himself if we drop by." Nick looked at his watch. "It's too late today, he's already left for the day. That's why I was trying to find you. We'll have to go the next time he's at work."

"That's disturbing," Megan said with a shudder. "I'm more unsettled now than ever."

"You should be, and you need to be careful until we figure out exactly what's going on."

"What am I supposed to do? I have things to do."

"Considering you don't have a car, I'm calling Luther. He can easily be your driver for a couple of days, and I'll feel better that someone I trust is with you when you're out of the house."

"Nick, that would be awkward," Megan protested.

"Nonsense," Nick said as he pulled out his cell phone and started texting. Within minutes, he received a reply and texted again. "I gave him your cell so you can text or call directly. Make sure you connect with him."

Megan heard her cell phone chime and looked at the text. Luther had sent a friendly exchange and encouraged her to call him anytime she needed him for driving or otherwise. He also expected her to contact him tomorrow. His schedule was open for her. Her face flamed red as she looked up at Nick. "This is so embarrassing."

"Promise me you'll call him," Nick said as he watched her. "I've already had a couple of scares with people trying to kill you." When she didn't answer, he repeated, "Promise me, Megan."

"Fine, I promise. Are you happy now?"

"Very happy," Nick said as he leaned forward and pulled Megan toward him. He kissed her and then gave her a squeeze. "I don't know what I'd do if something ever happened to you."

Megan was quiet as Nick started the car and headed toward Misty Manor. They were due to meet everyone at The Clamshell in an hour and Megan wanted to change before they did.

CHAPTER 32

The bar was dark when they walked in. They could hear Tommy and the band singing from the bandstand in the corner. They stood in the foyer for a few minutes to let their eyes adjust. Megan saw Amber waving at her from a table across the floor. She tapped Nick on the arm and started walking toward her.

Amber, Georgie, and Doogie were all seated and there was a platter of appetizers in front of them.

"Did you start the party without us?" Nick asked as he pulled out a chair for Megan and then one for himself.

"No, Tommy said he was starting early since it's Saturday and I drove here with him."

"Doogie and I were just hungry and wanted to eat so we arrived early as well," Georgie said.

Amber stood and handed plates and the platter of food over to them. "Here, have a bite. We waited to order dinner until you arrived."

A waitress arrived at the table and introduced herself. She wore black pants, a Hawaiian shirt and had a towel in her waistband. "Can I get anyone a drink?"

Megan and Nick looked at each other. "Are you on call tonight?"

"Thankfully, no," Nick said as he turned to the waitress. "I'll have whatever's on tap."

The waitress rattled off ten different beers and Nick chose one he would prefer. She turned to Megan and waited with pen poised.

Megan looked at Nick and shrugged. "You know, I think I'll have a Mai Tai."

"Oh, I haven't had a Mai Tai in ages," Amber said. "Usually I don't like rum, but I think I'll have one of those tonight."

"Make it three," Georgie echoed.

Doogie raised his hand. "I'll have whatever beer Nick is having from the tap."

The young waitress nodded and said, "Okay, I'll be back in a bit."

"This is so much fun," Amber said. "We haven't been out as a group in months. We need to make a pact that we'll go at least once a month."

"Sounds good to me," Georgie said as she popped a chip in her mouth.

Megan laughed. "We used to follow Tommy's gigs but he's so busy becoming famous that he's stepping up his venues."

Amber gave a large smile. "Sounds great to me."

Doogie looked over at Megan. "So where do we stand with the salt marshes and the zoning board meeting."

"I went to the library and found some nice graphs on predicted loss of marshes due to development."

"That's great," Doogie said. "I think we can extrapolate and point out the potential cost to the town depending on the number of units they want to build. The sewer costs and potential damage from flooding are important as well. There are costs for road maintenance especially if the town must pay to build them. I can put all that together for you."

"I'd appreciate that very much," Megan said. "Lindsey is putting all the information together for me. Perhaps, you can pick it up from the library?"

"Sure, no problem."

"Teddy is also pulling information and seeing if he can contact any of the environmental agencies in the state. He'll try to invite them to the meeting. Perhaps I can have him call you so you can collaborate? The stronger the argument, the better our chances."

Doogie nodded. "But we all know that we don't always get the results we want."

"Well, we're going to try as hard as we can," Megan said.

Nick reached over and squeezed her leg. "Which is why I don't plan on leaving your side until this is settled." He then turned to her. "And maybe not after that."

Megan gave a weak smile. She had almost forgotten Nick's theory of her being a target of this finance group. She still couldn't believe there would have been poison at a public event, but stranger things have happened. Megan hoped Chen got the rest of the results back soon.

"Nick, I have to run some errands tomorrow."

"That's fine. I'm working. What time do you want Luther to pick you up?"

Megan paused. "10:00 a.m. would be fine. Although I feel so funny about this whole thing."

"Better to feel funny then not at all," Nick said as the waitress arrived with a tray full of drinks. She passed them out to each guest with practiced skill. When she was finished, she collected the empty appetizer plate and took their dinner order. Tommy planned to join them on his break. Megan picked up her drink and decided she was glad she had ordered a double rum.

CHAPTER 33

Luther pulled the black SUV into the Misty Manor driveway at 9:55 a.m. He was wearing a pressed black suit, with a white button-down shirt, skinny black tie and his best pair of shades. He was happy for the job, but he would have done anything for Nick. It wasn't difficult to tell he was ex-military. His training and physique were still sharp.

Nick told him that Megan had asked for help as her car was in the shop, but Nick had given him orders to protect her as well. He was to be as covert as possible but that was his mission while they were out of the house.

He walked to the front door and knocked to let her know he would be waiting in the driveway. She could take her time and come out whenever she was ready.

Five minutes later, she made her way down the walkway. Luther was leaning against the black SUV and opened the back door for her.

"Miss Stanford," he said as he gallantly helped her into the back seat.

"Luther, this isn't necessary. I'm not famous or anything. My car just won't start."

"Miss Stanford, you could be as poor as poor can be. It doesn't make you any more or less special in my eyes."

Megan was touched and speechless by his comment. She felt her face flame from embarrassment. By trying to be humble she had demonstrated judgement. "Thank you, Luther. I appreciate you helping me out today."

"It is my honor and pleasure," he said as he made sure she was buckled and tucked in and closed the door. He made his way to the driver's seat, then put his seatbelt on and looked into the rearview mirror.

"Where are we off to today?"

"I need to go to the bank," Megan said. "I have some business at Shore Community Bank."

"The one on Main Street?"

"That's the one Luther. Thank you very much."

"You got it." He started the car, put it in gear and slowly headed away from Misty Manor.

Megan still felt awkward sitting in the back. Should she make small talk or stare out the window? Thankfully, Luther solved the problem by commenting on the weather.

"It's a lovely day," Megan responded. "I tend to enjoy the fall beach weather more than the red-hot summer. The water is warm, the sun is comfortable, and the beach is not as crowded."

"I agree with liking things less crowded." Luther pulled up to the curb and made his way around the SUV to help Megan out of the car. Megan would have popped out on her own but knew it wouldn't make a difference at this point. Luther was still coming to help her.

"I'll have to move the car down the block," Luther said. "This is a yellow curb right here."

"Of course. I'll look for the car when I come out and I'm very capable of walking."

"Yes Ma'am," Luther said.

Megan spun around to face him. "Okay, enough is enough. I didn't say anything when you called me Miss Stanford, but Ma'am is just too much. If you want me to accept your help, I want you to be a friend. You are not a hired hand. Call me Megan or I'll walk home."

Luther started to laugh. "Yes Ma'am, ah, I mean Megan."

"That's better," Megan said and turned toward the bank. "I should only be ten minutes or so. I just have to sign a check for one of the charities."

"You got it. I'll be waiting down the block," Luther said as he went to move the car.

As Megan walked into the bank, she didn't see the two men standing on the corner across the street. One was the town mayor, and the other was the nasty man from the Pure Horizons public meeting. If she could have heard them, she would have been upset to hear them ask who she thought she was now that she had a driver dropping her off in a shiny, black SUV.

True to her word, she left the bank ten minutes later and almost slammed directly into the Misty Point Mayor, Andrew Davenport.

"Well, Miss Stanford. It's a surprise running into you here and I mean that literally."

"Mr. Davenport," Megan said without a smile. "I'm not sure what you mean by that."

"I thought you let your lawyer, Theodore Harrison Carter, do all your dirty work for you like banking and harassing people."

Megan tilted her head at his rudeness. "Excuse me?"

"Just saying I'm surprised you're here in person."

"You're a very rude man," Megan said shaking her head. "Teddy serves as counsel, but I approve everything that goes forth. Unlike you, I actually have a moral compass."

"Yes, I'm sure you feel entitled to that as well."

Megan felt herself flame inside. "You'd better watch yourself, Mayor. If I were you, I'd spend a little more time deciding what trash came out of my mouth."

"Excuse me, Miss Stanford. Is this man bothering you?" Luther appeared out of nowhere. His bulk and strength indicating a no-nonsense demeanor.

"He bothers most people, Luther, but he was just moving on," Megan said as she took a deep breath.

"Excellent, let me walk you to the car."

"Thank you, Luther." The pair pushed through the Mayor and walked to the car. Luther stayed between Megan and Andrew Davenport until she was safely inside the rear passenger seat of the car. He then made his way to the driver's side and got in."

"Are you okay?" Luther asked as he looked at her in the rearview mirror.

"Yes, thank you for coming to get me."

"I couldn't hear what that guy was saying, but the body language looked heated."

Megan snorted. "Believe it or not, Luther, that's our esteemed mayor. He is corrupt, rude, and incredibly obnoxious."

"Oh, is that the dude?"

"You've heard of him?"

Luther nodded. "Yes, his name has come up in certain circles and not in a positive way."

"He's usually a jerk but today he was particularly bombastic."

"Sorry about that but I'm glad I was here to help."

"Me too, thank you."

"Where to?" Luther asked with a grin.

"I was going to stop at a market for a few things, but I'm not sure I feel like going now."

"With all due respect, that's exactly what you should do now. Don't let that jerk change your plans. He's not that important and don't let him live in your head."

Megan laughed. "You're right, Luther. To the market."

Luther nodded at Megan in the mirror. "My pleasure."

CHAPTER 34

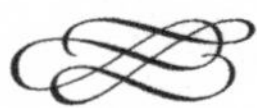

Luther pulled into the driveway of Misty Manor and helped Megan out of the car. He opened the trunk and carried her packages up to the front door. She opened the door and turned to thank him.

"I'd like to pay you for your time, today," Megan said.

"That's not necessary."

"It absolutely is," Megan insisted. "Otherwise, you will never drive me around again."

"You look like you would hold to that."

"If you think I'm kidding, you don't know me very well. Come in, please." Megan turned and walked into the foyer. Luther placed the packages on the marble foyer table and turned as Megan opened her wallet. After a moment, she removed several large bills.

Luther surveyed the foyer and let out a large whistle. "Wow, this place is as impressive as they say."

"Who says?" Megan asked.

"Just talk around town," Luther said. "But all good talk. You have a wonderful reputation, just like your grandmother did."

"I'm glad to hear that. Grandma Rose was adamant that the Stanford Foundation help to support the different needs of the community and we're going to keep doing that as long as we're able."

"Wonderful to hear," Luther said. "One day you can thank me with a tour."

"It would be my pleasure," Megan laughed.

"Will you need to be going out again today?"

"I don't think so, but I'll need a ride to pick up my car when it's ready." Megan quickly checked her phone. "Apparently, the dealer hasn't called to have me approve the repair so it's not going to be ready today. Are you available tomorrow?"

"You have my number. Call or text me and I'll make sure I'm available whenever you need me. That includes creeps that bother you. Nick knows I have training in Special Forces. If you don't call me, he will, if necessary."

"I get it," Megan said. "And thank you, Luther." She pressed the bills into his hand. "I'm sure you'll find that will more than compensate you for your day."

Luther placed the bills in his pocket without looking at them. "Thank you. I'll be on my way, now."

"Have a great day, Luther." Megan said as he turned and waved. She closed the door and picked up her packages. She walked the food to the kitchen and put away the refrigerated items.

Megan carried her other purchases up the three flights of stairs to the landing and walked toward her room. Dudley, Bella, and Smokey came running down the hall.

"What have you three been up to?"

Dudley wagged his tail and jumped onto the bed. Bella followed Dudley. Smokey also jumped up but was more aloof. Megan sat on the edge of the bed and rubbed Dudley's head when he nudged her. He licked her arm several times and panted with his tongue out of the side of his mouth. Bella watched with interest.

Megan stood up, made sure she scratched the cat behind his ears. Smokey purred as he enjoyed the attention.

She then unpacked her things and laid on the bed. The animals were more than happy to settle themselves around her. She pulled out her cell phone and dialed Teddy's private cell. He had one phone for colleagues and friends, but another private cell restricted to certain people and she wanted to make sure he answered.

"Teddy?" Megan said when he picked up.

"Yes, it's me. Is everything alright?"

"Yes, but there are a few things I wanted to discuss with you. First, you will probably be getting a call from a man and I told him to ask for you or Ellen."

"Who is this man?" Teddy asked

"He's the manager of Fiona's apartment building."

"Why will he be calling me?" Teddy asked.

"The manager was deciding what to do with Fiona's things once the police were done with her apartment. I couldn't let him just throw them out so I asked if we could purchase them and give them to someone in need."

"I see and is there any other reason for this?"

Megan paused. "Well just in case we need to look through them later."

Teddy stayed silent at first. "I hope you are not meddling."

"Teddy, Nick cannot know that I made this arrangement. That's why I didn't give my name. Please do this for me just in case we need to look through her things later. There's no other way I could do it."

Megan took his silence for consent. "I also wanted to let you know that I bumped into Andrew Davenport at the bank and he was particularly nasty today."

"Did he bother you?" Teddy's voice was full of concern.

"He would have continued to be obnoxious, but I had a driver who came to my rescue."

Teddy paused. "Why did you have a driver?"

Megan sighed. "My car is in the shop. I'm not sure if you met Luther but he drove us to the food tasting that night."

"No, I've not met him, but Nick spoke of him."

"He was my driver today while I don't have a car. Nick insisted because he also found out something about Fiona's death. I'll tell you but you must keep it secret."

"Dear me," Teddy said. "What could be that shocking?"

"It appears that Fiona Cochran died from poisoning."

"What?" Teddy sounded surprised.

"Victor Chen doesn't know if it was accidental or murder, but as soon as he comes back to his office, we're going to speak with him and find out." Megan realized her story sounded worse by the minute.

After a pause, Teddy responded. "I think Nick may be right on the money. Perhaps you should retain this man as a permanent driver if he can secure your safety."

"I don't know about that," Megan responded. "But I wanted to call and see if you knew of any reason that Davenport would be particularly nasty. There was no hesitation on his part to verbally accost me and he made a comment about you doing my dirty work including harassing people."

Teddy chuckled. "Ah, I get it now. I had a conversation with someone who is charged with the legal protection of the environment within our state. He was genuinely concerned when he heard of the plans for the salt marsh and mentioned that he would be putting out some feelers for information. This man is not someone to ignore and I'm sure word of his interest got back to the mayor."

"I see," Megan said. "I was wondering if something had happened."

"That's all I'm aware of but I'm concerned he was so vocal and aggressive. This project would mean loss of millions of dollars to their financial group, but they never should have assumed it would go through without a hitch unless the good mayor promised something he shouldn't have."

"Makes sense to me," Megan said.

"Just please stay away from him," Teddy said. "Don't provoke him. We don't want him to have any ammunition at this meeting."

"You don't have to worry about that," Megan said as Dudley nuzzled her side. "Thanks, Teddy."

"You are very welcome but please be careful. That man is unhinged."

"I will," Megan promised and disconnected the call.

CHAPTER 35

Nick called later that evening. "How did things go today?"

Megan stiffened for a moment before she asked, "Hi, Nick. Why do you ask?"

Nick paused for a moment. "I was wondering how things worked out with Luther as your driver. Were you able to get anything done?"

Megan didn't know how to answer him. She had her suspicions that Luther called and told him everything about her altercation with the mayor. On one hand, she felt mild irritation that she was being watched, but on the other hand, was grateful Luther was there for her. Megan assumed his reporting to Nick would be due to concern, not any other reason. She knew Nick worried about her and it was true her life had already been threatened several times and she had been in the hospital twice.

"What did you hear?" Megan asked nonchalantly.

Nick started to laugh. "Okay, you win. Luther called and told me about your run-in with Davenport. Besides that, I'm genuinely concerned and worried about you. I'm out of my mind that I can't be with you myself."

"Well, since you put it like that, yes I did have an unpleasant exchange with him and I'm grateful Luther was there. Davenport is such a jerk."

"At least he's consistent with how he treats everyone."

"He was so nasty," Megan said. She spent the next ten minutes telling Nick about what Davenport said to her. "I called Teddy since he named him, and he thought that Davenport was likely receiving push back from someone in the state about the marsh project."

"I'm glad Luther was with you," Nick said. "Have you heard anything about the car? You haven't mentioned anything."

"Now that I think about it, I haven't heard yet. I'll definitely call them tomorrow. The evaluation should be done. They should have called and given me the estimate."

"Make sure you let me know before you approve anything."

"Will do," Megan said. "Thanks for checking up on it."

"Just want you to be safe," Nick said. "Why don't you let Luther continue to drive for you for now? I know I would feel better."

"That's nice to hear, Nick."

"I also wanted to tell you that I got a message from Chen. He said he could meet with us tomorrow afternoon. Are you free?"

"You bet I am. The sooner we figure this out, the better."

"We?" Nick asked.

"You, I meant mostly you, but of course I do have some curiosity since the woman died right in front of me."

"I get it and if it weren't for that, I wouldn't be bringing you with me at all."

"I have no doubt of that," Megan said.

"I'll pick you up tomorrow at 2:30 p.m. and we'll drive over together. Maybe we can grab a bite after we're done with Chen."

"Sounds great, Nick," Megan said and smiled.

"It's a date. Not my idea of a great date, but a date nonetheless."

Megan chuckled and they spent the next hour talking about more pleasant things.

CHAPTER 36

The next morning, Megan called the Misty Point Country Club and made an appointment to speak with Julie and Mark Darcey about her event. She called Luther to make sure he was available, and he agreed right away. She wanted to go to the meeting and be back in time to change and be ready for Nick.

Luther arrived within the hour and knocked on the front door. Megan was ready to go and was waiting for him to arrive. She grabbed her purse and hurried out the door. They walked to the driveway and Luther opened the back door. With little hesitation, she jumped in, buckled her seat belt and waited for Luther to start the car.

"I'm still not use to this back seat driving arrangement and I'm not sure I like it," Megan called up to him.

Luther grinned. "We'll have to give it more time and see what happens. We're on our way to the country club?"

"Yes, I have to go over some arrangements with them."

"Will you be awhile?"

"I'm not sure, but you can leave if you have to. I don't want you to sit around waiting for me," Megan said. "I can text you when I'm done or even start walking."

"It's no problem. I'll be there when you get out," Luther said as his eyes flicked up to the mirror. "I just wanted to know which podcast I should start listening to."

Megan grinned and shook her head as she glanced out the window.

They arrived at the country club and Luther insisted on opening her door for her in grand style. Megan was embarrassed but Luther hoped someone was watching. She walked to the front door which was open early in the day for customers. Cleaners, decorators, and deliveries were directed to the back entrance.

Megan stepped into the foyer to complete silence. She took a couple of steps, looked around and said, "Hello? Anyone here?"

Within a minute, both Julie Bratton and Mark Darcey walked into the foyer to greet her. "Good morning," Mark said with a director's smile.

"Good morning," Megan nodded. "It's amazing how quiet it is without a party."

"Very true," Mark said. "It shows the life of the party is in the guest list, but a great venue helps to bring it alive."

"Hi, Julie," Megan said. "How are you?"

"Fine," Julie replied. She appeared sullen today and was dressed in rumpled jeans and a T-shirt. Her hair was lank. Megan was sure that Mark wanted to include Julie as she had originally toured Megan through the facility, but probably felt uncomfortable with her complete handling of the event.

They walked into Mark's office and he invited everyone to take a seat at a small conference table. "Can I get you anything? Coffee, tea, or a soft drink?"

"No, thank you," Megan said as she made herself comfortable. "Before we start, I want to say once again how sorry I am about what happened to Fiona. You must be upset."

Mark sat with his hands steepled before him. "Yes, to be honest, I'm still not sure what happened." He pointed to Julie and himself. "We're not family so we can't ask any questions. We haven't touched her office yet because I haven't gotten a final go ahead from the police, but she was a damn fine event manager, and we will miss her very much."

Julie stiffened next to Megan as she turned to her. "This must be upsetting for you to experience."

Julie shrugged her shoulders and looked away. Remembering how Julie had stepped right in when Fiona was pulled out by Bridezilla, Megan wondered if there was some competition involved. Although Julie would have to up her game if she wanted to take over part of Fiona's responsibilities.

Megan turned back to Mark. "Just out of curiosity, and I realize it's inappropriate to ask, but what's going to happen to the wedding Debbie Goren was screaming about that night?"

Mark gestured to Julie and smiled. "The wedding will happen this weekend and I'm sure that the reception will be beautiful. Many times, there is a lot of angst leading up to these things but when the actual day comes, everything turns out fine. We don't often speak of events about our other guests, but Julie has been able to handle her questions and concerns up to this point. If Ms. Goren has any other concerns about the wedding, she is certainly welcome to speak with me as well."

"Thank you for saying," Megan said. "I'm sure she will have a wonderful event. It's a shame it was so stressful for Fiona."

Julie rolled her eyes and Mark waved her off. "No problem, but let's turn to your event. If you wouldn't mind starting fresh, I'd like to talk about some of your goals and expectations."

Megan thought he was exceptionally smooth at his approach and although he probably hadn't had direct conversation with clients in a while, he was able to easily glide right back into that role.

"Of course, Megan smiled. "As you probably know, my grandmother was Rose Stanford. She set up a large foundation which supports and champions many charities in our town and the state. When Grandma Rose passed, I became the new Chair of that foundation. One of the non-profit groups we are proud of is the Pure Horizons Environmental Group. Our work has been a positive influence on the beach and helps to keep the streets and boardwalk clean."

Mark nodded. "And I applaud you for that. A clean beach helps our venue as well."

"Yes," Megan said. "We have an annual event to raise funds and awareness about the environment. Our event for this year is already scheduled, but I was looking to schedule for next year as I understood you are booked far in advance."

"That is correct and thankfully, Fiona's death has not impacted our reservations at this point."

"That's good to hear," Megan said. "When I was here the first night, Fiona and I had started talking in the ballroom and she was called away when Debbie started yelling in the foyer. Julie continued with a lovely tour of the entire facility. I booked a potential date with Julie, but we never got to the details with everything that happened." Julie half grinned at Megan's words.

"I see," Mark said as he stood and leaned over his desk. "I have the event planner right here. Let's recheck the date and make sure everything is set." He looked at Megan and Julie. "Can I please ask what date you held?"

Julie didn't answer so Megan jumped in. "We put in a reservation for next August. We've already put some ideas into play for the community for the next beach season, but we like to meet at the end of each summer and identify any new concerns or discuss how we can continue to improve."

Mark continued to turn pages until he reached the following August. He placed his finger on the page and scrolled down. "Yes, here it is. Your event for August 15th is written in."

"I spoke with several members of the board after the unfortunate food tasting and they agreed we would like to continue with that date and have our charity event here as long as we agree on the price and the details. I am authorized to leave a deposit as well."

Mark smiled. "Excellent. Why don't we discuss a few things such as number of guests, type of food service, entertainment and décor? You don't have to make any final decisions until next summer, but just to have a basic idea of your expectations."

Megan spent the next fifteen minutes discussing their planned event. Pure Horizons hoped to have approximately 200 people attend the charity event. She would go back to the committee and discuss specifics such as food and entertainment. Her décor would center around colors reminiscent of the ocean and beach, but she wasn't sure how elaborate they wanted to be with flowers or centerpieces. There would be an award ceremony and a few fundraisers such as a silent auction and they would need a separate room for that. She assured Mark that she would provide answers as soon as she had them.

"That sounds great," Mark said as he stood and extended his hand to Megan. "We are honored to be able to host next year's event for you."

"Thank you very much," Megan said. As she shook his hand, she offered a large smile. "You know, when I discussed things with Fiona, I gave her a folder with some ideas which were suggested by the committee. With all that happened, I never got the folder back and I was wondering if it would be an imposition to look for it. I'd be happy to do it myself since you don't know what it looks like. Would you be able to let me into Fiona's office for a few minutes?" Megan was worried that Nick would be upset with her if he ever found out about her ruse, but she was hoping she might see something, anything, that would help give answers about Fiona's death.

Mark paused for a few minutes. He looked up at Julie and asked if she was available to guide Megan to Fiona's office. Julie shrugged and reluctantly said, "I'll take her."

"It would just be for a minute. My folder might be sitting right on top of the desk," Megan lied.

"What color is your folder?" Mark asked.

Megan had to think fast. She recently started using purple file folders in the office of Misty Manor and that's the first thing she thought of. "Purple. It was purple."

Mark leaned back and pulled a ring of keys out of his pocket. He identified a specific key and handed it to Julie. "Here you go." He looked at Megan. "Please be quick about it and as far as I'm concerned it never happened. The police didn't say I wasn't allowed to go into the office, and I believe they've retrieved whatever they thought was important.

"Thank you, thank you very much," Megan said as she zipped her fingers across her lips.

Megan and Julie left the room and made their way to Fiona's office. Julie unlocked the door and then walked into the office with Megan. She looked around for a few seconds. "Do you see it?"

Megan shook her head. "No, but maybe I can just flip through the desk papers quickly?"

Julie's cell phone rang, and she answered it. She gestured toward the desk and then turned and walked out of the room. Megan quickly ran around to the other side of the desk and quickly looked through drawers, papers and Fiona's appointment calendar. Nothing of importance popped out at her. There were no medication bottles in the office, but if there had been any she was sure the police would have already collected them. She turned to the computer and started tapping on the keyboard to see if she could bring the computer to life. Maybe, if she was lucky, there would be a screen with information. She typed but only a screen saver appeared, and Megan clearly did not have the necessary passwords to unlock it. Megan jumped when she heard Julie's voice outside the door. She quickly swiveled her chair to face the desk so Julie would find her there when she walked in.

"Did you find it?" Julie asked as she thrust her cell into her denim pocket.

Megan shook her head. "No, I didn't. I'll have to go back to the board and recreate it. We have time before we make any final decisions. I was just trying to give her some idea about the different ways we had discussed to raise funds, and we wanted to add some charm to the fundraiser."

Julie shrugged. "Well, I never saw it so I can't help you out there."

"Thank you, Julie. You've been so much help already. Do you miss Fiona? She must have been a good mentor for this type of thing."

Megan was surprised when Julie frowned and said, "Not really. She tried to keep all the glory to herself. Maybe it would have been nice if we worked as a team more often."

"Yes, that can be hard," Megan nodded. She walked to the door and over the threshold. Julie pulled the door closed and locked it with Mark's key.

Together they walked toward the front door and Megan spied Luther standing in the foyer.

"I wonder who that is?" Julie asked.

"Oh, that's Luther. He's a friend who drove me here today. My car isn't working so he was kind enough to offer."

"Gotcha," Julie said with a head nod.

Megan walked forward. "Luther, thanks so much for waiting. Are you ready to go?"

"Ready when you are," Luther said as he looked over the foyer once last time. He put his aviator glasses on and opened the front door. He held it until Megan was outside, nodded briefly at Julie and walked outside, closing the door behind him.

They got into the car and Luther began to drive away. "Everything alright in there? The mood didn't seem too jovial when I saw you walking toward the door."

"It was fine," Megan said. "It's been a weird vibe ever since Fiona died. It's the first time I sat and talked with the director and Julie. He's very smooth and she's just too young to finesse the job. I'm sure she'll get more experience over time."

"I don't know," Luther exclaimed. "That's twice I brought you here and twice this place has creeped me and everyone else out. That's got to mean something."

Megan laughed as she turned and looked out the window to watch the ocean as they flew by.

CHAPTER 37

Nick arrived an hour later. When Megan opened the front door, he smiled and pulled her to his chest for a tight hug. "Hello, beautiful."

"Hello," she cooed as she enjoyed the strong hug from Nick. He was still in uniform, but off duty for the rest of the day.

"I want to get over to see Chen right away. With our luck, he'll get pulled for a new homicide and I want to know what he found."

"I'm ready," Megan said. "Let's do this." They both walked down from the deck and to Nick's car in the driveway. "I appreciate you letting me come along."

Nick looked at her as he drove. "Well, I'm still ambivalent about that, but since you were involved from the beginning, you may have a different perspective."

"Thanks," Megan said dryly. "I'm glad I can be of assistance."

Nick laughed. "You are always of assistance."

Megan crossed her arms and scowled at him.

Nick continued driving down Ocean Ave and then inland to Main St. and to the gray building which housed the ME's office. They parked and went into the building where they were stopped by someone manning a reception desk, but the security officer recognized Nick and the two made small talk for a few minutes. When Chen was free, he buzzed the front desk and asked for Nick and Megan to be sent to the back office.

When they arrived, Dr. Chen stood up and shook hands with Nick and Megan. He invited them to be seated in the plastic chairs while he sat behind a small desk as they spoke.

"Thanks for seeing us, today," Nick said. "I'd like to wrap up this investigation as soon as possible so whatever you can tell us would be great."

Chen nodded. "I understand. I'm eager to close this case, but it gets stranger as each day goes by." Chen sorted through some papers on the desk and found a small folder. He opened it and pulled out several large prints. He handed them over to Nick. "Here, I want you to look at these morgue photos." Megan's eyes went wide as she considered whether she wanted to view Fiona's last images. Nick quickly shuffled through and handed them to Megan. He nodded and encouraged her to take them.

Megan looked through the photos. Although she had expected a lot of gore, she saw photos of Fiona's hands. She looked through the lot, handed them back to Chen and said, "I don't understand."

Chen took the photos and placed them back into the folder. "What you're seeing is something called Mees lines. They're a discoloration of the nail that runs across the nail bed. That's why they're distinctive. They're horizontal, not vertical. It's rare for a patient, live or dead, to have them unless something significant happened with their health."

"Like what?" Megan asked, trying to understand as she looked at her own fingernails.

"Some causes of Mees lines are heavy metal poisoning such as arsenic, thallium or other heavy metals." Chen paused before he continued. "Plenty of other diseases can cause Mees lines as well, but they're all serious such as leprosy, tuberculosis, treatment with chemotherapy, kidney disease, malaria, carbon monoxide and others. I can tell that something serious had gone on just by looking at her hands and taking fingerprints."

"Did you find anything else on the autopsy?" Nick asked.

Chen shook his head. "Nothing on a gross level which is why I leaned toward the heavy metal poisoning. I had to take tissue samples and send them out for analysis. I got positive results which is why I called."

Megan leaned forward with eyes wide open. "And?"

"The result showed that she was poisoned with thallium."

No one responded for a few moments.

"Thallium?" Nick asked as he shook his head. "What is thallium?"

"It's a heavy metal that's found in the earth and in large doses can cause acute poisoning, or it can build up over a longer period of time and cause other symptoms."

Megan looked at Nick and then Chen. "What does that tell us?"

Chen shrugged. "If we knew a little more about how she was exposed, we could come to some conclusions."

"Like what?" Megan asked.

Chen looked at Megan for a second before answering. "Like whether she was murdered or died of accidental poisoning."

"What about the chocolate?" Nick asked. "Could the thallium have been in the chocolate?"

Chen nodded. "Of course, it's possible. The tests haven't come back yet, and I just called the lab and told them to make sure they test for thallium in both desserts."

"How long do you think that will take?" Nick asked.

"I told them to put a rush on it, so hopefully it will be within a few days," Chen said as he shrugged. "But I don't have to tell you that priority cases get the fastest results. They'll do the testing but if a hot case comes in, they'll drop this case to complete the other."

Nick nodded. "Yeah, I get it. I just hope they work it this week. I'm worried because if this was murder, we don't have a clue where to start. We don't even know that Fiona was the intended victim," Nick said as he looked at Megan.

"That's true," Chen said as he watched Megan squirm in her chair.

Chen's cell began to ring. He answered and listened for several minutes before he responded. "Okay, I'm here. Just tell the driver to ring the bell and we'll open the back gate for him to bring the body in." He disconnected the call and looked up at Nick and Megan. "Sorry, I've got more work to do tonight."

"Anything I need to know about?" Nick looked for an answer.

Chen shook his head. "Nah, this was an elderly patient who was found at home by a neighbor. Looks like he probably had a heart attack. He was sitting in his easy chair looking relaxed. Of course, the police were called so I'm sure there's a report somewhere, but it doesn't sound like there were signs of foul play."

"Okay, good."

Chen looked at the pair. "Listen, I'm sorry I can't give you a complete discussion on thallium, but it's easy to research. I would encourage you to do so because you might identify something that would make sense in this case. When I have the results from the chocolate, I'll let you know. If the chocolate is positive, we'll have a clear-cut case of murder because you would never find thallium in a chocolate dessert for natural reasons. But if the chocolate is clean, we may never know what happened here. I'll have no choice but to rule the death an accidental poisoning on the death certificate."

"Understood," Nick said as he stood up and shook Chen's hand. Megan did the same and the pair turned and left the room. They walked out past the reception desk and got into the car.

Nick sat with his hands on the steering wheel and stared past the parking lot into the street. "That is not what I expected to hear."

"I'm more confused than ever," Megan said. "The police searched her office, didn't they, Nick?"

"Sure did, but in light of this report, I'm going to have to send them back to give it another look. Maybe they missed something obvious. We didn't release the room yet, so it should be just as we left it unless the staff has been going in there."

Megan's stomach clenched. Nick would not be happy if he found out she was in Fiona's office. Not only was it closed, but if Fiona had been murdered, Megan could have ruined potential evidence.

Nick started the Camaro and put the car in gear. "On to our next stop. Where would you like to eat?"

Megan shook her head. "To be honest, I'm feeling a little nauseous right now. I'll go with you to pick something up, but I'll probably just watch you eat."

"Are you sure?"

"Yeah, my stomach is off a bit and has been since this afternoon." Megan wasn't sure if she was sick or it was Chen's revelations that made her nervous.

"Okay, let's run up to the boardwalk. Maybe I'll grab a sausage sandwich and if you decide you want a little something you can order."

"Sounds great," Megan said as she watched the scenery fly by.

"What are you thinking about?" Nick asked several minutes later. "I can smell your thoughts burning from here."

Megan turned toward him and smiled. "I was thinking about thallium. I'm going to do some research and see if anything stands out. I only met Fiona a couple of times and spoke with her on the phone, but there may be something we've overlooked."

"We?"

Megan laughed. "You, the police, you know what I mean. It's just research, on the computer," Megan added as she smirked at him.

"Yeah, the last time social media got involved the town was overrun with people digging for treasure."

Megan lightly punched his arm. "No social media, just good old investigative techniques."

"Now I think I'm getting nauseous," Nick said as he turned to her. "Just make sure you let me know what you find before you talk to anyone else."

"I will. It's a promise," Megan said.

"Famous last words," Nick said as he shook his head.

CHAPTER 38

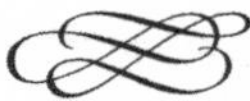

After a stroll on the boardwalk and a delicious sandwich, Nick dropped Megan off at Misty Manor. He offered to bring her to the door, but his cell rang with official police business, so she closed the car door and waved him off. Walking up to the porch, she felt melancholy and not quite ready to turn in for the night. She opened the front door and called to Dudley and Bella. They ran out from the kitchen as soon as they heard her voice. Marie also ducked her head out and Megan let her know that she was home but would be outside for a bit.

"C'mon guys," Megan said. "Let's get some fresh air." They walked onto the beach and took a slow walk near the water. Megan watched as the dogs chased seagulls and splashed in the waves at the shoreline.

She was having a hard time trying to digest the information they were given by Chen. He said Fiona died from thallium poisoning, but he didn't know how or where she was exposed. The poisoning could have been accidental, or it could have been cold blooded murder if the exposure were planned.

Nick worried that if it had been murder, Fiona may have been an accidental victim as the target could have been Megan.

Megan needed to make a list of who would want to see either of them dead. She didn't know much about Fiona's personal life and from what the police found in their investigation, it didn't appear she had much contact with anyone outside of work unless Nick was holding back information.

Clients like Debby Goren appeared crazy enough to kill and she was always a possibility, but Nick never mentioned whether the police interviewed her.

The police weren't looking for information about Fiona's friends when they searched her apartment. Megan decided she would call Teddy to follow up on whether the landlord had contacted him about her belongings. Nick would be upset with her if he knew she had decided to purchase the contents of Fiona's apartment, but it would be a good way to go back through the items in her desk to see if anything could give them a glimpse into Fiona's personal life.

If the poisoning had been an accident, Megan may be able to find out where she had potential exposure to thallium. Megan was more than determined to research the poison and find more information.

Megan picked up a stick Dudley had dropped at her feet and threw it toward the water. Dudley raced toward the water, grabbed the water worn stick and brought it back to her. She threw it again and watched the dogs run off. Dudley turned to look at her and appeared happy. There was a theory that dogs could smile. If it were true, Dudley was smiling. Her heart was heavy to think this poor dog had such an extended stay in a cage in the shelter. He had found his forever home now and she would make sure he was taken care of. Dudley liked playing with Bella as well.

As Megan walked back toward Misty Manor, her stomach clenched as she made a mental list of people who would want to hurt her. Top of the list would always be a Davenport. The mayor, Andrew Davenport, was a power-hungry man who believed the world owed him a living. She knew his family had been in Misty Point for several generations but that didn't mean he was owed anything. There were plenty of other residents who had lived in this town for many years.

The mayor's father had known and was involved with the death of her grandfather years ago. It was a shame that Grandma Rose didn't learn of that fact until right before her death. When the truth was exposed, Megan was lucky to escape death at the hands of Jeff Davenport, the mayor's son. She was certain he was still in jail, but she promised herself to check with Nick to be sure.

There were others who would not be upset if Megan had an accident. She had helped the police bring a few criminals to justice. She would ask Nick about them as well. She worked as an investigative journalist prior to being unemployed and moving back to her childhood home in New Jersey. Losing her job turned out to be the best thing for her. She had inherited her grandmother's estate and Misty Manor but that meant nothing compared with being able to care for her grandmother before she died.

Megan racked her brain to see if anyone she knew or investigated in the past could possibly be a threat to her now. Her job had been in Detroit. Shaking her head, Megan did not have any names.

Megan agreed to take the position of Chairperson of her grandmother's foundation. Her mission was to protect the environment and support the community. A private financial group, who would lose millions of dollars could certainly be a threat. She only knew what Teddy had told her of the members of the group. The Mayor, the obnoxious jerk from the meeting, the chef and the bartender from the country club were all part of the group. There may be others that Megan would consider a threat. She would have to talk to Teddy to see if he found any new information. The Mayor had certainly been rude after he was pushed by someone in the state about his environmental plans.

It seemed coincidental that Fiona had died while they were all together at the food tasting. Maybe both she and Fiona had been slated to die which would make the poisoning appear more like an accident then murder.

Megan's head began to pound. As she approached Misty Manor, she turned to call the dogs to her side. They ran to her, panting heavily. She was glad they enjoyed their foray to the water's edge but felt she hadn't given herself a solid direction to follow up. Yawning, she let the dogs and herself into the house and decided on a warm shower and bed.

In the morning she had some serious research she needed to accomplish.

CHAPTER 39

Megan slept well and jumped out of bed the next morning. She dressed, let Dudley and Bella outside to do their business and spent the next half hour in the kitchen making a strong pot of coffee. While she was waiting, she fed the pets and had a low-calorie yogurt. Bella was fitting right in at Misty Manor. She'd have to talk to Nick about his intentions with the dog.

Megan didn't like heavy meals before research or writing as they made her sleepy. Pouring the rest of the coffee into a thermos, she added cream and a small amount of sugar. She grabbed her favorite coffee mug and brought everything into the library with her.

She made sure the coffee was placed on a heavy blotter on the cherrywood desk and when she was settled, she opened her laptop. Typing in the keywords she was looking for, she had pages of information within a short time. She printed out page after page and placed all her thallium related information into a special folder to read later. If she were going to look for a source of poison, she would need to know what she was looking for.

The phone startled her from her work. She pulled it from her pocket and placed it to her ear without looking at the caller ID.

"Hello?"

"You'll mind your business if you know what's good for you."

Megan was stunned for a moment.

"Who is this?"

"That's not important. What you need to know is that if you value your life, your dog, your friends or your house, you'd better mind your business." The call disconnected before Megan could respond. Her heart was pounding in her chest and her forehead covered with sweat as anxiety set in. She looked down at her phone but didn't recognize the number. Her hands shaking, she immediately called Nick.

"Officer Taylor."

Megan was relieved to hear his voice, even though it was his officious police personality.

"Nick?"

"Megan? What's happening? Are you okay?"

Her voice shaky, she responded. "Yes, but I was just threatened."

"By whom?" Nick shouted into the phone. "Where are you? Are you alone?" Questions tumbled out of him.

"I'm fine, Nick. I'm at Misty Manor and Marie is here, somewhere, I think."

"What happened?"

"I got a call from some man who threatened me. He told me to mind my own business if I value my life, my friends, my house..," Megan paused as she felt her hands shake.

"Give me the number," Nick said.

"What?"

"Look at the phone and give me the number. I'll have someone try to track it down."

Megan looked at her call log and rattled off the number. Dudley whined and placed his head on her knee. She stroked his fur as she spoke with Nick.

"Thanks," Nick said as he rustled papers nearby. "I'm on my way. Lock the door and windows and don't go out until I get there."

"Nick?"

His voice softened. "It's okay, probably a jerk associated with the salt marsh project. But lock all the doors, check on Marie and the animals and stay put. I'm five minutes away."

The call disconnected and Megan stood up. She and the dogs walked to the foyer to check the front door which thankfully was locked. Next, they went to the kitchen and passed Smokey stretched out on the dining room rug. "Marie? Marie, are you here?"

Megan immediately went to the back door and found the door locked. She then went around the entire first floor and made sure all the windows were fastened and the alarm Nick had installed months ago was activated. Initially, she had turned it on every night, but recently she had been complacent and hadn't activated it for the last several weeks. She knew Nick was right. As the owner of Misty Manor and Chair of a large foundation she was and always would be a target, but the one thing she loved about living near the beach was the ability to fling open the front door, walk a short distance and feel alive.

Whenever she needed to focus, to feel free, to realize her problems were minuscule in comparison to the world, she ran to the ocean for comfort. She would be horrified if she always had to watch her back, but she should be more careful.

Within minutes she heard a noise at the front door. Peeking out the side window, she saw Nick staring back. Relief washed over her as she disengaged the alarm and opened the door. He opened his arms and crushed her to his chest. After a minute or so, he kissed her on top of the head, and she looked up at him.

"Are you okay?"

"I am now," she said trying to smile.

"I walked around the house, looked at the beach and the back of the property. I didn't see anyone or any cars."

"What about the phone number?"

"Turned out it was a burner phone. Not a big surprise there." He leaned down and kissed her lips as he continued to hold her against him. Megan's thoughts were no longer on the phone call. As he pulled back, he said, "I don't know what I'd do if something happened to you."

Megan looked into his eyes but stayed silent as he continued.

"I'm worried about you out here. It's one of the most beautiful places on the Jersey Shore but you're very isolated. Don't you ever get nervous living in a mansion by yourself?"

Megan took a deep breath and shrugged. "I have Marie with me most of the time. Dudley is by my side and Smokey is always lounging somewhere. Bella is very lively. It's not like I can just ask people to come live with me, Nick." Megan rubbed her temple. "C'mon, let's go to the kitchen. I'll make a fresh pot of coffee."

Together they walked into the kitchen. Megan set about filling the pot with water and pulling pastry out of the refrigerator while Nick placed utensils and plates on the table. As Megan waited for the coffee, she turned and watched him.

"What?"

She shook her head. "I was just thinking how comfortable we are together."

"Like a married couple?" Nick asked.

Megan felt a quick knot in her abdomen.

"That's another conversation I want to have," he said as he looked directly into her eyes. "But now is not the time."

"Hello?"

They both jumped when they heard Marie's voice.

"Oh, I'm sorry. Did I interrupt anything?" She stood at the door holding two bags of groceries.

"No, of course not. Come in," Megan babbled as she turned to the coffee pot and began to pour. "Would you like a cup of coffee? We were just having a bite."

"I'm fine," Marie said as she walked to the counter and put the content of her bags away in record time. "I need to go up to my room and organize a few things." She flew out of the kitchen and up the stairs.

Megan chuckled as she pulled out her chair. "See? I'm not alone."

"You didn't know where she was," Nick said. "And if it wasn't for Dudley, we may never have found you locked in that secret room several months ago."

They drank their coffee and concentrated on taking a few bites of their food. Nick wiped his mouth with a napkin and reached out to take her hand.

"Listen, I know you'll hate when I suggest this. I'd like to ask Luther to watch the place. He's a great guy. I can't assign town police to come here and do it. It would be awkward, and I don't want anyone to accuse either you or me with abusing town funds. Are you comfortable with him?"

Megan nodded. "He's very nice. A little too formal, but hopefully he'll relax at some point. What do you have in mind?"

"I don't know, exactly," Nick said. "I need to talk with him and see what his schedule is. He's trained and he has people he works with."

When Megan opened her mouth to protest, Nick put his hand up for a moment. "I'm not saying we need someone all the time, but maybe we can have someone keep an eye on you and Misty Manor. At least until all this business with the salt marsh is settled." Nick shrugged. "I don't know. If we win and they lose this business proposal, maybe we'll have to keep an eye on you for a while more, but you're too exposed by yourself. When is the meeting with the zoning board?"

"I don't know. I must call Teddy. He was taking care of that for me."

"Well, then call him and find out," Nick said. "I'm going to talk to Luther."

"Can't you just check on me or move in for a week or two like you did before?"

Nick looked at her and took her hand. "Megan, you have no idea how much I would like that, but honestly I'm struggling a bit."

"What does that mean?" Megan asked, panic in her voice.

"C'mon, let's take a walk." Megan followed Nick to the front door. They called Dudley and Bella who followed them outside and ran off toward the weeds. After locking the front door and setting the alarm, Nick took her hand and pulled her toward the water.

Megan was filled with dread. Finally, she turned to him. "Alright, out with it. What's on your mind?"

Nick turned to her and took a deep breath. "Okay, here it is. When I was called to Misty Manor the day you returned, the first time I had seen you in seven years, I could barely breathe. You know I've always been in love with you. I still am and ever since we've started dating again, I've been afraid everything will come crashing down the minute you realize I'm just a small-town guy."

Megan tilted her head. "What? What are you talking about?"

Nick spread his hands. "This, I'm talking about all of this. You own more than half the town and a landmark Grand Victorian Mansion. You're the Chairperson of a large foundation which supports half the charities in the county. Me? I'm just a plain guy living on a cop's salary."

"So what?"

"I'm still living on the other side of the tracks, Megan. How does it look if I suggest I move in to protect you? Everyone is going to think I'm taking advantage of you and your money."

Megan was stunned. When she was able to speak, she put her hands on her hips and was furious. "First thing, Nick Taylor, you and I started dating again before I was rich, before I owned Misty Manor or had that position. Everyone assumed my father would be the one to inherit Grandmother Rose's estate, including me, so no one could accuse you of asking me out just to get close." She started to point her finger at his chest. "You're damned right! This is me and I'm not changing. I don't care how much money I have. No one even knows how much money I have, except for Teddy. I'm insulted that you think having money makes me any different that I am. I'm me, and that includes my anxiety, my curiosity and getting into trouble. Take it or leave it. And by the way, who gives a damn what other people think anyway?"

Megan started to tear up and turned around.

Nick grabbed her by the shoulders and spun her back. "Megan, I love you more than anything. I never stopped loving you even when you refused to go to the prom with me back in high school. You don't realize how many men would love to marry you and be in your so-called inner circle. I know you don't see yourself that way, but you're a powerful woman and I never want you to second guess my intentions for loving you or moving in if I have to protect you."

Megan hiccupped with sobs and Nick pulled her into his chest again. He stroked the back of her hair and whispered in her ear. "I love you so much."

After a few minutes, she calmed, and he dried her face with a handkerchief. He pulled her hand and they silently walked to the gazebo near the water. They went inside and sat for a few minutes with Nick holding her close. She let her head rest on his chest as she watched the water crash to shore. Closing her eyes, she concentrated on the wind in her face, the smell of the brine and the sound of the gulls circling overhead. She could have stayed in that position for hours and easily fallen asleep, but Nick's radio sounded, calling for him to contact the station.

"And that's another thing," Nick said with a sigh. He reached up and grabbed the mike, answering with a curt reply that he'd be back at the station in a few minutes. Megan stood up and started walking the beach toward Misty Manor. When they reached the steps, she turned to him. "Be safe, Nick."

He grabbed her and kissed her hard on the mouth. When he pulled back, he said. "This is me, Megan. I want you to think about us and make sure you know what you want, because very soon, I won't be able to walk away without being destroyed." He kissed her again and smiled as their foreheads touched. "I think it's too late already, but I want to make sure you're dedicated to this relationship with your eyes wide open."

Megan looked up and kissed him on the cheek. "Go to work." She spun around, called to the dogs and let them both inside the house while Nick watched from the bottom step.

CHAPTER 40

Megan watched as Nick walked away. Her heart felt heavy and part of her wanted to run outside and beg him to stay. She knew he had to work, and he'd always have to be on call for the police station as long as he worked there. Nick would never want to feel as if he'd been kept, even if she convinced him they would be financially independent.

"Is everything alright?" Marie asked with a worried look from the grand staircase.

Megan looked up. "Yes, but it's been a day. There was another nut who called and threatened me on my cell phone today."

"Oh, dear," Marie said as she put her hand up to her face.

"Nick is suggesting we have someone patrol the grounds on occasion. He feels we're too isolated out here."

"He's got a point. It's an awfully big house for just one or two people and no offense, but you've already had a couple of issues since coming back from Detroit."

"I know and he's right. He wants me to hire Luther and his team to keep an eye out here. Nick can't ask the police to do it again. It's awkward."

"Luther? Luther Tucker?" Marie asked.

"Yes, nice guy," Megan confirmed. "He drove us to the food tasting."

"I know his mother, Esther," Marie said. "She's such a wonderful and spiritual woman. They go to the Baptist church on the end of Main Street. I would trust Luther. If Nick trusts him, I think you should follow his suggestion."

Megan nodded thoughtfully. "Marie, I have a bit of a headache. I'm going to go upstairs and lie down. Right now, the alarm system is on."

"I noticed when I arrived with the groceries."

"Nick would like us to keep it on forever," Megan said with a chuckle. "He asked me if you were here this morning and I wasn't sure. Just to be safe, let's make sure we keep in touch about our schedules."

Marie nodded. "Yes, Megan. I think we need to get another couple of dogs as well. What is Nick doing with Bella? I know she has been here lately, but who watches that dog when he's at work? It would be a shame if she's stuck at Nick's all by herself. Why don't we let her live here and then Dudley could have a friend as well?"

Megan smiled as she climbed the stairs. "I'll mention it to Nick the next time I speak with him."

Dudley and Bella bounded up the stairs behind her and together they entered her third-floor bedroom and flopped on the bed. Megan pulled the coverlet over all of them and they cuddled together for a while. Megan had grown up in this bedroom and Grandma Rose had kept it exactly as Megan left it when she went to college. When she moved to Detroit for her job as an investigative reporter, Rose refused to allow anyone inside. When Megan returned to New Jersey to take care of Grandma Rose, Megan chose to stay in her childhood bedroom and continued to stay there despite her inheritance. She loved being on the top floor and so near the glass room in the attic. Maybe one day, she would move to the larger, master bedroom on one of the other floors but her childhood bedroom still provided her comfort and reminded her of Grandma Rose.

Megan tossed as she rehashed her conversation with Nick. He had no idea how much she was worth, but tongues were wagging about her being wealthy around town. Megan would never let that information become public if she had any choice in the matter. That kind of information easily destroyed relationships and created dishonest friends.

A while later, Megan startled when she heard her cell phone and realized she must have dozed off. She nervously checked the caller ID and immediately connected when she saw Teddy's number.

"Hello?"

"Megan? It's Teddy. How are you?"

"Fine. I'm glad you called," Megan said as she sat upright in bed and pulled the coverlet higher.

"Are you alright? You don't sound like yourself."

"Yes, I'm fine. To be honest, you just caught me in the middle of a nap. I'll be awake in a moment."

"Good," Teddy said. "I called to let you know that the town moved the zoning board meeting to Tuesday night. They put the notice out today. I wanted to make sure you were aware so you can gather everyone and your research together for the public portion of the meeting."

"Oh, great. Thanks, I'll let the others know. Will anyone else be showing up to support us?"

"I don't want to promise anything, but I do believe we'll have a few representatives from the DEP to hear what their attorney plans to present."

"That's great," Megan said. "I was going to call and ask when the meeting was. I wanted to tell you that I had a threatening phone call this morning from a man telling me to mind my business if I valued my life, or that of my dog or my home."

"Megan, that's serious. Did you report it?"

"Yes, Nick came over and the police department found it was a burner phone so that wasn't a help. Nick wants to hire Luther Tucker to arrange some security patrols around the property."

"I think that's an excellent idea," Teddy said. "As a matter of fact, I believe I'll get in touch with Officer Taylor and make things official."

Megan groaned on the inside. "Nick doesn't know anything about the furniture from Fiona's apartment. Please don't tell him. Did the landlord call you?"

"Yes, he called Ellen. He was in a hurry to empty the apartment and get paid. We arranged to have everything stored. I believe it arrived today and the landlord has been compensated."

"Thank you," Megan said. "Please do not let Nick know."

"I won't unless it becomes necessary for some reason," Teddy said.

"Have you gotten any calls from the moving company?"

"Not that I'm aware of. I believe we received the key to the storage locker several hours ago. Why are you asking?"

"There's something else I need to tell you."

Teddy waited with a pregnant pause.

"Nick and I spoke with Dr. Chen. It turns out the poison that killed Fiona was thallium."

"Really? I don't believe I've ever heard of that."

"Yes, but Chen doesn't know if it was intentional. He hasn't declared if it was accidental poisoning or homicide. If it was murder, Nick is wondering if the intended victim was Fiona or myself since the dessert platter was made especially for us. The toxicology results haven't returned yet, so we don't know if the poison was in the dessert."

"Megan, this is frightening and not to be trivialized," Teddy said.

"I know," Megan said. "Do you think anyone from the financial group, especially the members who were at the food tasting, would go as far as trying to poison me before this planning board meeting."

"I certainly would hope not," Teddy said. "If the zoning board does not approve the deal, they would lose a substantial amount of money, but it happens all the time in business."

"Don't get upset. We don't know anything yet. If Fiona was the intended victim, I was worried there may be some poison mixed in with her apartment items. That's why I asked about the moving company. Or the poison could be in the chocolates. I'm planning on doing some research as soon as I get up. That will give us a better idea of how this poison works."

"Megan, please be careful. I have every intention of calling Nick as soon as we hang up to authorize that security. This is very concerning."

"I agree which is why I told you about it. I'm not sure how this man got my private cell, but I think I'm going to change my number as well."

"I will make arrangements for a new private cell and send it to you. Don't give the number to anyone except your close friends and myself. We'll take care of your current number and make sure you're not receiving any direct calls. I can have someone take care of all this immediately. In the meantime, do not answer any call you don't recognize."

"Thanks, Teddy. I won't, but I will let you know what I find out when I research."

"Excellent, and I will be in touch as well. Stay safe, Megan."

"I will," she said as she disconnected the call.

CHAPTER 41

Megan settled herself at the library desk and started her day once again. Dudley and Bella were situated on the comfy dog bed by the side of the desk. Megan turned on her laptop and navigated to search for more information on thallium poisoning. Although she had printed some information earlier in the day, she hadn't had time to read any of it. Before she started, she wanted to get information from as many different sites as she could. She continued to check sites, scan articles and print anything which appeared significant.

Once again, her cell phone rang. She stared at the phone. Although the number looked familiar, she wasn't sure who it was, so she let it go to voicemail as she continued to research. Megan spent two additional hours looking up facts about thallium, reading articles and wishing she had concentrated more in high school chemistry.

As she stretched backward in the desk chair her phone rang once again and she recognized Nick's number. She quickly picked up the call. "Hello?"

"Hi, beautiful."

"Hi, yourself," she whispered into the phone and waited for his response.

"What are you doing tonight?"

"Nothing that I know of."

"Would you care for a little company?"

"Sure, of course. That would be great." Happy that Nick called, she was excited at seeing him later.

"Mind if I bring a few friends?"

"No, I guess not," Megan said. "Anyone I know?"

"Yes, the gang. Teddy called me and told me about your talk. Then Doogie called to ask me to check something he found while researching. Anyway, one thing led to another and we'd like to come to Misty Manor for a pizza party."

"That sounds great," Megan said. "Is everyone coming?"

"As far as I know. We're bringing the pizza and the beer and whatever else anyone picks up."

"I'd better tell Marie, so she doesn't put on a big dinner."

"Sounds good. We'll see you around 7:00 p.m."

"Great. It will be nice seeing everyone. I feel like it's been weeks even though it's only been a couple of days."

"I feel the same way." Nick said. "I'll see you later."

"Can't wait," Megan said quietly.

"Love you."

"Love you, too." Megan hung up the phone but couldn't help smiling to herself. She had been back to Misty Point for more than a year now and couldn't imagine anything being different or being with anyone else than she was right now. She was in love with Nick Taylor and it was high time she acknowledged it.

Megan popped up from the desk and found Marie in the kitchen. She let her know about the impromptu pizza party. Marie was ready to cook and said she would make a few extra snacks for the group as well. Realizing that cooking was therapeutic for Marie, Megan welcomed whatever delicious food Marie would whip up for them.

Megan passed the next hour reading the material in her folder then ran up to her room to shower and change for the evening. She had just finished dressing and was at the top of the staircase when Marie called up to her.

"You had a delivery."

"I didn't order anything," Megan called down.

"You'll have to check it out when you get down here," Marie said with a small smile.

Megan bounded down the stairs and turned toward the marble table in the foyer. There she spied a large bouquet of two dozen roses interlaced with baby's breath. A smile immediately formed on her lips.

"There's a card in the flowers. I'll have you know, I'm proud of myself for not opening it," Marie said with a knowing glance.

Megan pulled the card and opened the back flap. Inside was a message with the following sentiment. "Megan, I love you more each day." The card was signed from Nick. Megan turned to Marie, "They're from Nick."

"I would hope so. We'd be having a different conversation if you were getting two dozen roses from someone else. Let me place them in the conservatory. I assume you'll all congregate there tonight."

Megan nodded. "Thanks, Marie."

CHAPTER 42

The front doorbell rang later that night. Megan opened the door to find her friends on the porch. They arrived with pizza, beer and her favorite chilled wine. There was laughing and hugs all around.

"Where the heck have you been?" Georgie asked as she stepped over the threshold with Doogie in tow. "We haven't heard from you since you left the beach."

"I know," Megan said. "I've been a little crazy lately."

They walked in and turned toward the conservatory. Megan looked back at the porch and found Nick looking in at her. He was dressed in pressed black jeans and a tight fitted shirt which emphasized his chiseled body. Bella and Dudley ran to greet him.

Megan smiled as the dogs ran past and said, "Thank you for my roses. They're lovely."

"You're welcome." Nick grinned and crossed the threshold. He curled his free arm around her waist and leaned in for a kiss. "You look beautiful."

"Bet you say that to all the girls," she teased.

"You're the only one for me," he said as they followed the others into the conservatory.

They made quick work of opening the pizza boxes and pouring drinks. Marie had laid out appetizers as well as plates, napkins, silverware, glasses, and ice on the sideboard. She then turned in for the night with the animals to keep her company.

"I'm pouring," Tommy said. "Who wants what?"

"I'll take a beer," Doogie said.

"You got it," Tommy said as he pulled out a cold beer and handed it to Doogie with a glass. "I'll pour the wine."

Tommy handed glasses of chilled wine to the ladies as the group filled their plates and sat facing the ocean. The lights in the room were dimmed and the French doors were opened so they could enjoy the salty breeze, the sounds of the surf and the evening sky as if they were on the sand.

They spent the next thirty minutes eating, enjoying the company and the view. When they finished, they cleaned up and placed everything on the sideboard for later. Nick refreshed the drinks, and everyone grabbed a seat to relax.

"I didn't get a chance to tell everyone, but Teddy called today to say the town meeting was moved up to Tuesday night. He wanted to make sure we knew about it, so we had the weekend to get our research together."

"I'm ready," Amber said as she sipped her wine. "I made up large boards to show what would happen to the environment if commercial buildings were allowed in that area. I have everything on a PowerPoint as well in case they want to go with a digital presentation, but I wasn't taking a chance of not being able to present."

"That's great," Megan said. "Teddy said a lot will depend on the attorney's presentation for the financial group. But he also said he thinks someone from the state will be able to attend the meeting as well. There may be some legislation we're not aware of that would nip the whole thing in the bud."

"Doogie and I have the beach presentation ready. We can talk about the impact to the beach including threats to marine life if there is any type of water pollution. The marsh interacts with the ocean through the tidal waterway so any problem there will wash directly over to the beach."

"Thanks, I think that's a very important impact to consider." Megan sipped her wine.

Nick spoke up next. "I had a long talk with Teddy. He's going to make sure the financial impact to the town is discussed. Depending on the number of units, the sewer hook ups, the cost to the police department and other town obligations, the financial cost may not be covered by taxes or other revenue."

Megan smiled. "Knowing Teddy, their attorney better have done a lot of research in that area."

"That's great," Georgie said. "We also have a lot of community support. There are a lot of residents who are planning to come to the meeting to hear about this proposal and whether there will be any benefit to the town. The summer generates enough traffic and crowds. We enjoy our slower months and don't want crowds year-round. I can guarantee the discussion will be lively."

Megan nodded. "The more discussion, the better to let them know the community has a concern about their future."

"Anyone want another beer?" Tommy asked from the sideboard.

"No, but I'll take more wine," Georgie said as she held her glass high in the air. "This has been a hectic week and I'm happy to drink to its passing."

"Cheers to that," Megan said as she accepted a refill as well.

Georgie sipped her wine and sat up a bit. "So, I have a question. While keeping my ear to the ground, I heard a rumor that Fiona Cochran died of poisoning. Is that true?" She looked from Megan to Nick. Megan turned toward Nick as she didn't know if she should comment or not.

Nick shrugged at her and turned toward the group. "It's true. She died of thallium poisoning, but we don't know if it was accidental or a homicide." He held his hand up in the air. "And before you ask, we don't know where or how she was exposed to the poison."

"Well, that's a little scary. She dropped right in front of us at the food tasting. What if we were all exposed?"

Nick shook his head. "I don't think so. I spoke to Chen about that in anticipation of questions when the news broke. No one else from the affair has reported feeling sick or having a problem. If anyone else was acutely poisoned, they would have had symptoms by now."

"The last thing she ate was that chocolate truffle," Doogie said. "The chef sent that silver tray out to Megan and Fiona."

Megan swallowed and took a gulp of her wine. "Thankfully, I was distracted and never tasted that dessert."

Nick held his hand up. "Normally, I would never discuss an ongoing investigation, but I know there was a reporter asking Chen some questions, so I'll tell you not to worry. The police do not think there's any danger to the public, but we haven't figured it all out yet. It may just be an accident. It happens from time to time."

"Well, I can tell you this," Tommy said. "I went to talk to some guys in the band before we left. First of all, Tommy and the Tunes are going to be doing a few gigs there in the near future."

"That's great," Megan said. "I hope you'll be free to do our event next year. I booked the date and gave them the deposit so it's all set."

"Definitely," Tommy said. "Anyway, I happened to be near the Mayor, the bartender and the chef as well as the obnoxious guy from the Pure Horizons meeting. I overheard their conversation for a while and I can assure you, that chef was no fan of Fiona Cochran. Apparently, the events she managed were very well planned and occasionally the staff had to make some concessions to meet the expectations of the guests. The chef and bartender did not like being told what to do." Tommy turned to Nick. "If anyone was looking to bump off Fiona, I'd be questioning those two."

Nick nodded. "Yes, they were on the investigation list, but I can't discuss what happened."

Georgie laughed and spoke up. "No offense, Nick. Please close your ears. This is just a friendly gossip session by a group of people who watched a woman die in front of our eyes."

"Yes, we all love you, Nick. We're just talking," Amber said as she turned to the group. "If I were going to bet on anyone, I'd wager on Bridezilla. What was her name? Debbie something. Remember how frightened Fiona looked when she ran into the bathroom? That woman could definitely have pulled something as well."

Nick rolled his eyes and got up to add wings to his plate.

Megan tried to soothe the group. "Honestly, we don't know anything about Fiona. She may have been accidentally exposed to something. If she were murdered, it could be something totally unrelated to the people in that room. We just don't know enough about the situation."

"True, but it's fun discussing suspects," Georgie added as she turned to Megan. "Now if you were the one they wanted, who would I suspect?"

Amber and Georgie looked at each other. In unison they sang, "Mayor Davenport, of course."

"Hey, let's not be too hasty to discuss me as a victim," Megan said with a laugh.

Amber jumped up and hugged Megan. "Oh, we're sorry. That was insensitive and scary if it were true. I'll feel better when this meeting is over and done with."

"Me too," Georgie said, and she hugged Megan as well.

Everyone took a moment to refill their glasses and grab a small snack. Megan sauntered near Nick and he hugged her to his side. The breeze kicked up a notch and whipped around the room.

"This is a perfect room," Amber said. "All the benefits of being on the beach but we're still able to be inside. I would have my bedroom here. Can you imagine waking every day to the beautiful ocean?"

Megan laughed. "Yes, but it's all glass so there's no privacy and it can get pretty hot in the summer."

They wandered back to their seats and made themselves comfortable.

"Let's not get back to that last discussion, but I'd like to say something about thallium if I may," Doogie said as he sat forward.

"Of course," Megan said. "You would know more about that than any of us."

Doogie smiled and gave a slight nod. "Thank you. Thallium is an interesting heavy metal. It comes from the earth and was discovered around 150 years ago. It's a byproduct of coal-burning and smelting and stays in the air, water and soil for an extremely long time. As a matter of fact, it's absorbed by plants and can build up in fish and shellfish. We need to find out more about this. I hope it's not related, and I certainly hope she didn't accidentally get poisoned by anything in our waters because we would have a much bigger problem on our hands. Also, it's not commercially available so accidental poisoning is not as accidental as it was fifty years ago."

Nick looked up, suddenly interested. "Chen did say that if he declared her death an accidental poisoning, there would have to be follow up by someone in the state."

"I think I can shed some light on that," Megan said. "When I found out Fiona was poisoned with thallium, I did some research. You're right about the fact that thallium is not commercially available so if it was intentional, it's probably murder."

"Tell us m

ore about your research," Nick said as he encouraged her.

"What I read today, suggested that thallium was used as a medical treatment for things like gonorrhea, syphilis and tuberculosis years ago. They used it for ringworm as well. Believe it or not, it was also used as a depilatory. Hair loss was one of the signs of chronic poisoning. Victims with acute poisoning died too quickly to lose their hair."

"Goodness," Amber said. "I wonder when people started waxing. I'll have to look that up myself. I hate using creams."

Megan started laughing. "Waxing's been around forever."

"We talked about her hair loss in the bathroom," Amber said. "I remember I wanted to tell her about a great shampoo for thinning hair."

The group shook their heads and Megan continued. "Yes, she did have bald spots. Anyway, they eventually started using thallium in formulations like rat poison and ant killers. People started dying in the early 30's so they started to keep track and report on it. The commercial use of thallium was banned in the United States in the mid-seventies."

"That's frightening," Amber said as she shivered.

Doogie looked interested. "You said commercial use. Is it still being used?"

"It sounds like it," Megan said. "But only for manufacturing of electronics, and optical materials as well as other business equipment. It was used for some medical procedures as well. The scary thing is that it's odorless, tasteless and water soluble so any residue can be absorbed through your skin. There are occupational workplace guidelines to protect workers but as Doogie said, you can get poisoned from eating contaminated shellfish or living near a waste site. Certain drugs such as herbal remedies, cocaine and heroin can be contaminated with thallium. Since it can be ingested or absorbed without difficulty, the exposure can be difficult to trace."

"The person who is poisoned doesn't know?" Tommy asked as he listened to the conversation.

"Not unless they see a physician and even then, it's difficult to trace at times. It all depends on whether it's chronic or acute poisoning. Initially, a patient would have severe nausea and vomiting several hours after being exposed. The next symptom would be a nerve type pain, called neuropathy, in the hands and feet. If the exposure is chronic, presumably in small doses over a period of time, their hair would start falling out. The symptoms of chronic poisoning are similar to many other diseases, so it's very rare to diagnosis it without specific testing. Most would feel fatigue, headaches, depression, loss of appetite, leg pains and skin changes."

"That could be anything from viral diseases to thyroid or just life in general," Doogie said as he nodded. "So, what's next in Fiona's case?"

Nick shrugged. "Pretend you didn't hear this from me, but we continue our investigation. We need to go back and interview any potential suspects. We need to check her office and her apartment again to see if we can find anything. For that matter, we need to check and see if Megan had any other chance of exposure as well." Nick turned to Megan. "You mentioned you were nauseous last night?"

Megan nodded but didn't add her stomach was doing flip flops thinking about how mad Nick would be if he found out that she and

Teddy had appropriated all of Fiona's apartment to a storage locker. Megan also didn't want Nick finding out she was searching Fiona's office the other day. Could she possibly have exposed herself to poison? She prayed that Julie and Mark kept their mouths shut. "Yes, but I'm feeling better today. I don't know if it was the stress of this week or something I ate. Who knows?"

"That's exactly the point," Nick said as he placed his beer bottle on the table.

"But if Megan had eaten the chocolate, she would have been sick that night," Doogie pointed out.

"Yes, if both Fiona and Megan were ill, it would be obvious it was a deliberate poisoning. The question would be who was the actual target and who was the foil to make it look accidental? At any rate, the chocolates have been sent for testing, so the next step is to wait until the toxicology report is back. First, we rule out homicide, then we can follow up on accidental poisoning. To your point, Doogie, we would have to notify someone from the Department of Health to do some testing and tracing."

Doogie nodded. "I follow the beach reports regularly. There's been no reports of multiple seafood poisonings or concern over crabs like there was years ago."

"I read those reports as well," Georgie said. "They're always testing the water, not for thallium but for bacteria."

"And if there was a problem with the local fish or shellfish, we'd probably be hearing about more cases in the local hospital or doctor's offices," Doogie added.

Nick stood and held his hand up. "Okay, everyone listen up. Right now, we have not confirmed anything about Fiona's death except for the presence of thallium. We don't know if it was accidental, murder, the local fish or anything else. You must promise me, and I mean double promise me that none of you will say anything to anyone outside of this room. We don't want to cause any unnecessary panic or have anyone wondering about their food until we have enough evidence to worry."

"That's true," Megan said. "Can you imagine if the local businesses were impacted. It would be irresponsible to tell anyone."

"Promise?" Nick asked again as he looked at everyone in the room.

They all nodded in agreement. "I guess I'll be eating a lot more pizza. I don't think I'll be eating fish until you figure this out," Tommy said. "I'm working at the docks this week, so I'll keep my ears open to see if there's any concern."

"Like we mentioned, no one else at the food tasting has been ill so it may not be the fish, Nick said.

"I'm not sure any of the food at that tasting was local. Those lobsters were not from around here, so it may not be a good example anyway," Doogie pointed out.

"True enough," Nick said as he turned back to the table.

Georgie stood up. "On that note, I think it's time we were going. Doogie and I have some beach time scheduled for tomorrow morning. If anyone wants to watch older lifeguards try to surf, you're more than welcome to join us at Twentieth Street."

"We'll come with you," Amber said as she and Tommy rose as well. "We're lucky Tommy didn't have a gig tonight."

"Thanks for coming," Megan said. "I needed to see all of you. I'm sorry this was not as exciting a night as we've had in the past."

"It's okay," Georgie said. "It was great having the gang get together, but next time let's hit the boardwalk. We can try to win this year's big prize and have some ice cream."

"It's a promise," Megan agreed as she and Nick stood together near the door. They followed everyone onto the porch. Nick put his arm around Megan's shoulders as they watched their friends drift toward the boardwalk and walk home.

CHAPTER 43

When they were alone, Nick turned to Megan, pulled her close and kissed her. He then wrapped his arms around her tightly and held onto her while they stood on the porch. Megan kept her head against his muscular chest and relaxed in his arms. She pulled back and looked into his eyes. "I'm really glad you're here tonight, Nick."

"I'm glad to be here. I was worried all day I wouldn't see you again." He pulled her tighter. "I've wanted to talk about us for a while."

"Oh?" Megan smiled at him.

"Yes, but every time I start, I get tongue-tied."

"Practice makes perfect," Megan teased.

Nick laughed as he looked at her. "Okay, that makes sense."

They both jumped when they heard a loud voice.

"Get your dirty hands off me."

"All in due time," someone answered.

"When you do, you'd better duck because I'm going to knock you on your ass."

"You and what army?"

Megan and Nick turned to look out toward the beach. "What the hell? That sounds like Luther."

"Nick? Is that you on the porch?" The voice asked.

"Luther?"

"Yeah, it's me." As he spoke, he walked into an illuminated area off the porch. He was with a man who had his hands zip-tied behind his back. He pulled him forward and the man fell to his knees in the sand in front of the stairs.

Dudley and Bella began to bark wildly from the foyer and Megan could hear them scratching at the front door to get out. She turned to Nick. "What's going on?"

Luther straightened, put one foot on the lower step and his hand on the rail. "I was taking a lap around the house and found this man hanging near your back door. He was on your private property Ms. Stanford and looking for trouble. Possibly breaking and entering. Do you know this man?"

Megan looked at the man at the base of the stairs. Nick put his arm out so she wouldn't walk down the steps. "I recognize him as a very obnoxious guest at one of the last Pure Horizons meetings. I don't know him, and I certainly have no clue why he would be near my home tonight."

"Funny, I asked him that. Said he was just taking in the sights," Luther snorted.

"At midnight? I highly doubt that," Nick said derisively. "And what sights would he be taking in at the back door of Misty Manor?"

"My thoughts exactly," Luther said as he prodded the man's shoe. "At minimum, it sounds like trespassing to me. Anything you want to add?"

"I don't need to say a word. You'll be hearing from my lawyer soon enough and then you'll get yours," the man said.

"Is that a threat?" Nick asked as he heard a siren in the distance. He looked at Luther.

"I called the station. Up to you what you want to do, but I figured you'd at least want to see if our friend here has a record."

"True enough," Nick said as he turned to Megan. "Does his voice sound familiar? Could this be the caller that threatened you earlier?"

Megan slowly shook her head. "I can't be sure, Nick. The voice was muffled."

"Please check your phone and turn on the full porch lights. See if there were any other calls."

Megan did as he asked. She opened the front door and had to slip inside so Dudley wouldn't run out. Marie was now at the door with the other animals, concerned about the noise. "It's okay, Marie. There was a man at the back door. The police are on the way. Please keep all the pets inside for now."

"Of course, as long as you're safe."

"More than safe, I have Nick and Luther outside protecting me and a patrol car is on the way." Megan grabbed her cell from the foyer table and offered a weak smile.

Marie nodded although she didn't look happy as she clutched her robe around her.

"I'm going outside to give Nick some information." Megan walked onto the porch and pulled up the recent call list and voicemail. Noting the call from earlier, she showed the phone to Nick. "Should I play it now or do you need to do something first?"

"Go ahead and play the voicemail, but put it on speaker," Nick answered.

Megan hit play and turned the volume up so everyone could hear. A chipper young voice began speaking. "Good morning, Ms. Stanford. This is Mandy from your car dealer. We just wanted to let you know your car is ready. Everything was covered under your warranty so there's no charge. When you arrive, just go to the service desk and ask for your keys. I hope your service was to your satisfaction and if you don't mind, there's a little survey about us. We'd appreciate the highest rating possible. Thanks again."

Megan gave a nervous laugh. "Sorry about that, but at least my car is ready." She cleared her throat when no one responded.

Hearing a noise on the drive, Nick and Luther turned toward the side of the house and saw an officer cautiously approach. Nick recognized him. "Peters, it's Nick Taylor. We have a visitor near the stairs. He was trespassing near this home."

Luther pulled the man to his feet and Nick turned toward Megan.

"I had such high hopes for tonight but I'm going to have to go the station until we identify this gentleman."

"What will happen to him?" Megan asked.

"He'll receive a warning after we check to see if there are any warrants." Nick put his hand on Megan's arm. "I know your car is ready, but I'd like you to let Luther continue to drive you around. This meeting will be here before you know it and I want you to stay safe. Let Luther take you to pick up the car tomorrow but then let him drive you anywhere you need to go until the meeting. Please don't be alone for the next week. Promise?"

Megan looked up into Nick's concerned face and nodded. "I promise."

"Good." Nick smiled and gave Megan a peck on the cheek. He turned and nodded toward Luther. "No go inside, lock the door and put the alarm on."

Nick watched until she was safely inside, with the door locked, and then bounded down the steps. Megan watched as Nick, Luther and Officer Peters walked the intruder to the waiting patrol vehicle.

CHAPTER 44

The next morning, Megan texted Luther to see if he was available. She needed to retrieve her car. She promised Nick she wouldn't go out without having Luther as an escort, but she wanted the ability to drive if she needed to in an emergency. He quickly answered her text and asked her when she wanted to be picked up. He agreed to meet her in twenty minutes and drive her to the car dealer.

Megan poured another cup of coffee and sat down in the kitchen with Dudley at her side. Nick let Bella stay at Misty Manor for now and currently she and Smokey were at Marie's feet. "What was that all about?" Marie asked as she sat at the table.

Megan took a sip of coffee before she responded. "The person near the door was part of the financial group that wants to build in the marsh. I don't think it would have been anything more than intimidation tactics but what do I know?"

Marie shook her head. "The world is crazy right now. Don't assume anything."

"I won't and can't. I promised Nick I would let Luther be my bodyguard for the next week. He's going to drive me to the dealer to pick up my car and then stay nearby. The big meeting is on Tuesday but there could be hard feelings on either side depending on the outcome."

Marie poured herself a cup of coffee, stirred in sugar and cream and sat down again. "What are we going to do?"

"Exactly what Nick told us to do. Right now, you keep the house locked up and the alarm on, especially if you're here alone. We establish some sort of communication system, so we always know who is here or wherever just to be safe. Things will calm down eventually, but we need to be safe."

Marie nodded. "I can do that, and I'll have the dogs with me." She looked over at the cat and smiled. "Smokey can protect me too. He just has his own ways about him."

Megan laughed. "I've heard about a lot of cats who have helped or warned their owner about mischief."

Marie toasted the animals all nestled on the floor and took another sip from her mug.

CHAPTER 45

"Thanks for being there last night." Megan smiled at Luther when he called to collect her at her front door.

"No problem, Megan," he said with a smile as they walked toward his SUV.

"What was he doing back there?"

"When I caught sight of him, he was peering through the window. Had his hands up to the glass, trying to get a better look inside, then he tried to knob. That's when I tackled him." Luther shook his head. "Don't know what his plan was, and he wasn't admitting to anything, but he did have a lock pick in his back pocket."

Megan's stomach clenched. She felt vulnerable and frightened for herself and Marie.

Luther turned onto the main street which led to the car dealer. Their conversation was light but strained as they drove. Luther's eyes flashed up in the mirror and watched her looking out the window.

"Don't worry. My team and I will be watching the house and probably you for the next week at least. I just want to warn you not to be frightened if you see a strange man following you around, because there will be someone. Hopefully, if we're good at what we do, you won't see us."

Megan turned to watch his eyes in the rearview mirror. "But if someone approached me, how could I be sure it was one of your team and not someone who's trying to kill me?"

Luther pursed his lips and nodded. "Good question, important question. My team will have a code for you. If you're not sure, just ask them what the code is. Don't say anything else. Just simply ask them what the code is."

"And what is the code?"

Luther started to laugh. "I'll tell you, but don't get mad now."

Megan squinted and frowned at him in the mirror. "Luther?"

"Okay, okay, your code name is Princess."

"Princess? What the hell?"

"Well, we didn't want to call you something rude like 'the package'."

Megan rolled her eyes and stared back at the road. They were a mile or so away from the car dealer.

Luther cleared his throat to gain her attention. "I'll be coming in with you to collect your keys. Then we'll go out to the car together and once you're on your way, I'll follow you to Misty Manor." Megan didn't answer right away which caused Luther to look up at her in the rearview mirror again. "I get the feeling you're not saying something important. You were going straight back to Misty Manor, correct?"

"Well, I was going to make a quick little stop."

"Where?" Luther asked as he watched her and tried to drive at the same time. Megan didn't answer directly until he cleared his throat and frowned. "You do know, I'll just follow you, whether you see me or not. There's no way I'm letting you out of my sight. Nick will have my head, for sure."

Megan chuckled. "That's probably true. Okay, I'll admit to you, I was thinking of driving by the storage unit that Fiona's things were moved to."

"You have Fiona's things? Does Nick know?"

Megan fidgeted in the back seat. "Not exactly."

Luther slowed the SUV to make the turn into the driveway of the car dealer. "Didn't this woman die of poisoning?"

Megan stared down at her hands. "Yes, that's true."

"And what were you planning to do? Look for a big bottle with the word Poison written across the front?"

"I don't know. I just wanted to make sure everything arrived and was in storage."

Luther slowed down but didn't park because he wanted to continue the conversation. "Listen, I'll follow you to wherever you want to go. I'm not sure what good any of that will do and if there's poison there, I guess I can drive you to the emergency room, but I'm coming with you."

"Fine, Luther. I'll give you the address when we stop and retrieve my car."

"You got it," Luther said as he chose a parking stall and parked. He got out of the car and walked inside the service area next to Megan. The attendant picked her keys off a large board and proceeded to explain what was serviced to Luther. Megan tapped her foot and placed her right hand on the counter for the keys. The clerk handed everything over to them after Megan signed the service form.

When they were outside, Megan belted herself in and started her car. She drove by Luther in the SUV who pulled out right behind her. At the end of the drive, she put on her signal and turned onto the highway. Within minutes, she was speeding along with Luther right on her tail. After making a few turns, she turned into the storage facility and used the code Teddy had given her to gain entrance. The gate lifted and she rolled through. She parked and got out of her car but jumped when she ran into Luther's chest.

"What the hell? You scared me."

"Sorry, but I didn't want to miss you. In case you didn't notice, you forgot to give me the code. I had to park and run up."

Megan smiled. "Sorry about that."

"I'm sure you are," Luther said dryly.

"Well, if you're coming, let's go." Megan turned and walked into the facility. When they reached the storage unit Teddy had given her, she used another digital code to open the door. The furniture was covered with plastic. Boxes were stacked in high piles around the furniture.

"Find what you're looking for?" Luther asked. "You're not seriously going to unpack every box and look for poison, are you?"

Megan sighed and shrugged. "No, I guess not. I was hoping I'd be able to identify something that would be a clue, but apparently not. Teddy said no one who worked with the movers got sick, so there's probably nothing here anyway."

"Good, if you're satisfied, let's go. No wonder Nick doesn't want you left alone for now. You could easily find trouble."

Megan frowned in his direction as she closed the door and engaged the lock. They walked from the storage facility and drove back to Misty Manor.

Megan pulled into the driveway and parked her car next to the garage. Luther followed her in the SUV and as they were getting out of their cars, a Misty Point black and white SUV pulled in as well.

They both watched as Nick parked his vehicle and jumped out of the car.

"What's up?" Megan asked. "I didn't expect to see you so early."

Nick looked annoyed as he eyed the two of them. "I see you got your car back." Luther turned around and pretended to be interested in a mark on his car.

"Yes, Luther was kind enough to drive me to the dealer this morning."

"Hmm, interestingly enough, I went over to Fiona's apartment this morning. The landlord advised me that all her stuff was gone. Purchased by a young woman. The movers came and dragged it all away after the landlord was paid for it. You wouldn't know anything about that, would you Megan?"

Megan shot a look over at Luther who silently shook his head and held his hands up the air. "Yes, Nick, if you must know, the landlord was going to throw everything out. I'm sure he sold whatever he thought was valuable, but he let Teddy pay him a fee for the rest. Teddy also made arrangements to have it placed in a storage unit until we could donate it to one of the charities that could use it."

"What?"

"The police had released the scene and said he could do whatever he wanted with her possessions as long as he attempted to find family. No one came forward so we bought it to donate to someone else. Obviously, we didn't know about the poison then."

"You're really something," Nick said. "What if there is poison in her things?"

"Then Teddy would probably be hearing from some very cranky moving men by now."

Nick put his hands on his hips. "So where is it now?"

"It's in the storage unit up on Route 35." Megan refused to drop her eyes.

"Then please do me a favor and leave it there. Don't touch it, don't go through it. Leave it alone until we figure this out."

Megan paused and then nodded. "Okay, I'll do that. I don't want to give it to anyone if there's a chance it could be dangerous."

"Is that why you came here today?" Megan asked, her mouth firm.

"No, I wanted to let you know that Chen called. He told me to stop there today because he got the results of the chocolate."

CHAPTER 46

"He didn't even give a hint?" Megan asked as she watched Nick at the driver's wheel.

Nick shook his head. "No and he won't give results via text either. He doesn't want to take a chance that results can be compromised. He wants to have in person conversation."

"Okay, hopefully he'll be in his office when we get there."

Nick turned into the driveway for the medical examiner's building and found a parking spot. They both exited the car and went inside to the receptionist desk. After ten minutes, Chen came to the waiting area and beckoned them back to his office. He sat behind his desk and adjusted the glasses falling down the bridge of his nose.

"Hi, Nick. Hi, Megan," Chen said with a weary smile. "How are you both today?"

"So far, so good," Nick said as he grinned at his friend. "I got your message and wanted to hear what you've found."

Chen shuffled through a mound of papers on his desk and pulled out a report. He quickly glanced through it and then tossed it over to Nick who picked it up and immediately started reading.

"What does it say?" Megan asked as she anxiously watched his face.

Nick turned to her. "Here, take a look." He handed her the form. Megan began to scan the results and then looked up.

"Please explain this to us."

Chen took the report back. "Basically, they analyzed the two pieces of chocolate that Nick had given me as well as the box. They found some mold, insect parts and rodent hair but there was no thallium found in those desserts."

"That's disgusting. I think I'm nauseous. What's the significance of the bugs and other stuff?" Megan asked with a sick look.

Chen began to laugh. "Are you sure you want to hear about that?"

"Yes, if it's important."

"What was found was within the allowed amount of insect parts, rodent hairs and poop that is in our everyday food."

"What?"

Chen shrugged as he spoke. "We do our very best to keep food as clean as possible, but we eat mold, bacteria, insect parts, rodent hair and insect poop all the time. Whether you're eating pasta, jelly, coffee, or chocolate, insects and their excrement are the byproduct of growing and harvesting healthy food."

"Now I know I'm nauseous," Megan said.

"The mold is different. It's entirely possible there was no mold when the chocolate was sent to the lab, but it has grown since then. So, it's hard to conclude anything about the mold."

Nick turned to Chen. "I want to be sure I understand. You're saying there was no thallium or poison in the chocolate."

"That's correct," Chen said. "We ran a general screen for common poisons such as arsenic and cyanide which came up negative. We ran a specific test for thallium which also came up negative. Ms. Fiona Cochran definitely died from thallium poisoning, but it was not from eating chocolates."

Megan nodded, deep in thought.

Chen continued, "We also reexamined her stomach contents. She had no shellfish in her stomach, so the thallium didn't come from fish. As a matter of fact, she had very little food in her stomach except for the chocolate."

"I believe that," Megan said. "She spent most of the night running around trying to appease guests or close potential bookings."

Nick was lost in thought.

"What are you thinking?" Megan asked him.

"This is interesting information. I'm trying to see where it puts us in terms of the investigation." He looked at Chen. "Do you have something I can write on?"

"Sure, here you go." Chen tossed a yellow legal pad over to the other side of the desk. "What are we taking notes on?"

Looking at Chen, Nick said, "We made a hot list of what suspects were likely to poison Megan or Fiona, especially if the thallium was in the chocolate dessert the chef presented. The chef, along with the bartender, are part of a financial group that's trying to ram new construction down the town's throat. Megan and her Pure Horizons Environmental Group are going to try as hard as they can to block them. Fiona, on the other hand, didn't get along well with her work colleagues. In addition, she was given the other chocolates by a very unhappy bride. There are more people."

"The problem is we don't know for sure anyone murdered Fiona Cochran or that anyone was trying to murder Megan. To be honest, since the chocolate tested with no poison, I think we're back to accidental exposure. There may not be any murderer involved."

"That would be tragic, but a relief as well," Megan murmured.

"I think I mentioned when we first talked that Fiona had something on her fingernails which are called, Mees lines."

"Please remind me what they are again?" Megan asked.

"Of course," Chen agreed. "Mees lines are a yellow-white discoloration of the fingernails which appear as transverse bands on two or more nails. Transverse means side to side which would be across the nail. Mees lines are common in arsenic or thallium poisoning but can also be seen in patients who have certain diseases, some of which are quite severe. That was the reason we were looking for Fiona's medical history. She could have had renal failure or any one of several different cancers which would cause Mees lines," Chen continued. "If the Mees lines are from thallium, the exposure is considered chronic.

She may have been accidentally poisoned over a month or so, but we have no idea where she was poisoned. The problem is I'm going to have to make a decision soon and I can't find a good fit for murder."

Nick and Megan were silent at first. "If that's the decision, we'll have to accept it," Megan said as she looked at Nick. "But I still feel as if something was off. Her behavior seemed off. Is there anything else we can do?"

Chen shrugged. "Hard to say because we haven't proved anything either way. Remember, Mees lines can be the result of chronic illness or poisoning. We know she was exposed to poison, and the poison was most likely chronic so it can still be accidental or murder." Chen watched the pair take in the information. "You don't look convinced. I can wait a few more days if you think you can find any more information. Otherwise, next week I'll declare her death accidental."

Nick nodded and placed his hand on Megan's back. "Fine, that sounds fair. Thanks for the information and your time. I'm not sure we'll find anything new, but we'll review any tips we have one last time and see if anything pops up." He leaned forward and shook Chen's hand before he and Megan headed for the door.

CHAPTER 47

"What are you thinking? You have smoke coming from your ears," Nick said as he drove by the ocean on their way back to Misty Manor.

Megan shook her head. "I'm just trying to think through what Chen said. Going back to when I first met Fiona and trying to reassess her behavior."

"Are you coming to any conclusions?"

"Not necessarily. The first time we met, she did say she wasn't feeling quite right. She seemed tired and I did notice that her hair was thinning. I think she mentioned something about feeling nauseous."

"Then what?"

"She had to leave because the bride, Debbie Goren, was screaming in the hall about wanting lavender vases. Fiona went to calm her down and Julie Bratton finished my tour. Fiona called me later and sounded weary as well."

"When was the next time you spoke with her?"

"Not until the food tasting. We had gone to the ladies' room and she ran in there and hid from Debbie Goren. She may have been simply trying to hide for a few moments, but she locked herself in one of the stalls and we covered for her."

"Was she sick?"

Megan shook her head. "I don't think so. As far as I know she wasn't vomiting or sick to her stomach. She didn't admit to being dizzy or anything other than fleeing from Debbie Goren. The bride made a comment about her hair, but I think Fiona was just trying to hide. Anyway, we left to go back to the dining room. After that I saw her buzzing around the ballroom until she began to make her speech. I didn't see her eating a meal, so it makes sense there was no food in her stomach."

"Except for the chocolate," Nick pointed out.

"Yes, and I can't say she was looking forward to it. We were chatting and Skylar ran up to us with the platter from the chef. He said it was a new creation and he seemed immensely proud. Fiona sort of gulped it down and I never got a chance to taste it."

Megan was quiet for a few seconds as she swallowed hard. "The next thing I know she's clutching her stomach, falling to the ground and seizing. It was hard to watch, especially when the EMT's came in and started pounding on her."

Nick reached over and squeezed her arm. "It is a bit scary when you're not used to seeing that kind of thing and it's more unfortunate because they weren't able to save her."

Taking a deep breath, Megan said, "I just want to do our best. Either way, it's still a mystery and I feel bad this woman died without anyone knowing her or celebrating her life."

Nick was silent for a few moments. "Well, we do know she had a past and that's probably why she kept to herself."

Looking toward Nick, Megan said, "What else can we do?"

Nick shrugged. "Nothing much. I'll call the police station in New Paltz and see if there's anything else they can tell me. Sometimes you get new clues when you recanvas the investigation. The only other thing is to ask the country club staff and her landlord about the chemicals they use."

"No one but Fiona has been sick at the country club or apartments."

"Not that we know of," Nick said. "But we didn't ask about other tenants."

"Did you ever look at the employee list at the country club?"

Nick nodded. "We did. There has been little turnover, and we haven't found anyone past or present with a problem."

Frowning, Megan said, "I guess that's it then."

"Like I said, we'll go over the investigation one more time before we close it out. We have a couple of days before it's over."

"By then the town meeting will be over as well. I can't wait to move on from all of this."

Nick smiled and tousled her hair as he drove. "Let's just enjoy the ride and look forward to something else."

"Sounds good to me."

"I still want Luther to keep an eye on you until that meeting has ended. It doesn't look like anyone was targeting you with poison, but I'm not happy about the intimidation at Misty Manor."

"Oh, yeah. Did that guy ever check out?"

"Yeah, no priors. History of being a bully but no criminal record so we let him go, which is why I want Luther to be near you until after this meeting."

Megan turned to him. "I'm not looking for any trouble so that's fine with me. Luther can hang out until next week. He's a nice guy."

"I'm glad to hear you say that, but right now, Luther is off duty and you're with me. I intend to take advantage of my time so let's get back to the house and hit the beach for a little personal time."

Megan smiled for the first time as they drove back to the Grand Victorian.

CHAPTER 48

Tuesday morning began at the local bagel shop. The big day was finally here. The group agreed to meet to discuss strategy for that evening's meeting. Teddy called Megan early in the morning to make sure she had the time correct. He wanted a summary on everything they planned to present after researching salt marshes and the impact of commercial construction on the environment, beach, local taxes and utilities. The cost to the town would have to include any increased services that were needed to support those buildings such as police and fire department personnel. Megan reported that she had received the additional research from Lindsey at the library regarding projections of environmental destruction due to development in the state and Doogie had used that research for his presentation.

"It sounds like everything is in order," Teddy said. "Are you nervous?"

"A bit," Megan said. "I hate to go to contentious meetings, but I think it's important to protect the town, so we have to try."

"It will be fine," Teddy said as he tried to calm her. "After all the presentations are complete, I'll give a summary report and if we luck out, we'll have someone with a lot of experience ask questions of their attorney regarding research and plans for development."

"Thanks, Teddy. I realize this is not your normal area of expertise, but I appreciate all the support and guidance you offer."

"You are most welcome," Teddy said. "I'll see you tonight."

Megan wanted to share his perspective with the gang as they prepared for the evening. When she walked into the bagel shop, she saw Georgie, Doogie, Teddy and Amber at a table in the corner. She walked over with a smile and pulled out a chair. "Hi, how is everyone today?"

Amber laughed. "We're fine, but we're in the middle of the endless discussion of deciding whether to order a Taylor Ham or pork roll sandwich for breakfast."

"Uh, oh," Megan said. "Who's winning the argument?"

Amber shrugged as she looked at the rest of the table. "From what I see, it appears to be tied between the men. They're pulling out the Taylor Ham vs. pork roll map of New Jersey to try to settle the debate."

"It's all semantics," Megan said as she shook her head at the men. A bell jingled as the door opened and Nick walked in. He was dressed in uniform.

"Over here," Megan said as she waved her hand in his direction. He joined the table and pulled out a chair next to Megan. Leaning over, he gave her a good morning kiss on the cheek.

"How's everyone this morning?"

Megan tilted her head toward Doogie and Teddy. "They're having the Taylor Ham vs pork roll debate."

"Oh boy, I'm staying out of that one. Did everyone order yet?"

"Not that I know of. If we wait for them to finish their debate, we could starve to death."

Nick laughed as he looked up and caught the eye of the waitress. She arrived at the table with pen and pad at the ready.

"What can I get you today?"

They quickly placed their order for fresh fruit juice, coffee, and sandwiches. When the waitress was done writing, she tucked her pen behind her ear. She was back in a flash with paper place mats, silverware, thick coffee mugs, as well as a fresh pot of rich coffee followed by a pitcher of cream and a cup of sugar.

"Smells great," Georgie said as she enjoyed the aroma.

"I have to say, they always have great coffee here," Nick said as he fixed his coffee.

"Lucky for you since they are gracious to the local police with food," Georgie said.

Nick laughed as turned to Georgie. "No offense, we're more likely to be poisoned than to be sent gifts."

Georgie nodded in agreement. "I can see how that would be true."

"Speaking of which," Megan whispered. "Did you find anything new in the investigation?"

Nick shook his head. "No. We went back over the interviews of colleagues at the country club, difficult customers and her apartment complex. No one was ill recently, and no one seemed to have enough of a beef with her to have meant or planned any harm. The chef and bartender didn't like her but they like their jobs and were paid well. They have more of an issue with you, but that will bear out tonight at the meeting."

"That's comforting," Megan said with a frown.

"There are no local medical records indicating she was chronically ill, and we checked several databases in the area. No one has any knowledge of her not feeling well or complaining about illness other than the few conversations she had with you. So basically, we've got nothing."

Megan shrugged. "It's a mystery but a frightening one to think that there's poison around here somewhere and we have no idea where or how to avoid having another accidental death."

"Not much more we can do on our end," Nick said as he finished his coffee. "The only thing still pending is the full police report from New Paltz. I called and they said they would scan it over as soon as possible. Once I clear that, Chen will call it an accidental death."

"It certainly sounds like you went above and beyond looking for possibilities," Megan said as she watched the waitress arrive with a large tray of food perfectly balanced over her shoulder. "That's a real talent. I don't know how her neck and shoulders don't pain her at night."

"They most likely do," Nick said. "But she probably needs her job."

Megan couldn't help thinking of Fiona and the country club as she watched the waitress work and resolved to leave something extra in the tip. She also insisted on picking up the whole bill as this planning session was for the Pure Horizons Environmental Group.

Megan presented Teddy's comments and suggestions to the group as they enjoyed their breakfast. After some spirited discussion, the group wrapped up with their plan for the evening. "The meeting starts at 7:00 p.m. in the town chambers so let's all meet at 6:30 p.m. in the parking lot," Megan suggested.

"Great idea," Amber said. "Let's get the right seats so we can watch everyone's reaction to our presentations. I have a feeling this is going to be a long meeting."

"Group hug everyone, group hug." Megan gathered everyone into a huddle. "I love you guys so much for helping with the charity and keeping the town protected."

They broke up and headed for their cars. Everyone felt strong and ready to attend the meeting.

As Megan and Nick stood on the sidewalk and watched everyone leave, Nick received a text about incoming reports. "The New Paltz police report is in," Nick said to Megan as he scanned the text.

"What does it say? Anything interesting?"

"I can't access the report here. I have to go to the station," Nick said.

Megan was quiet for a moment. "Listen, I don't have anything planned and if I go home now, I'm just going to obsess about the meeting so can I come with you? If we're going to let it go, I'd like to know nothing else turned up."

Nick was thoughtful for a minute. "Okay, I can say you're helping me review this case. I'm letting you do this only so we can put the case to rest once and for all. We read the report and then let Fiona Cochran fade into the night. Tonight, we get through this meeting without anyone being arrested and move on with our lives. I have some important plans for the two of us." Nick said as he smiled and planted a kiss on her forehead.

"Oh really?"

"Yes, and I've waited way too long as it is. Let's go. Did you drive here?"

"No, to be honest, I jogged along the boardwalk. Don't get mad. I didn't call Luther but honestly this place is only a half mile from Misty Manor, and I needed to walk off some nerves today."

Nick lifted his eyebrows with a slight frown.

"There must be fifty people on that boardwalk. Whether they're walking, jogging or biking, I had a lot of company, so technically, I was not alone," Megan protested.

Nick shook his head and opened the car door. He gestured toward the seat. "My lady? After you."

Megan offered a small, satisfied smile and slid into the seat. Nick slid behind the driver's wheel as she buckled her seat belt. She opened her window as far as she could. It was a gorgeous day. She turned her face toward the fresh air and enjoyed the scent of the salty breeze, the warmth of the sun on her face and the sound of the waves as they broke on the shore. The day was going to be busy, but she resolved that she would spend a few days at the end of the week on the beach with Georgie and anyone else that could join them.

Nick put the car in drive and headed to the police station a few short blocks away. He pulled into his designated parking space and the pair made their way inside. Megan was told to stay in the small lobby until Nick could go inside and retrieve the report. Once he was set up, he called Megan inside the busy day room and guided her to a scarred wooden desk. He remained professional, polite and reserved in front of his fellow officers.

When they were both seated, he opened the folder and began to read through the paperwork. As he did, he softly read parts to Megan out loud.

"There is a Fiona Cockburn that lived or was registered to this address a while ago. According to the report she was considered the girlfriend of Ozzie Hawk. Apparently, he was not a law-abiding man and was the owner of a Ponzi scheme with which they cheated many people out of a lot of money. They were both scheduled to be arrested. They arrested Fiona first, but she didn't have enough evidence against her, so they let her go but not until she flipped on Ozzie. He was never arrested because he was found to be murdered when they went to pick him up. Fiona did not get along with Ozzie's mother or sister." Nick continued to read from the report. "Mother's name is Beatrice Hawk and sister is Cherie Bratton. I'm not sure whether she's alive or dead or what."

Megan had been listening and nodding as Nick shared the information. However, her head snapped up with his last statement. "Wait a minute. What's the sister's name?"

Nick looked back into the folder and grinned. "Good pick up. The sister's last name was Bratton. That's very interesting. We've talked many times with Julie. If there was a relation, why wouldn't that be disclosed?"

"I have no idea, but I have some time. Do you want to go check it out Officer Taylor?"

"I have an hour or so. Let me inform Davis where I'm going, and we'll take a quick ride. You go outside and wait. You shouldn't be going with me in case there's any danger. Putting a civilian in danger is one of the worst things I could ever do."

Megan leaned over the desk. "Listen, you wouldn't have caught the connection if I didn't ask the question. We're simply going to ask a few questions. You don't have enough evidence or information to arrest anyone. If anything happens, I swear I'll run outside immediately. We all want to put this whole episode to rest."

"And believe me, if this doesn't pan out, that's exactly what I'm doing. I'm closing the case today and I'm not ever going to discuss it again."

"I agree," Megan said. "This is the last thing we're going to do."

CHAPTER 49

Nick slowed as he approached the driveway of the Misty Point Country Club. He turned to face her. "I'd like you to stay in the car until I see what this is all about. People can do some pretty weird things when they feel they're being confronted about something, especially if they have something to hide."

"But Nick," Megan started.

"No buts," Nick said. "It's not right that you're here. You have no authority to be questioning anyone and having an untrained civilian in the process is just putting all of us in danger." Nick pulled out his phone and started texting.

"Who are you texting?" Megan asked as she watched him type.

Nick looked up, prepared for battle. "I wanted to see if Luther was in the area."

"What? To watch me?"

"Yes, that's what I was thinking."

"You don't trust me? To hell with that. I've done everything you've asked so far."

"That's what I'm afraid of. This is the part that normally gets you into the most trouble."

"I don't believe you," Megan said as Nick's phone chirped.

Nick looked down at his phone and said, "We're in luck. He happens to be home and only a block away."

Megan crossed her arms and scowled at Nick. "In case you don't remember, I'm not the criminal here. Let me get this right. You're asking a civilian to watch another civilian while you go inside and confront a potential killer or relative of a killer."

"First of all, Luther is a trained black op operative. He's had a little different experience than you have, although watching you, he may need his whole squad. What I'm doing is working my butt off trying to keep you safe. Why can't you understand that? I never should have brought you along."

A knock on the window caused Megan to jump in her seat. She turned toward the window. "Luther, you scared the hell out of me."

He grinned ear to ear. "Be thankful I wasn't sneaking up on you then."

Megan got out of the car and slammed the door. "I am humiliated that you were brought here to babysit me."

Luther stepped back with his hands up in the air. "I agree completely so let's make this as easy as possible. You and I will stay here and have a nice conversation about the beach while Nick goes in and takes care of business. No problems and later, you have my permission to scream at him all you want."

Megan grinned despite herself. "Thank you, Luther. I will take you up on that suggestion."

"Great. I didn't want to have to tackle you anyway. I have a feeling you would have won."

Megan started to laugh as Luther looked up at Nick and said, "Go finish your business and get back out here as quickly as possible."

"Thanks, brother," Nick nodded as he skirted the front of the car and went inside the Misty Point Country Club.

Megan leaned back against the car and crossed her arms in front of her. "I'm not happy with Nick and I'm not happy with you either, Luther Tucker. But I am not holding you responsible because I know you're just trying to help. Also, Marie knows your mother and if I need to, I'll tell her what you two were up to."

Luther let out a deep throaty laugh. "That's probably the harshest credible threat you can give me."

CHAPTER 50

Nick went up to the door of the Misty Point Country Club and let himself inside. Megan watched and silently leaned against the car which was parked near the garden to the side of the ballroom. She peered through the white lattice to look at the shrubs which were all trimmed with precision into hearts and other shapes. There were benches scattered throughout with a large marble fountain in the middle. Although not currently lit, white lights were scattered throughout the garden and would provide subtle lighting from the trees as guests enjoyed their drinks and wandered outside in the warm air to listen to the sounds of the ocean.

"Why don't you take a deep breath?" Luther smiled as he tried to distract Megan. "He's trying to keep you safe."

"Hmm," Megan said with a frown.

"You mean the world to him," Luther said. "You must know that by now. He'd go nuts if anything happened to you."

"I don't know about that," Megan said.

"Listen, be patient and he'll tell you about it himself."

Megan was about to respond when she saw the side door of the ballroom open and someone fly out. The woman ran through the garden and toward an exit on the other side. Right behind her was

Nick. He hit a chair which crashed to the ground and she slipped away. She ran towards the exit near Megan and Luther.

"C'mon," Megan said. "Let's cut her off."

"Who?"

"Julie Bratton," Megan said. "Nick needs to ask her some serious questions." Megan ran toward the exit and Luther followed, but Julie slipped through and ran toward a small shed at the end of the parking deck. Instead of running after Julie, Luther grabbed Megan and stopped her from following. "What are you doing?" Megan asked as she struggled.

"Letting Nick do his job," Luther said.

"But she's getting away. Can you at least follow him to see if he needs assistance? Then you can help him out instead of worrying about me."

Luther stared at her for a second and shook his head. "He's going to kill me for this. I know it." He let Megan go and followed Nick. Julie ran inside the shed and was rummaging around when Nick and Luther approached the door.

"Hands up," Nick said. "Let me see your hands."

Wild-eyed, Julie turned toward them. Sweat was pouring from her forehead and she had panic in her eyes.

"Come out of the shed," Nick said. "I just want to talk to you. I need to ask you a few questions."

"I'm not going anywhere," Julie said. She looked around the shed for an escape. There was landscaping equipment, bags of fertilizer, hoses, sand shovels, and volleyball nets surrounding her. Nick followed her carefully to make sure there was not a hidden gun in the shed.

Luther stepped back a few feet, so Nick could stand in the doorway blocking Julie's exit. To be sure, Luther quickly walked the perimeter of the shed to make sure there was not a hidden back door. Megan had edged up as close as she dared to hear what was going on.

"Julie," Nick began with a calm voice. "We want to ask you a few questions about Fiona."

"Like what?" Julie shrieked.

Nick stood with his hands up. "Are you related to Ozzie Hawk?"

Julie started crying but remained in a defensive posture. "He was my uncle. He was a great guy."

"So, you knew Fiona when you started working here? Why didn't you tell us?"

"Why should I? I hated her guts. She didn't even recognize me when I applied for the job although it had been a few years so I could understand that." Julie looked around the shed.

"Julie, what happened? Tell me what was going on," Nick said. "Did you poison her?"

Julie started to laugh. "She was so stupid. It was because of her that my uncle was going to be arrested and died. If she had kept her mouth shut, he would be alive today."

"I get it. You loved him," Nick said as he tried to negotiate.

"He was supporting us, my mom and me," she said. "He took care of us and when he died everything went to hell and it was her fault."

Trying to calm her down, Nick said, "Why don't we talk about it, all of it. Tell us what happened. I'm sure whatever happened to Fiona was an accident. It sounds like you were hurt and angry."

Julie could hardly breathe. "You..have..no..idea."

"C'mon, come outside and let's talk. You have nowhere else to go."

Julie picked up a sharp spade and threw it at Nick's head. When he turned to the side to dodge the gardening tool, she ran to the door with a bottle in her hand and sprayed a solution in his face. Nick began to scream, and Julie ran from the shed.

Megan immediately ran to Nick. "Are you okay?"

Luther took off behind Julie and within fifty feet tackled her to the ground. She continued to writhe as he held her to the ground.

Nick held his hands up to his face and screamed. "My eyes. It's in my eyes but don't touch me. I don't know what chemical she used."

Julie started to laugh as she looked back. "Make sure you say hi to Fiona when you get to hell."

Megan pulled out her phone and called 911. "I need an ambulance at the Misty Point Country Club. A police officer is down. He may have been poisoned and needs help." She turned to Nick. "I don't know what to do. Should I pour water on you." Nick was writhing a bit less but began to vomit. "Oh, no, what should I do?"

The dispatcher was trying to get her attention. "Excuse me, Ma'am. Is he breathing? Do you know what poison was used? Please stay on the line and try to stay calm."

"I don't know. I don't know if she used pesticide or poison. It could be thallium."

Megan watched as Nick rolled on the ground. She wanted to touch him, help him, provide some comfort but she had no idea what to do. Luther dragged Julie back toward the shed until he found some twine and bound her hands and ankles so she couldn't run. He then pulled out his phone to call poison control but by then the police cruisers and ambulance was turning into the parking lot.

Megan felt like she was in a surreal dream for the next hour as they tended to Nick, loaded him in the ambulance and left to transport him to the emergency room. They called in help from a biohazard team as they didn't know what to touch or where the poison was located. Megan watched as other officers arrested Julie, placed her in a squad car and prepared to take her to the station.

Tears ran down Megan's face as yellow crime scene tape was pulled around the area. Luther stood next to her and placed his arm around her shoulders. Davis showed up in the parking lot and scowled at Megan. When it was time, she told an officer what she knew about Fiona's death after which the police insisted, she and Luther were transported to the emergency room as well.

Megan turned to Luther in the ambulance. She shook her head. "I don't know what I'll do if anything happens to Nick. Luther, what the hell happened?"

CHAPTER 51

Megan repositioned herself in the chair. Despite being upholstered, it was one of the most uncomfortable chairs she had ever sat in. Once again, she waited for an emergency room physician to provide an update. Megan had now met Dr. Curtis Jeffries so many times, he felt like distant family. After what seemed like days, although it was only an hour, he approached her with his characteristic laugh and beautiful dreadlocks bound together with a black band.

"Megan Stanford," Dr. Jeffries said as he took her hand. "It's been a week since we last spoke about Fiona Cochran."

"Yes, and now I'm frightened," Megan said looking at him. "How is Nick?"

Dr. Jeffries nodded. "He's stable, but he's not out of the woods."

Tears dropped down Megan's cheek and she reached up with her fingertips to wipe them away.

He began again. "Let's go and talk to him together, but first I want to tell you that your tests all came back fine. You have no poison in your system so luckily you didn't touch anything or come into contact with anything covered by the solution. "Come with me." He pulled her up from the chair and together they walked to a cubicle. Dr. Jeffries pulled back the curtain and gestured for Megan to enter before him. When they were both inside, Megan leaned over the emergency bed and hugged Nick as hard as she could without dislodging his intravenous line. Her tears fell faster.

"Megan, please have a seat. Nick has asked me to explain his situation to you both so you could help understand what will happen."

Megan pulled away from Nick and sat on the edge of the chair by his bedside.

Dr. Jeffries cleared his throat and began. "Acute thallium poisoning is usually characterized by problems with your gastrointestinal, neurological and dermatological systems."

"I believe that," Nick said. "I'm feeling nauseous."

"That's expected." The doctor shifted as he spoke. "You may feel abdominal pain and have nausea and vomiting which may be followed by bowel issues. It's not guaranteed, but it's highly likely." Nick nodded his understanding.

"In another couple of days, you'll feel numbness and tingling in your hands and feet. You'll probably have pain in the soles of your feet and some weakness in your lower extremities. When the nerves are involved, you can have tremors, headache, even seizures and coma."

"But he's going to survive and be okay, right?" Megan leaned forward and was concerned.

"I'll get to that in a moment," Dr. Jeffries said with a small nod as he turned back to Nick. "You may experience double vision, abnormal color vision and your eyesight may suffer. It's common to lose the outer half of your eyebrows and have skin lesions on the lids."

"I don't understand," Megan said. "There is a way to treat this, right?"

"Yes and no," Dr. Jeffries continued. "The other symptom that is common with thallium poisoning is general hair loss, you may go bald and, in a month or so, you'll have something called Mees lines on your fingernails. Your tongue could swell and feel sore. You may also feel your heart racing and have some tightness in your chest."

Megan and Nick stared at the doctor without expression as they struggled to understand what he was saying.

"Normally, it takes time to come to a diagnosis like this, but we know for a fact you were sprayed with a large dose of rat poison directly into your face. The police were able to recover the bottle and send it to the hospital for testing. You and the bottle both tested positive for thallium. The police thankfully used special gloves, so they weren't poisoned."

"But I vomited," Nick said. "Did that help?"

"In this case, we induced more vomiting. Initially we check your breathing and if stable we make you vomit. That was followed by charcoal and something called Prussian Blue. That's why you're going to start passing blue urine and have some strange colors in your body. We also washed you thoroughly to make sure no chemical remained on the body. It's lucky for you that we were able to quickly identify the poison and start treating you right away."

"I'm going to look rather funny for the next month or so," Nick said with a deep breath.

"Maybe longer," Dr. Jeffries said. "You'll have to continue the Prussian Blue treatment until your tests show that the thallium level has dropped to a safe level and we'll be testing the thallium levels in your system three times a week until then."

"But it will get better?" Nick asked in a quiet voice.

"Early diagnosis and treatment lend to a favorable recovery. Some of the symptoms may take years, some never go away, but you'll live a normal life."

"Why did Fiona die?" Megan asked, fear etched on her face.

"Apparently her poisoning was slow and chronic which allowed the poison to reach much higher levels. Even with treatment, she would have had permanent symptoms." The doctor turned toward the curtain. "I'm going to give you some private time. We'll be seeing a lot of each other. You'll be moved to a private room for tonight. I'm sure you'll have more questions for me when I see you next." Dr. Jeffries squeezed Megan's shoulder on his way out of the cubicle. "He'll be okay with treatment."

When the curtain closed, Megan stood up and neared the bed again. "Nick, I'm so sorry this happened. All because I couldn't let it alone." She cried as she leaned down and hugged him.

He reached up and hugged her with his free arm. "It's not your fault. I am an officer, and I was doing my job. We take risks every day."

"Excuse us, please," a pleasant nurse said as she directed Megan from the cubicle. "We'll be taking Officer Taylor upstairs now. Perhaps you could come back a little later?"

"What room is he going to?" Megan asked.

"Third floor, 3002. It's a beautiful room," the nurse said. "We'll see you up there in a bit."

Megan wandered into the waiting room, unsure what to do. She called Georgie and explained she would not be able to make the town meeting tonight. She wished them luck and then called Teddy to let him know what happened and why she would be absent. He told her not to worry about the meeting and to take care. They would talk tonight.

Thirty minutes later, Megan was allowed into room 3002. Nick had been positioned in bed, his intravenous stabilized and side rails pulled up. Megan gingerly approached the bedside chair and took his hand. He looked at her and smiled despite having a green countenance.

"Thank you for being here."

"I wouldn't want to be anywhere else," she said.

"What about tonight? The meeting?" Nick asked suddenly.

"I called Teddy and the gang. They're going to handle it and let us know what happened. They have everything they need."

Nick was silent for a moment. He raised his head, and his eyes were teary. "Before this happened, I wanted to talk with you, about us. Now, I'm not sure you'd like to spend the rest of your life around a blue, balding man with numb arms and legs."

Megan chuckled. "Is that a proposal?"

Nick shook his head. "No, not yet, not until I see where this poison leads." Nick held up his hands and gestured toward his body.

Megan leaned over and kissed him on the cheek. "Nick, one day at a time. I . . ."

"Hello, Hello," the pair were interrupted when Luther strolled into the room. He looked at Nick and said, "I gotta tell you man, next time you want me to spend fifteen minutes with your girlfriend, don't ask."

His comment broke the tension and they all smiled. Luther continued, "They checked me out in the emergency room and let me go about an hour ago."

"Was everything okay?" Megan asked as she squeezed Nick's hand.

"My test came back free and clear of that damn poison. How about you?" Luther jutted his chin toward Megan.

"My tests were normal as well."

"Glad to hear that," Luther said. "They had that woman, Julie Bratton, in the cubicle next to mine. She was going on for a while." Luther turned to Nick. "Your buddies were there trying to get details out of her, and she admitted the whole damn thing. They were checking her for poisoning and talking about giving her some blue stuff. I made it a point to hang around and talk to your buddies and some of the nurses as well. They think she was getting agitated from the poison because she had some chronic exposure. Said something about her damn fingernails."

"Really? So, what did she say?"

"As far as I heard, her mother was the sister of some guy named Ozzie Hawk. Seems Ozzie was taking good care of them, but he was a bit of a grifter. He and Fiona got into a legal scrape and they both were tagged. Fiona was arrested and eventually got off, but Ozzie was murdered by someone he fleeced before he was arrested. Once Ozzie died, there wasn't enough money for Julie, her mother or the grandmother. Julie sounds like she got pushed out of the nest and was on her own while mom ran off with another winner. Anyway, Julie moved down to New Jersey and started looking for a job. She ran into Fiona accidentally, but I think she came to Misty Point after hearing Fiona was hiding down here. It was probably eating at her all that time.

"Fiona didn't recognize her, and she was mean to the kid, so Julie wanted to get back at her. Last time Julie visited her grandmother in New York, she was pecking around the basement and found the old container of thallium they used up there to kill rats and ants. What I overheard Julie say is that she didn't want to kill Fiona, she just wanted to make her feel sick from time to time. She took a significant amount of the poison and made it into a solution which she kept in a glass bottle. When Fiona told her to clean, Julie was more than happy to get her "special solution." She made sure she sprayed an extra dose on her keyboard on a regular basis so every time Fiona spent time at the computer for her schedule or looking things up, she would feel nauseous the next day. The nurse said this stuff gets absorbed by your skin or you can eat or drink it. The kid probably slipped it to her a couple of different ways, but the keyboard thing was pure evil. None of us clean our keyboard that often. Who would think they could have a poisonous keyboard? Anyway, Fiona started losing her hair and had tingles in her fingers."

Megan swallowed hard as she remembered she had been at Fiona's keyboard and then felt nauseous that very night. "Thank goodness my thallium test was negative. I was in her office a couple of times. I guess Julie didn't spray the chocolates or we would have thought that Debbie Goren was a murderer."

"Nope, I guess the thing Julie didn't realize with this poison is it doesn't wash out of your body easily." Luther looked over at Nick. "Sorry buddy, I didn't mean to get you anxious. Anyway, enough poison must have built up that it finally overwhelmed Fiona and she died."

"That's frightening," Megan said as she listened to Luther's story. "I can't believe someone could be so evil to slowly kill someone that way."

"Like I said, she may have just thought she was making her sick on occasion. I'm not so sure she realized she was killing her."

"Unbelievable," Megan said as she shook her head. "What's going to happen to Julie?"

"It sounds like she has to go through a series of tests just like Nick here. From what I overheard, she's going to have more medical problems than Nick because she's got chronic poisoning. Since they were able to wash Nick out, and give him a whole bunch of antidotes, he'll be fine."

Megan turned and squeezed Nick's hand again. "Thank God for that."

CHAPTER 52

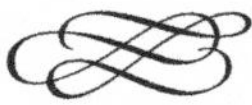

An hour later, laughter erupted in the hall. Georgie and Amber bounced into Nick's hospital room, followed by Doogie, Tommy and Teddy. The crowd was beaming. They had balloons, flowers and ice cream.

"You all look happy," Megan said. "Do you have good news?"

"Nick first," Georgie said as she placed her hand on the end of the bed. "How are you feeling?"

"Not too bad," he said with a shrug. "Just very nauseous."

Georgie looked up at Megan for confirmation.

"He's going to be okay, but he's got a lot of tests and medications in front of him." Megan placed her hand on his shoulder and smiled at him.

"As long as everything works out, that's great news," Georgie said with a grin.

Doogie and Tommy walked over and grabbed his hand. Georgie tied the balloons to a peg at the bedside while Amber began to remove large cups of ice cream from a bag.

"That looks delicious," Nick said.

"It should, it's from The Cone Cove, and I got your favorite flavor as well," Amber said. "Cherry Vanilla with hot fudge sauce and sprinkles."

A smile lit Nick's face. "Thanks, it's the best thing to happen to me today. I hope I can keep it down."

"And this is for you, Megan." Amber gave her a large cup of chocolate almond brownie ice cream covered in hot fudge.

Although Megan thought she was too upset to ever eat again, her stomach growled at the sweet treat.

Georgie passed out ice cream to the men while everyone relaxed and enjoyed their dessert.

Megan ate half of her dessert and wiped her mouth clean of hot fudge. "Okay, you all look pretty happy so out with it. What happened at the meeting?"

"Teddy, you should do the honors," Amber said. "After all, you saved the day."

Megan smiled as she looked at him. "I knew he would."

Teddy shrugged. "It was nothing."

"It was masterful," Amber gushed. "We went into the meeting and everyone took their places." She turned toward Megan and Nick. "You should have seen the smug faces on those financial guys and especially their lawyer in his fancy three-piece suit."

"For the record, Andrew Davenport, our illustrious mayor, rolled in with the chef and the bartender from the Misty Point Country Club. They snubbed us from minute one and took their seats. By the way, the Mayor did not recuse himself. Go on, Teddy, you take it from here," Georgie said.

As Teddy opened his mouth, Amber broke in and said, "They went first and presented their whole evil plan for the commercial real estate. Can you believe they suggested a six-floor commercial building? They thought they would toss a bone by placing a high-end fancy restaurant on the roof which would allow views of the ocean on one side and the bays on the other."

Georgie spoke next, "But then Teddy and his friend walked in. We listened to everyone's presentations and they were about to wrap it up before Teddy stepped up to the plate and asked to be allowed to make some comments and introduce someone to the board. Mr.

Dilworth was from the state and he made some interesting comments."

"Like what?" Megan asked as she turned to Teddy at last.

"He presented some of the latest research. It turns out that the sea level has risen in the last hundred years, but much faster in New Jersey, at almost double the rate. It also seems that the rate of rise is accelerating even faster due to melting glaciers and warming of the ocean. That would indicate increased coastal flooding in the future, which means towns will have to be creative in land use, building development and emergency management. Certain projections show that New Jersey is prone to significant erosion depending on coastal conditions. Development must try to relocate away from the shore and adjust to current occupancy by protecting existing infrastructure. Buildings, roads and existing development make those protections hard to accomplish. Superstorm Sandy was a significant event in New Jersey and there are areas that are still not restored to their pre-storm habitat."

"Sounds impressive," Megan said with a nod.

"We simply pointed out that a building of that size in a salt marsh prone to flooding and potential harsh weather conditions would put a strain on the community resources, the infrastructure as well as the natural environment. We also asked that should another Superstorm Sandy come along, who would be responsible to bear the cost of cleaning up a building disaster such as that. Insurance is much harder to obtain now."

Megan smiled as she realized his argument was sound.

Teddy finished. "I think the board realized the potential problems were not worth the taxes and revenue the building may bring in, not the mention increased traffic, crowding and crime."

"Is the decision final? The building won't go through?" Megan asked with fingers crossed.

"The board has to meet again, and they gave the financial group some time to offer another proposal which would have to address all the issues that were brought up today, but I think you'll find that won't be financially sound."

"That's fantastic," Megan said as she pulled everyone in for a big group hug. "You're the best friends we could ever have."

After a few more minutes of friendship and celebration, the group left Megan and Nick to themselves.

Nick yawned and Megan straightened out his blankets taking care not to disturb his intravenous. The hospital lights were turned down low and Megan pulled the bedside chair closer to the siderail.

"How are you feeling?"

"Tired," Nick said as he settled himself deeper in the bed. "Nauseous. I couldn't finish the ice cream."

Megan reached over and grabbed his hand. "It's been a bad day, Nick. You're going to feel lousy for a couple of weeks, but the best news is that you'll heal. You'll get better. Julie may live but then she'll be in jail."

Nick swallowed and adjusted his pillow as Megan turned off the light over the head of the bed. The television played softly in the corner.

"I still can't imagine killing someone by spraying a rat poison over their keyboard and mouse. We use our phones and devices all day long. You can bet I'll start cleaning mine properly."

Nick laughed as he took her hand. "It's a good thing we never know half the stuff we're exposed to."

A nurse appeared in the doorway. "I hate to break this up but visiting hours will be over soon. As much as you'd love to stay, it would probably be better for both of you to go home to a soft bed and a hot shower so you can rest."

"Thank you, I'll leave in a few minutes." Megan watched the nurse walk away. The hall lights were dimmed and the quiet of evening fell over the hospital floor.

"She's right," Nick said as he turned toward her. "Tomorrow's another day."

"Yes, it is, and there will be another tomorrow after that and another one after that."

Nick's face turned serious. "Megan, I wanted to tell you..."

Megan placed her fingertips on his lips. "Rest now. You could have died today but we got lucky. I love you Nick Taylor and I'll always love you. We'll have plenty of time to talk and I want to make sure you're feeling well and rested when we do."

Nick smiled as he held her hand. Together, they watched the night view from the large hospital window as the ocean waves gently kissed the shore goodnight and waited for a new dawn to begin.

ABOUT THE AUTHOR

Linda Rawlins is an American writer of mystery fiction best known for her Misty Point Mystery Series, including Misty Manor, Misty Point, Misty Winter and Misty Treasure. She is also known for her Rocky Meadow Mystery Series, including The Bench, Fatal Breach and Sacred Gold. Her independent novel, Midnight Shift was released in 2019.

Linda loved to read as a child and started writing her first mystery novel in fifth grade. She then went on to study science, medicine and literature, eventually graduating from medical school and establishing her career in medicine.

Linda Rawlins lives in New Jersey with her husband, her family and spoiled dog. She loves spending time at the beach as well as visiting the mountains of Vermont. She is an acting member of Mystery Writers of America. As a member of Sisters in Crime, Linda was the President of the Central Jersey Chapter for 2020, 2019 and the VP in 2018.

Visit Linda at her website at lindarawlins.com and sign up for her mailing list to be the first to know about new releases, appearances and more.

ALSO BY LINDA RAWLINS

The Misty Point Mystery Series

Misty Manor

Misty Point

Misty Winter

Misty Treasure

The Rocky Meadow Mystery Series

The Bench

Fatal Breach

Sacred Gold

The Elizabeth Brooks Mystery Series

Midnight Shift

Made in United States
Orlando, FL
20 February 2022